HAUNTING PARIS

HAUNTING PARIS

A NOVEL

MAMTA CHAUDHRY

Nan A. Talese DOUBLEDAY *New York*

All rights reserved. Published in the United States by Nan A. Talese/ Doubleday, a division of Penguin Random House LLC, New York, and distributed in Canada by Random House of Canada, a division of Penguin Random House Canada Limited, Toronto.

www.nanatalese.com

DOUBLEDAY is a registered trademark of Penguin Random House LLC. Nan A. Talese and the colophon are trademarks of Penguin Random House LLC.

Jacket design by Emily Mahon
Jacket photograph: Paris © Roger Viollet/The Image Works

Library of Congress Cataloging-in-Publication Data
Names: Chaudhry, Mamta, author.
Title: Haunting Paris : a novel / by Mamta Chaudhry.
Description: First edition. | New York : Nan A. Talese, [2019]
Identifiers: LCCN 2018031772 | ISBN 9780385544603 (hardcover) |
ISBN 9780385544610 (ebook)
Classification: LCC PS3603.H386 H38 2019 | DDC 813/.6—dc23
LC record available at https://lccn.loc.gov/2018031772

MANUFACTURED IN THE UNITED STATES OF AMERICA

1 3 5 7 9 10 8 6 4 2

First Edition

For Daniel

Il me reste d'être l'ombre entre les ombres . . .

For me all that remains is to be a shadow among shadows . . .

—Robert Desnos, poet and *résistant*, born July 4, 1900, Paris; died June 8, 1945, Theresienstadt concentration camp, Czechoslovakia

They call us revenants, those who return. Restless for this world, we pass each other in mute recognition, for to be silent and solitary is our essential condition. But death doesn't end our thirst for a human touch, a human voice calling our name.

And so I haunt these familiar quays, this familiar river. Music drifts down from Sylvie's window and I linger until it comes to an end. The scent of lilacs on the breeze stirs dormant phantoms to life, but music is sorcery more potent; though bound to time's measure, it exists on a plane beyond time, where there is no past and no future, there is only the present in which the dead revisit this world.

Night after night I wait until the last notes fade away and Sylvie comes to the window at last. I retreat into the shadows as one after another the beautiful mansions along quai d'Anjou spring to light, transforming those in the gloom below into a throng of ghosts. Occasionally a passing figure pauses in a pool of lamplight, to light a cigarette or glance at a watch.

Squandered time! The most enduring of regrets. In the end, a lifetime is not enough, the heart yearns for more. Who can reason with desire?

The heart has its reasons that reason cannot know.

Sylvie stirs uneasily in her sleep. Hearing a noise next door, she thinks it must be Julien working late, trying hard not to wake her though he knows she can sleep through anything. *The sleep of the just,* he says. *Chéri,* she calls out. Coco barks and she realizes of course it can't be Julien, it must be the Americans. Though her body wakes into the present, it takes her mind a few moments longer to absorb the shock of knowing that she will never hear Julien's voice again.

So the Americans are here finally, much later than expected. A good thing she had left the key downstairs with Ana Carvalho; the concierge is agog with curiosity about them. Sylvie herself plans to stop by in the morning, see that they're properly settled in. Not too early, though, they must be tired after the long flight from Florida, how long did Fabienne say it was, nine hours, ten? It never seemed to bother her friend, but then Fabienne was a force of nature. She had pushed Sylvie to divide the large apartment in two, and before the paint was even dry she had located Sylvie's first renters, a couple of professors from her college. With Fabienne nothing is *moderato,* everything always *presto, prestissimo.*

At one time Sylvie would have panicked at the prospect of dealing with strangers, but now her shyness seems the relic of a vanished self. When she was a child, her parents often acted surprised that they had produced someone with her shrinking temperament, and Fabienne said if schoolgirls had sobriquets like kings, she would be Sylvie *la timide*. The nickname had stuck to her through school, but when she mentioned it to Julien, he smiled and said that on the contrary, to him she was Sylvie, *coeur de lion*.

Sighing deeply, Sylvie turns over in bed. Seeing her unconcerned about the intruders, Coco tucks his head down into his paws. Sylvie has a harder time going back to sleep and wishes now she hadn't thrown away the pills that brought her respite from the sleepless nights when she paced the apartment till dawn. During the *nuits blanches* of the past winter, she had considered visiting Fabienne in America, had even booked a ticket at her urging. But in the end she had backed out because she couldn't bear to leave Julien behind. Not so lionhearted after all.

Yes, you are, Julien insists, encouraging even in death.

For so long she had felt as if the brightly lit banquet of life was being carried on behind closed doors, and she was entitled only to crumbs from the feast, not to a place at the table. She had felt it again at the house on rue de Bièvre, when Isabelle had seated her next to Julien. Then one day Isabelle's husband had risen from that table because of her.

Julien's love had turned her life into a vista of open doorways, like the grand enfilade at the neighboring Hôtel de Lauzun. Sylvie could not remember what her life had been before him, nor imagine what it would be after. But she no longer has to imagine it, she lives every day with his absence.

Even the smallest thing is a painful reminder that she will never see him again. A few days ago, when she and Ana Carvalho were moving Julien's desk from his study, they jostled open a secret drawer and a folder fell out to the floor. The concierge was beside herself with excitement about the discovery, but the shock of it hit Sylvie like a blow. She could not explain why she felt there was something fateful about it, though it looked no different from the stacks of such folders with his case notes filed away at Maison Chenizot. But when she opened it, she found a checkbook from an unknown bank and a sealed envelope with the initial *M*. Without a word, Sylvie quietly replaced the folder in the desk.

Opening the envelope or going through the checkbook feels like a trespass, something forbidden, as if Julien has sealed off part of the life they inhabited together and left her forlorn outside.

On their side of the apartment, Will throws open the door to the terrace. Alice is already under the covers, but he stays up for a while to shake off the irritations of travel—a delayed flight, a damaged suitcase—and wonders how Alice remains unruffled by it all.

At least the apartment on Île Saint-Louis has turned out better than he expected, none of the ghastly patterned wallpaper the French seem to love. But Fabienne had assured him it was a *bonne adresse*, one of the best in Paris, on the very street where Baudelaire created his imaginary paradise, *luxe, calme, et volupté*. She had also confided her hopes that their being on the premises would draw Sylvie out of her shell; she's become quite reclusive since Julien's death last fall.

Will wonders how exactly she expects them to lead a stranger out of her grief. They'll do what they can, of course, for Fabienne's sake, if nothing else. Amazing the way she had arranged the trip for them, even scoring some coveted tickets for the bicentennial parade. His misgivings suddenly vanish as he steps out to the terrace and sees the lights of the city spread before him, brightness rising like mist off a river.

My curiosity about the Americans is too mild to make me linger in their company. It's only by coming into Sylvie's orbit that they have attracted my attention at all. But she is now asleep and I hasten away, lest I trouble her dreams.

As a professional interpreter of dreams, there was one I encountered repeatedly: "All of a sudden I came across an unfamiliar door in my house, and my heart was beating loudly as I pushed it open and discovered a whole new wing, a secret part of the house where I had lived all this time unknowing, unsuspecting." Though I never had that particular dream myself, it's what death felt like to me, an unfamiliar door in a familiar house, which I pushed open to find myself forever outside.

In this twilight world between the living and the dead, I walk till the sky lightens from black to cobalt, my favorite hour, the blue hour, when the blur of mystery still clings to things, a mystery that the sun will burn off soon enough to reveal them as plain as day. I am tired, yet it is not fatigue, for the ailments of the body have been shrugged off like a cumbersome garment. But weariness does not belong to the body alone, and it is then, when I am past caring or thinking or feeling, that the buildings around me dissolve into ruined castles on a hill and the haze over the city is like the burning vines in winter, while far off I hear the mournful howl of wolves.

At the sound of footsteps behind me I spin around and find myself ambushed. Familiar faces transformed by hatred spit out the age-old curse: Sale juif! *Then a rock strikes me sharply across the temple and blood gushes from my eye. I am shocked by the taste, warm and coppery. But when I raise my hand to touch my face, there is no blood. Yet the pain, I feel it still under the cobalt sky, where for a moment the centuries stay their ceaseless glissade. Then the sun resumes its unrelenting course as I look around to find castles and fires and wolves all fled, and I am alone again, no longer a man but a ghost in a ravishing city where all that remains of what was once my life are some spectral ruins, which I try to piece together like the vanishing fragments of a dream.*

Though it's not yet light outside, Sylvie forces herself to get up, to boil water, measure coffee into the press. She closes her eyes, and Julien comes up the stairs with a brioche from the *boulangerie. Chérie*, he says, and she holds out her arms, but there's no one there, no warm and steady hand, no aroma of fresh bread. Blinking away tears, she pours the coffee, which she has made too bitter. She swallows it with a grimace, reminding herself to stock up on provisions; she doesn't want another scolding from Ana Carvalho about how poorly she eats.

She goes downstairs with Coco trotting ahead, his tail wagging excitedly, as if the morning walk is an unexpected treat instead of a daily occurrence. Watering the plants in the courtyard, the concierge calls out, "So your Americans have come, Madame Sylvie."

Your Americans. Sylvie smiles and shrugs. The Taylors are people she has never seen before, and after this summer will likely never see again. Perhaps there will be a thank-you note, then a Christmas card, then silence.

Sylvie is disappointed that Fabienne herself won't be coming this summer. *At the faculty concert someone told me, "Break a leg," which I promptly did*, she'd wired, *but luckily the cello suffered no damage, the insurers say it's worth a lot more than I am.* She wishes Fabienne had never moved to America. Now, more than ever, she feels the need of her friend's presence, someone who knows her so well that she can offer comfort just by being there, without saying a word.

Returning from her walk, Sylvie goes up to her landing and draws a deep breath. Best to get it over with sooner rather than later. Fabienne had assured her the Taylors were both *sympa*, but nice or not, Sylvie doesn't expect to see much of them after this; she has put in a separate entrance so they can come and go as they please. She knocks on their door, and as soon as it opens, Coco trots into the apartment, sniffing the room with a proprietary air. His black eyes glint with interest at the strangers. The first human touch the dog had known was a man trying to drown him, but he does not hold that against people in general, considering them for the most part capable of kindness. He goes right up to Alice and rests his wiry head trustfully against her knee, puzzled at first by the different layout of the room. Madame's piano is not in its accustomed place, nor Monsieur's desk. But Coco is philosophical about change. He knows that as long as there is a table, scraps will fall.

Sylvie notices the delicacies she had put out for them— pastries from Gérard Mulot, confitures from Mariage Frères— are untouched. Not fond of sugar, the Americans. Well, she'll know better next time. After a few pleasantries, Sylvie leaves them to their breakfast and returns to her own side of the apartment. She waits until she hears the Taylors go out, then sits down at the piano, the music on the stand turned to Schubert's last sonata. The beautiful opening melody ripples like light on water, but then an ominous trill sounds the dark undercurrent of loss. The notes blur before her eyes and Sylvie plays on from memory, tears rolling down her cheeks until Coco can bear it no longer and jumps on the stool to lick her face.

Making her way up to Sylvie's, the concierge encounters the Americans on the landing and stops to size them up in the broad light of day, her curiosity unsatisfied by a brief glimpse the night before. At least the man speaks fluent French, what a relief, she needn't break her jaw with English.

Everything about the Americans shines, their teeth, their nails, their skin; do they scrub themselves daily with pumice? And naturally they've got on tennis shoes, Americans wear them everywhere, even indoors. Ana Carvalho has watched many American programs on television and considers herself an expert on their peculiarities. No wonder they all come to Paris on holiday, what is there for them to do at home, nothing but autoroutes everywhere and wild creatures running loose on the streets. Armadillos. No, that's Texas, these people are from Florida. Alligators, then, and sharks, which explains why they're all bristling with guns. Thankfully, there's nothing like that at the beach in Hossegor, where she goes for her own vacation.

Ana Carvalho hopes their presence won't *dérange* Madame Sylvie too much, but on the other hand, a little bother might shake her out of her misery. At least she's no longer wild with grief; the look in Sylvie's eyes after Monsieur Julien's passing had given Ana quite a turn. Many a time she had gone upstairs to make sure Sylvie was all right, to keep her company through the dark watches of the night. Hopefully, that phase is over, but even if she no longer fears the worst, Ana still frets about Sylvie, the way she's shut herself up in the apartment like an old woman, as if fifty-three is any age at all, a mere girl compared to herself, long past retirement age and still working her fingers to the bone.

Ana enters Sylvie's apartment and finds her sitting in the dark. *Oh là là là là*, not again. It's enough to sink anyone's spirits, playing lugubrious music all day long. And that little dog listening at her feet, it's a wonder he hasn't succumbed to melancholy as well. Give her a gay little tune, something to set one's feet tapping. *"Quand on s'promène (pum pum) au bord de l'eau,"* she sings as she puts on a pot of coffee, *"comme tout est beau (pum), quel renouveau (pum)."* Now *that's* a song, and sure enough, Coco is up on his hind legs, didn't she say he was musical? She'd taught him to dance like that, by holding a biscuit just out of reach. A cowering little mite he was then, but look at him now, ready to take on anything, even the great big Rott down the street.

Ana Carvalho wonders if Sylvie has done anything about the checkbook that fell out of Monsieur Julien's desk last week. A bit of money, perhaps, like winning the lottery. Well, *she* certainly wouldn't turn down a windfall, it would be a welcome addition to the nest egg put by for retirement in Hossegor, with maybe a small patch to grow thistle and nigella for her darlings, it's highway robbery what shops charge for birdseed these days. Ana continues to hum as she throws open the shutters, admiring the pale pink of the leafing sycamores, the blue sky reflected in the river, the *bateaux-mouches* droning past quai d'Anjou. Their bright lights rake her ceiling at night and their amplified commentary breaks into her dreams, but she is used to the hubbub of the tourist boats now, rather likes it, in fact.

While Ana finishes cleaning up and wrings out the mop, Sylvie prepares lunch, marinated quail and wild mushrooms bought from the grocer that morning. On her own she would have been satisfied with bread and cheese or an omelet, but she always tries to have something especially nice on the days Ana Carvalho comes to clean.

The concierge wonders where the Americans are eating. Some shockingly expensive place, no doubt. Made of money, the people from America, but do they know value? For them there is nothing between the Love Burger and the Tour d'Argent. She'll drop a hint in their ear about the bistro across the bridge. *Impeccable!* An honest kitchen, where the food is fresh, the prices correct. Ana Carvalho is a notable *grippe-sou* and enjoys pinching pennies on other people's account as well as her own.

At the other end of the island, the Taylors linger over coffee and Will remarks that Sylvie is younger than he expected. Fabienne had said her friend was a woman of *a certain age*, which he, like Byron, understood to mean *certainly aged*. Not that he can peg anyone's age anymore, even his graduate students look no more than twelve, despite Fabienne's tales of their flings with middle-aged professors. But then scandals are to Fabienne what truffles are to pigs, she can sniff them out anywhere. Difficult to picture her and Sylvie as friends, but lucky for him, he would never have found this place otherwise, all the hotels and apartments booked months in advance for the bicentennial. And certainly not at the price, several thousand francs cheaper than other apartments on the island, but that might be because there's no elevator, it's a wonder he didn't get a hernia carrying luggage up five flights of stairs. Will signals for the check, and he and Alice stroll by the river, enjoying the mild spring weather.

On the towpath, several men have their lines in the water. A man reels in his catch and Will goes down to the lower verge to watch. But Alice is afraid of the water ever since the incident at Ginnie Springs. She had gone diving with a group of friends when a sudden panic spread that one of them was missing. Her best friend swam frantically back to the cave to look for Ben, but he was waiting for them on the bank; it was Katy who drowned. For years afterward, Alice had nightmares of being trapped in the cave, watching in horror as the water rose around her.

Even now, if she closes her eyes she can feel the water lapping at her ankles, rising to her knees. Abruptly she turns away from the river. There's no point dwelling on it, the past is the past.

Sylvie finds it harder to leave the past behind, it shadows each step she takes. Every morning, she and Julien turned left to pass the bread makers' syndicate with its lingering aroma of warm bread, and she takes the same route now that she is alone. Coco trots ahead, barking loudly at the Rottweiler in front of the Hôtel de Lauzun before adding to the pile of droppings under its gilded balcony. He zigzags across the narrow street chasing down smells, but when he comes to rue des Deux Ponts with its speeding cars, he waits for Sylvie and they walk down quai de Bourbon all the way to the tip of the island. When they reach the footbridge leading to Notre Dame, Sylvie turns and retraces her steps.

Every evening, as she did with Julien, she turns to the right, admiring the circular gallery of Hôtel Lambert, where the two of them had once spent an evening with the Rothschilds. As she passes the square Baryé with the NO DOGS sign affixed to the gate, she thinks how Julien found it *illogique* that dogs weren't allowed in parks but had free run of the streets. After the quiet stretch of quai de Béthune, she again crosses rue des Deux Ponts, this time into the livelier quai d'Orléans. At the crowded footbridge, she turns back once more.

When they walked around the island together, she'd say to Julien, *One fine day*. Luxuriating in the feeling of time stretching before them, she'd repeat the words. *One fine day*. He'd nod, waiting for the next part. *When you retire*, said Sylvie. And they both laughed, knowing he never would; there'd always be another lecture to give, another patient to see.

Italy, she said. *Florence.*

La Réunion. He kissed her hair. *Or Florida, if you like.*

She knew he was only saying that because on gray winter days he'd seen her looking longingly at Fabienne's photographs of palm trees silhouetted against a cloudless sky. But she didn't care *where* they went, as long as it was together. In any case, like true Parisians, they always took their vacations in August, always on the rocky coast of Brittany, where Julien ran into the waves with the vigor of a man much younger than his years. The thought makes her happy and she closes her eyes, feeling the sun on her face, smelling salt spray on the rocks, and when she opens them again she is alone on the streets of Paris, with only the dog to keep her company in the encircling gloom.

*In the dusky light we call "the hour between dog and wolf," not
quite day, not quite night, I am jolted at the sight of Sylvie standing
alone in a pool of lamplight. My breath catches in my throat as she
turns her head, searching for someone in the shadows. I say that as
if I still have breath, as if I still inhabit my body, when I am now
incorporeal. But no language exists for how one apprehends the
world as a spirit, our emotions remain too strongly tied to the body,
things are still "heartbreaking," "breathtaking," even when there is
no heart, no breath, but only their phantom habits.*

*Strange how these habits linger, how I still feel the throbbing
of my scarred eye, still smell the pipe smoke clinging to my beard.
Death has not transformed me into a spirit floating in ether, I
remain as firmly grounded as when my feet touched the earth, when
I listened to my patients and tried to decipher the hieroglyphs of the
human mind. What remains at the end is what makes us human,
not our bodies but that deepest part of us—some call it mind, some
call it soul—whose secrets are impenetrable even to ourselves.*

*No longer an actor in my own life, I am now only a spectator
to the lives of others as I wander the streets and watch scenes play
out in lighted windows, from the concierge's lodge at street level to
the grand windows of the* bel étage, *from the modest middle-class
panes to the stingy dormers of the attics. Small wonder that when
the Lumière brothers premiered the first moving pictures in Paris, we
were instantly smitten, they reminded us of the darkened theater of*

the streets where you can remain solitary in a crowd, cloaked in the anonymity that night confers upon us all.

But sometimes a fissure opens between these parallel realms, when a moving image projected on the screen looks out into the audience with sudden recognition, a recognition fatal for the living. Those firmly in the grip of life have nothing to fear; even animals with their heightened perception remain insensible to our spectral presence. Any danger from the restless dead is only to those wavering between life and death until one or the other claims them. That's when they are most vulnerable to subtle shifts in the atmosphere, to a current of air on a windless day, to seeing visions that, once seen, they cannot unsee.

The door between two worlds opens only in one direction: I cannot cross the threshold back to Sylvie, and I'm terrified of her willfully stepping over it toward me. So when Sylvie turns her head, I press myself deeper into the shadows to avoid detection. But just as the persistence of vision creates a fluid whole from the disconnected frames in a film, so the persistence of memory dissolves separate moments of strong emotion into a dreamlike continuum. Like Dalí's melting clocks, time runs together as I find myself inhabiting two different decades at once, this mild summer evening in 1989 when Sylvie lingers alone near the Street of the Headless Woman and a similar night some thirty years before, when she came to dinner at the house on rue de Bièvre.

Sylvie, too, is thinking of that dinner in the distant past. She hasn't set foot inside the house on rue de Bièvre for thirty years, but she's convinced it remains just as she remembers, the celadon walls, the priceless tapestries, the mirror frames dulled to a soft gold, everything lustrous yet muted by the patina of time. The dinner invitation was an unexpected kindness, she was only the piano teacher, after all. She had worn her good black dress and arrived much too early to find Madame Dalsace putting peonies in a vase. Isabelle looked startled and asked Sylvie to excuse her for a moment while she gave the maid some last-minute instructions.

Julien Dalsace came in fastening his cuff-links and stopped short on seeing Sylvie. She blushed, realizing she had caught her hosts unprepared by arriving punctually, and cast about for something to say, her fund of small talk limited, but Isabelle returned and took up the slack with a flow of conversation that required little from either her husband or Sylvie.

The doorbell rang, announcing the other guests. Odile was the last to arrive, trailing a chiffon scarf and a smug young man. Isabelle sent for the children and they came down to shake hands, kiss cheeks, and give perfunctory smiles as people exclaimed at how much they had grown. They turned gratefully to Sylvie, who didn't talk to them in the bright, artificial tone adults reserved for children, and Alexandra whispered that she had practiced her Clementi all afternoon, she was sure to play better than Charles tonight. Alexandra was fiercely competitive, she couldn't bear to be second best. Her brother shrugged. "It's not a contest," he said, but Sylvie could see how much the recital mattered to Alexandra.

Sylvie clasped her hands nervously when they sat down at the piano, but Charles and Alexandra got through the duettino without any obvious mistakes. "*Bravi*," Odile's young man called out, a little louder than necessary, to show he had said it correctly, in the plural. Isabelle nodded, taking it as a compliment to herself. Charles was coming along quite well, she said, but Alexandra needed to work harder, Sylvie was too lenient with her.

Noticing that the child was biting her lip to keep from crying, Sylvie got up at once and moved to Alexandra's side, whispering words of encouragement in her ear. When she straightened up, she noticed Julien's eyes fixed on them, his face marked with an unaccustomed frown.

"Since you're up, mademoiselle," Isabelle said, "perhaps we can persuade you to play?" Isabelle's commands were always framed as requests. Sylvie's hands turned clammy at the thought of performing for strangers, but to draw attention away from Alexandra, still red with mortification, she promptly seated herself at the piano.

Though no one could have found fault with Sylvie's playing, she sensed that something was missing, some essential thing that transported her at times into a different sphere, where she was unaware of anything except the music, unaware even of that, because she and the music were no longer separate but dissolved into one.

Certainly I did not find anything to criticize that night. Listening to the depths she explored in the familiar piece, I thought she had known sorrow perhaps though still so young, and at the thought of suffering and youth, my thoughts turned, as they often did, to Clara, and I was taken aback at how easily I would have given up everything in that room, in the world even, to ask her pardon that I had survived the war and she had not, to kiss again that smooth forehead or glimpse once more that beloved face. Then with a frisson of amazement I realized that in fact Sylvie bore a passing resemblance to my sister, not her coloring, but the contours of her face in the lamplight.

It brought me solace to imagine Sylvie as a child during the dark days of occupation, when streets were made unfamiliar by the flags of an occupying army, by menacing signposts in German, by children who disappeared without a trace from this indifferent city. I pictured Sylvie at her parents' kitchen table, her head bent over her homework. An ordinary sight, a child preparing her lessons, but what comfort I draw from the scene, a reminder of the loveliness of quotidian life which hatred had all but extinguished in Paris.

I shook off those somber visions and listened to Sylvie until the music came to a close. Once the piano lid was lowered, the children returned to their rooms and the rest of us resumed our broken-off conversations. Isabelle and Odile spoke in undertones about some scandal at the Jockey Club, and Sylvie must have felt like an eavesdropper as she glanced uncertainly around the room.

Seeing her so clearly panicked at the prospect of small talk—an extreme case of shyness, in my professional opinion—I drew her into the circle where Max Gouffroy was praising a recent performance of Rigoletto. "That quartet in the final act, I've never heard it sung better, really quite sublime."

Sabine Gouffroy laughed. "Two women in love with the same man, no surprise the story ends badly."

"My dear Sabine," Isabelle said, in her clear, carrying voice, "the surprise is that it ends at all. For Gilda to sing so long after she's stabbed, it's really quite absurd."

"No, no, Isabelle, you're wrong," protested Max. "It's not absurd at all, opera has its own logic, just like dreams."

Isabelle raised her eyebrows; she seldom heard the words "you're wrong" directed at herself. From the door, Berthe signaled to madame that dinner was served, and Isabelle led the way to the dining room.

"I hope no one is superstitious," said Sabine Gouffroy, "we're thirteen at the table tonight." An awkward pause followed, and I thought how much better it was to remain silent than to blurt out the first thing on the tip of one's tongue.

Sylvie looked around in wonder at the vaulted cellar cleverly converted into a dining room, with a fire burning in the fireplace to take off the chill. Its flickering light burnished Isabelle's bare shoulders, her golden hair. *Like a painting*, thought Sylvie admiringly. Then she noticed that the maid had to negotiate the narrow stairs laden with tureens and platters, but it didn't seem to worry Isabelle as she constantly rang her silver bell for Berthe.

At first Sylvie thought the company ill-assorted; Julien's colleagues from the hospital had little in common with Odile and her "protégé" or with the famous photographer and his young model, so androgynous-looking that Sylvie couldn't tell if the name was René or Renée. The only thing they shared was their appetite for talk, they would rather be hungry than bored, Sylvie thought, listening to them feast on aphorisms, banquet on irony. But as the truffled pâté was served and champagne glasses refilled, she realized the guests were not mismatched at all but carefully chosen—composed, in fact—so that their conversation had the zest of surprise. Even the disparate crockery was artfully random, like plants in a cottage garden. Everywhere Sylvie looked, Isabelle's sure hand was visible. Sylvie's mother always used to say that was *la classe, la vraie classe*! Looking at the glistening pâté, it seemed surreal to Sylvie that in another part of the same city, her mother complained daily about inflation, how turnips had gone up by fifty percent, to say nothing of *haricots verts.* And here was Isabelle apologizing because she hadn't found white asparagus, they would have to make do with green.

Unlike his wife, Julien rarely voiced an opinion, but listened courteously while his guests unfurled like ferns in the generous warmth of his attention. Only once, when Freud was mentioned, he cleared his throat. "When I met him in London . . ." he said, as everyone fell silent, "we spoke to each other in German, though he knew French quite well from working at the Salpêtrière with Charcot. By the time I saw him, he had great difficulty in talking, his jaw eaten away with cancer from his cigars. But his sense of humor was intact and he shook with laughter when I told him how I had been misled by an unfamiliar British accent, when someone introduced me as the young man from Paris, I protested, *Non, monsieur, I am the Freudian, not the Jung man.*"

Sylvie thought everything about the evening coalesced like a well-orchestrated piece of music. But at some point her sensitive ear picked up a discordant note which she couldn't pinpoint. Noticing her silence, the photographer turned to Sylvie and asked about her favorite composer. She hesitated, clearly taken aback by the question, one you would address to a child; so many people mistook shyness for stupidity. The conversation paused, ready to flow around her hesitation like water around an obstacle. She murmured that it was hard to single out a favorite, but she was drawn to the Romantics—Chopin, Schumann, Schubert.

"Schubert," said Odile, catching the last word, "oh, that is all finished, the young people think only of jazz."

Berthe struggled down the stairs with a large copper *turbotière*, and when she lifted the lid, the aroma of shallots and bay leaves filled the air. Julien reached over to refill her glass, but misjudging the distance, he spilled wine on the fine linen tablecloth and Sylvie noticed for the first time that he was blind in one eye. Odile quickly sprinkled salt on the stain, but Isabelle said, "Oh, don't bother, both wine and heirlooms improve with age."

"Heirlooms," said the playwright, "that's the trouble, people want precious old things handed down to them, they won't take a chance on something original." An aggrieved flush spread over his face, from which both hairline and chin receded as far as they could without actually disowning him.

Odile said, "I've told Arsène *I'll* back his play if no one else will."

"What's it about?" someone asked.

Arsène, who had waited all evening for this moment, swallowed his food hastily and pushed away his plate. "It's called *Intolérance en trois actes*. Act One: Toulouse, 1761. The curtain rises on a bare stage. A young man's body hangs from the rafters, an old man clings to the corpse. A crowd gathers, someone shouts, *'The father did it.'* Jean Calas is arrested and tortured. He insists to the end that his son's death was suicide, but they hang him for murder all the same. Scene ii. A spotlight comes up on a dark corner of the stage. Voltaire is writing his challenge to the judges to produce their *secret evidence* or confess they condemned a man based on nothing but *the yell of brutes*. Thanks to Voltaire, the dead man's name is cleared."

People murmured politely, although the story was familiar to everyone. "Wait, wait," the playwright said, raising his hand. "Act Two: Paris, 1895. The curtain rises on a courtyard at the École Militaire. A soldier is stripped of his rank, guilty of selling military secrets to the enemy. Scene ii: Dreyfus, in solitary confinement on Devil's Island, writes to his wife: *Darling Lucie, when they find the real traitor I shall return vindicated to France and to you.* Scene iii: Again, a spotlight on a darkened corner, where Zola is writing his famous *J'accuse.* Dreyfus is also cleared."

Arsène stopped to wipe his shining forehead and sip some wine. Nobody said a word. More than fifty years later, the heated emotions surrounding *l'affaire Dreyfus* had not cooled. Not only were the national schisms between right and left deeper than ever, but family breaches caused by the "affair" had not yet healed. Wherever did Odile find these tedious young men?

People were shifting in their seats, and the playwright's voice rose to compensate for their flagging enthusiasm. "Act Three: Île d'Yeu, in our own century. A white-haired prisoner says his dying wish is to be buried with his troops where they held the citadel at Verdun. But it seems the country has forgotten the first war, they talk only about the second and throw *le handshake* with the Führer in his face. Pétain pleads, '*O you writers who defended a Protestant draper and an Alsatian Jew, will no one speak for a Catholic patriot?*' The stage goes dark. This time, the spotlight comes up on me. '*Yes, Maréchal,*' I say, '*me voilà.*'"

A stunned silence followed his allusion to the Vichy anthem that schoolchildren were taught to sing during the Occupation, still painfully fresh in people's minds almost two decades later. The playwright took a deep breath to launch into an impassioned defense in the final scene, but before he could utter another word, the photographer drawled, "Perhaps, my dear Arsène, you should change the play's title from *Intolérance* to *Intolérable.* Pétain was no innocent, and if you will allow me to say so, you are not exactly Voltaire or Zola."

Taken aback at the hostility, Arsène looked at Odile. In a low voice she said Julien's sister died at Auschwitz. She didn't need to say more, everyone knew Pétain's role in sending the Jews off to certain death. Arsène muttered that he meant no offense, he had no idea Isabelle's husband was not a Frenchman but a "foreigner."

At that, Julien rose to his feet and very deliberately turned his back on Arsène. The playwright's face reddened. He looked around the table but no one would meet his eyes, except Sylvie, who stared at him with grave amazement. Arsène appealed to her, "A truly original work always seems shocking at first, doesn't it, look how the audience jeered Stravinksy on the opening night of *Le Sacre du Printemps.*"

All eyes were on her, and though Sylvie turned pale, she did not hesitate. *"Shame on you,"* she said, *"shame on you!"*

Julien drew in his breath. Sylvie looked as if she might faint, and he took a step toward her. But then Isabelle also rose and drew her arm through Julien's. "Shall we go upstairs for coffee?"

Still shaking with emotion, Sylvie marveled at how adroitly Isabelle had managed to both stand with her husband and extricate her guests from an embarrassing situation. *La classe.*

It was late by the time they finished coffee, and Sylvie would have to run now to catch the last metro. Docteur Gouffroy and his wife offered to drop her home, and Julien Dalsace lit his pipe as he walked them to the car. Sylvie breathed in the aroma of tobacco mingled with the scent of roses. She had never imagined a street in Paris could be so fragrant.

Once I came back into the house, Isabelle threw up her hands. "Well, tonight was a disaster. First the awkwardness with Sylvie, and then that deplorable scene at the table."

I replied drily that it wasn't Sylvie who created the scene.

"Oh, Arsène's just as bad, I grant you, hard to imagine why Odile parades him around, he's the worst of the lot so far. She's getting less fussy about her lovers, and about her appearance, for that matter, it's shocking how she's let herself go."

I thought how hard it was to live up to Isabelle's exacting standards. But I did not wish to discuss the evening further, Arsène had raked up too many painful memories. Clara was never far from my thoughts, but tonight had put me in mind of her husband. Bernard had joined the Résistance and been caught. No doubt he was tortured, and keeping silent under those circumstances was heroic; but so many others had kept silent out of cowardice or opportunism when they should have spoken up. It sickened me to hear Arsène whitewash the hard truths of those dark years, disguising complicity as patriotism and expecting the audience to applaud.

Finally Isabelle asked the question I knew would come sooner or later. "And Max?"

"I turned him down."

"How could you!"

I knew she was disappointed, she had her heart set on my taking over as director of the department. It would allow her to shine in the official role of hostess, more fitted for it than Sabine Gouffroy, who had used a knife for the turbot instead of a fish fork, just the kind of slip that Isabelle would notice. And although she wouldn't mention the directorship again, I knew her pique would go underground and that "How could you!" would resurface in other ways.

Isabelle shrugged. "In any case, the evening was already ruined."

I could not fathom what had left her so disgruntled. Surely not the lack of white asparagus, or the awkwardness caused by Sylvie, or even Arsène's appalling play. No, something had struck a deeper nerve, and suddenly I realized what it was. Isabelle considered it ill-bred to make a scene, but still she had felt herself shown up by Sylvie. "Shame on you!" It would have been the merest nothing for Isabelle, so sure of herself, to have rebuked Arsène. But for Sylvie to be the lone voice at the table to utter those words was an act of extraordinary courage.

Long after Julien had already left his wife for her, Sylvie was mortified to realize how thoroughly she had misread the dinner, a misreading that was to affect the rest of her life. Still, that night lingered in her memory like a banked fire whose coals she would stir again and again for warmth, even though she now knew her presence at the table was accidental; she hadn't been invited to dine, but merely to play for the guests. Isabelle's surprise, the scuffling activity, the thirteenth chair jammed around the table—everything finally made sense. The only discordant note in that well-orchestrated evening was herself.

At the time, I thought it was a night like many others. Charles and Alexandra played a duet before going back to their Tintin *comics. Isabelle locked away the silver and went up to bed while I stayed in my study, looking over notes for my lecture. But I could not rid myself of the memory of Arsène as he was leaving, taking out his ill humor on Odile. He grumbled that her friends had cut him off before he could explain that Pétain's people had made a pact with the Nazis, they could have Jews who were stateless as long as they kept their hands off French Jews; remarkably enough, only five percent of Jews who were French were killed in the camps, compared to ninety-five percent from other countries.*

That astounded me more than anything he had said earlier. "Only five percent!"

They say those who forget the past are doomed to repeat it. But those who falsify it condemn us all. "Only five percent!" Arsène's claim that French Jews fared better in the death camps is merely a sleight of hand, a legerdemain. Because if you tally among the dead the thousands whom the Vichy government had first stripped of their French citizenship, then in fact ninety-five percent *of French Jews also did not survive.*

When the survivors straggled home—so few, so pitifully few—I was stupefied by their vacant eyes, their blackened teeth, the numbers tattooed on their emaciated arms. But what struck me most was their silence. It made for uneasy consciences. Overnight there wasn't a single collaborator to be found, as if the entire city during occupation was one heroic underground.

What might be a figure of speech elsewhere is literally true here: We stand on a yawning pit. Riddled with caves and quarries and cellars, the city's aging bones are brittle as a confectioner's gauffrettes. *Some years before a revolution shook France to its foundations, there was a premonitory collapse when a sinkhole opened up on these streets. While shoring up the city's crumbling hulks, a visionary architect seized the opportunity to create the catacombs, a subterranean metropolis as grand as anything aboveground, and when the overcrowded Cemetery of the Innocents disgorged its rotting contents, a hollow city was ready for the restless skeletons. So no one knows better than we that however deep you inter them, the dead do not stay buried.*

When the sealed envelope fell from Julien's desk, Sylvie's heart had beat faster. A message from beyond the grave! Every secret crackles with electricity, but this one seemed doubly charged, as if Julien's death had galvanized it into a life of its own. Yet she hesitated to open something not intended for her eyes; it seemed indecent to violate the secrets of the dead.

Even though Julien's work meant that he dealt with people's most intimate disclosures, he seldom spoke of his own great sorrow, and Sylvie had respected his reticence, the fiercely proprietary nature of his grief. She knew only the tragic outlines of the story, that as a young doctor Julien was invited to work with Ernest Jones in London; it was the chance of a lifetime, to turn down Freud's great disciple would be like saying no to the master himself. With both their parents dead, Julien had worried about leaving Clara alone in Paris, but there was no particular reason to fear for her safety under a Jewish prime minister, and small appetite among the French for another war. Even after Léon Blum fell and the new government's appeasement policies failed, people were not unduly alarmed when Germany attacked, regarding it as a *drôle de guerre*, a sham war; Parisians continued to flock to the opera and whistle lighthearted airs from *Carmen*. The mood darkened under occupation, but Julien knew his sister was safe, married now to a gentile and living with Bernard's devoted aunts. Sylvie couldn't imagine the blow it must have been for Julien to learn that despite everything, Clara and her daughters had been rounded up during *la grande rafle* of 1942.

The fact that Julien had escaped a similar fate felt like both a blessing and a curse. Survivor guilt, Freud labeled it, that endless self-reproach. Mercifully, Freud had not lived to hear that his sisters, too, had died in concentration camps the same year Clara perished at Auschwitz.

Julien said that whenever he dreamt of his sister, it was always as a child, vivacious, carefree. "She loved nothing more than playing hide-and-seek among the vines, calling out in her sweet piping voice, *Come find me, Julien, come find me.* And waking or asleep, I feel I'm looking for her still, I've never stopped looking."

Sylvie did not have the heart to probe further. What good would it do to reopen the wounds of the past?

But now the discovery of the folder seems uncanny, as if something long hidden has come to light, some unfinished business connected to Julien. Convinced she's been entrusted with an important message, she hurries down a familiar street to deliver it, dimly aware that the street sign is wrong, it can't be rue de Bièvre, which is remarkably short and straight, but she continues to run down the long and twisting road, at the end of which the streetlamps stop and darkness begins. All at once she notices the mingled aroma of roses and tobacco and turns her head eagerly, but she's alone on a deserted street. She wakes up with her heart pounding and tries to grasp the remnants of the dream, but they've dispersed stealthily, like pickpockets on a train. All but one. The letter, being real, does not vanish.

Yet Sylvie cannot bring herself to open the sealed envelope, to look through the checkbook. It's not decency that holds her back but dread. What if it concerns herself? Is there a new will, as Isabelle suspects, or something much darker? In any case, the discovery has raked up all her old insecurities.

Like the time with Alexandra, all those years ago. Sylvie had overheard her complaining to her father, and Sylvie knew without hearing the words that it was about her. Julien's daughter hadn't forgiven her and made no secret of the fact that she thought Sylvie lacked birth, breeding, beauty, so unlike Isabelle in every way, how could he leave them for *her*! With the unerring cruelty of children, Alexandra had struck where Sylvie was most vulnerable, aware that in Isabelle's world she was only the daughter of a housemaid.

Her friend Fabienne always scolded Sylvie for letting the brat walk all over her, but Sylvie said she was too harsh on Alexandra, the child was only eight, and naturally she was upset.

"My poor Sylvie, you're even more naïve than I thought. Read *Bonjour Tristesse* sometime, you'll see how this ends. The little monster wants you dead so she can have her father back."

Sylvie had laughed off her friend's warning, reminding herself that Julien *chose* to be with her, thankful to find happiness, as he put it, *in the autumn of his life.*

"Not autumn," she had corrected him quickly. "It's still midsummer."

Seeing the look on his face, she would have willingly sacrificed the years between them to grow old with him. Julien had left the house on rue de Bièvre for her sake; if only she could do something equally bold for him!

But there's nothing she can do for him now. If the children

were here, they could decide together, but she'll have to wait till they return. How thankful she is that somehow they had made it through that rocky patch, that the children are still in her life. But they won't be back till September, and the summer stretches endlessly before her.

For Will, the days are slipping by much too soon. He's making scant progress on the manuscript his editor is impatiently awaiting. And well she might, she's practically a coauthor at this point, the only page free of her corrections is the title page: *Shakespeare and "The Whirligig of Time"* by Willoughby Taylor.

He looks up as Alice asks him a question. She's leaving for her French class, hoping to improve her language skills. As it is, she says everything in the present, making it hard to carry on a conversation for any length of time, especially with her limited vocabulary. What is *sensible* skin, she wants to know; whatever it is, she probably has it, there isn't a square inch of her that isn't sensible. Will says it's another of those words the French call *faux amis*, false friends; *sensible* is not sensible at all, it means sensitive.

"Well, that lets me out, then." Alice goes up to the kitchen window and exclaims, *"Merde, il pleut!"* The present tense is perfectly appropriate for once.

The rain starts up in earnest and Will murmurs, *"Why didst thou promise such a beauteous day, And make me travel forth without my cloak."*

Just like him, Alice thinks, spouting poetry instead of helping her look for an umbrella. She finds one, finally, in the hall closet. "Shakespeare," she says on her way out, and Will nods approvingly. As if she's one of his graduate students, Alice thinks. He still hasn't figured out that it's her standard answer, and she's right nine times out of ten.

Will pours another cup of coffee and returns to his pages. In theory it was a grand idea—to revise his manuscript on the legendary street where Ford Madox Ford published *The Transatlantic Review*—but he's discovering that what should work in theory is quite another story in practice; just like the *minuteries* that *en théorie* are timed to keep the lights on till one reaches the next landing, but which frequently switch off halfway up the stairs. Scribbling notes in the margins, he thinks never in his life has he sat in more uncomfortable chairs, straight-backed and spindly. Perfect for the French, who always sit erect, but they make no allowance for the sprawl of American limbs. Gingerly he tilts the chair back to read through what he has written, when out of the corner of his eye he sees a movement on the terrace. The rain has stopped and a tiny orange bird is flitting around the balcony, pecking at crumbs. Will runs to get his camera, and when he returns, the bird is in the kitchen, hopping about on his papers. Hardly daring to breathe, Will presses the shutter. With an alarmed chirp, the bird flutters in the air for a moment, then streaks out again. Will leans out of the window but feels the iron railing shift beneath his weight and quickly steps back. He must remember to warn Sylvie about the rotted window frame.

Just then he hears music through the dividing wall and realizes it's Sylvie at the piano. He comes out to the landing to listen and is struck by her playing, brilliant— no, more than brilliant— sublime. Seeing her door ajar, he creeps closer and peers through the crack. Coco bounds up and wags his tail, but immersed in the music, Sylvie remains oblivious of his presence.

Since she first learned to play, Sylvie has drawn solace from an invisible listener whose presence steadies her in a world where she so often feels an outsider. That familiar presence had calmed her as she performed on the night of the dinner at rue de Bièvre; but, alert to the slightest disturbance in the atmosphere, even then she had sensed a distant storm.

After that night, Julien avoided her and Isabelle remained aloof. Better that way, Sylvie had thought, kinder to keep her at a distance from a world she could never enter, a life she could never inhabit. And if she minded, then more fool she. Better to focus on Alexandra's trills. *Like this, Alexandra, liquid, flowing, don't tack it on like a frill, weave it into the fabric.* She nodded at Alexandra, see, like this, a hand trailed in water, and then the lovely undulating bit, a gondola rocking gently. As the low rippling notes of the barcarolle built to a swell, Sylvie drew up from their depths obscure yearnings, inarticulate desires. Her thoughts turned wistfully to Isabelle, lucky to have all this, her children, her husband. Sylvie imagined Julien bending to kiss that beautiful face, but what flashed into her mind was his lips on her own, and her cheeks burned as she played the final octaves.

Alexandra jumped up to embrace Julien, standing silently in the doorway. "Papa," she said, "you're home?"

Startled, Sylvie glanced up and met his eyes before she had

time to mask the emotions which the music had stripped bare. With a rush of love she thought, *I know you, I have always known you*. She had played for him so long in secret and he had listened so long concealed.

Shaken to my core, I went that evening to my study and looked
at my papers without taking in a word. At the dinner table, I ate
without tasting anything. In bed, my tossing and turning woke
Isabelle, who wondered if I was coming down with the flu. I threw
off the covers and went downstairs, where I opened a window and
heard a bat's high-pitched squeak in the deep silence of the night.
Roses in luxurious bloom released their perfume into the air. I pulled
a branch closer, inhaled its fragrance, the petals velvety against my
face. Deliberately I crushed the branch in my hand until a thorn
pierced my skin and blood oozed into my palm. I thought ironically
of what I might put in my case notes if one of my patients had
spoken of this self-inflicted wound. In the kitchen I bandaged my
hand with one of Berthe's immaculate white towels. It stanched the
bleeding, but my hand continued to throb as I went back to bed.

Even when I closed my eyes, all I could see was a slight girl
with a steady gaze, no different from the throngs of young women
coming out of the metro or walking by on the street, not a face one
would pick out in a crowd. But her appearance seemed beside the
point, I was drawn so strongly to her spirit. Sylvie was half my age,
it was unsuitable, unseemly, it didn't make sense. But the heart
has its reasons that reason cannot know, I thought wryly, and the
fact remained that illogical as it might seem, I had fallen in love
with her.

Still I hesitated to say the words that would end my marriage.
When I had returned after the war, it was to a changed Paris, where

I felt dispossessed at once of family, friends, and country, and it was Isabelle who had sustained me through that dark homecoming, had made a life here again seem possible. If I was unhappy with Isabelle, surely it was no one's fault but my own. And as for happiness with Sylvie, it was a remote possibility based on nothing but an unguarded expression on her face.

For weeks I wrestled with myself in silence and Isabelle put my abstraction down to work; she saw my professional success as a credit to herself. I wondered when it was that her passion for me had changed to possessiveness, she spoke of "my husband," or "the father of my children" as she would talk about her paintings: "my Daubigny." Indeed, my absorption in my work helped me to avoid looking too closely at the state of my marriage, but on the night of the dinner things suddenly came into sharp focus when I observed Isabelle, certain of always being in the right, criticize our child in front of others; and then Sylvie, shy and unsure of herself, rose to shield the girl from further humiliation. For some reason, that juxtaposition crystallized the situation for me, and when I was seated next to Sylvie at dinner it struck me suddenly that in a couple of years I would be fifty and I wanted more from life than merely going through the motions.

Abruptly I left my study and went into the drawing room. Isabelle's head was bent over her needlework, and I thought there was still time to retreat, to reconsider. But then the words were out, creating their own hard reality.

"Moving out?" Isabelle was silent for a moment. "You've taken a mistress?"

I stared at her in astonishment. The word seemed so incongruous in connection with Sylvie. No, I said, I had not, but surely Isabelle had sensed it, too, that emotionally we were already living apart.

"Look, you don't need to justify it, I won't interfere with your amusements. Just rent a place for her until it's over." Her voice was steady, though her hands trembled as she folded up her embroidery.

If only it were a question of amusement! I felt as if something momentous had happened, something terrible.

"Please don't exaggerate, men your age go through this all the time, it's banal. Who is she? Someone I've met?"

"Sylvie," I said quietly, knowing how she would react. And indeed she physically recoiled, as from a blow.

"Sylvie! Don't be absurd." After twelve years to leave her for that common girl, how could he! Her voice shook now with mortification. "Leave if you must, but there's no question of divorce, the marriage will end only when one of us dies."

As if death ended anything. Clara had been dead for more than fifteen years and I tried not to dwell on her fate, mindful of Nietzsche's warning: When you look long into the abyss, the abyss also looks into you. But sometimes, when the steam rose from a plate of choucroute, it would carry me back to my mother's kitchen in Alsace. From there I could see the neat vineyards, the ruined châteaux on the hill, the landscape I visited faithfully in my dreams, like the storks returning there year after year to nest on the chimneys. Little Clara would run out of the house to welcome the birds, amazed they had found their way back from Africa. As the storks circled over the roof, their outspread wings seemed to shade her face like a benediction. Yet Clara was murdered. Why?

Unanswered questions: the enduring legacy of the dead.

Away in London, I had been shielded from the naked horror of the roundups in Paris. Only later did I painstakingly fill in the details. A July night in 1942. Footsteps turning into rue des Rosiers, then up rue Elzévir. The peremptory knock on the door. Relief at the sight of French uniforms. *Not Germans, thank God, not the Germans. The little girls, roused from their sleep, staring at the* gendarmes *in their living room.*

Why did they give the enemy even more than they had asked for? For the love of God, why hand over the children?

The abyss did not answer. But I kept asking, all the same.

No, death did not end the conversation, it just made it one-sided. And you had to live as best you could in that great shadow, to glean what happiness still remained.

When Sylvie arrived one Thursday for Charles and Alexandra's piano lesson, Berthe told her that madame had taken the children out. Sylvie asked if she should wait and the maid shook her head. Madame left a note for you, she said. An apology, thought Sylvie, but when she opened the monogrammed envelope and pulled out Isabelle's card, she was stunned by what she read. Seeing her expression, Berthe asked if she was unwell, would she like to sit down. Sylvie shook her head and walked out in a daze.

I regret to inform you your services are no longer required. That was all. Not a word of explanation, not even a signature. Dismissed as abruptly as if she were a servant caught stealing. She was still humiliated and resentful when she received a message from Julien a few weeks later, asking her to meet him at his office. Sylvie had half a mind not to go. For the life of her, she could not figure out why she had been treated with such contempt.

It had revived a memory from her childhood that even after all these years still made her cringe: another long-anticipated evening followed by abject humiliation. She'd been so excited about attending one of Madame Wanda's musical evenings, though her mother warned her to be as quiet as a mouse and not stir from the kitchen. But Sylvie had no wish to venture out of the servants' domain with its warm and fragrant ovens, the laughing banter of the staff as they went about their tasks. Her mother grumbled that *les riches* liked to have the kitchen a long way from the other rooms to keep out the smells of cooking, but when she carried the tureens down the drafty corridor to the table, Monsieur always complained that the food was cold.

The chef, deftly fashioning *pâte d'amande* into *petit fours*, said, *"Open wide, chouchou,"* and popped pieces of bright green marzipan into Sylvie's mouth. "Nothing but the best for Madame," said the cook, "she did all right for herself, didn't she? A penniless *émigrée* and look at her now, dripping with diamonds and *tout* Paris crowding here for her candlelit *soirées*. What she spends on candles could feed an entire village for a month, but they can afford it, can't they? Monsieur's factories profited from the war, made him a fortune."

Ewa shot him a warning glance as Monsieur's valet came in; Pierre was known to carry tales, he could get them both dismissed. Pierre lifted an eyebrow at finding Ewa's daughter in the kitchen, and Sylvie cringed at her mother's obsequious smile, at her voluble excuses. But after Pierre left, Ewa defended Madame, with whom she felt a kinship despite the difference in their stations; as Poles, they were both outsiders in Paris, and she always made it a point to refer to the countess by her Polish title: "Monsieur may have the money, but it's not for him that *tout* Paris comes, it's for *Hrabina* Wanda. She's the one who has class, real class."

The cook laughed as he stirred the sauce, watching it like a hawk. Lifting the saucepan off the flame at the critical moment, he said, "I never met an *émigré* yet who doesn't claim a title, but *la comtesse* certainly married up, that's one way to climb the social ladder—horizontally." There was general laughter, and then the servants got busy with their tasks; once the music was over, they'd be on their toes till midnight.

Sylvie heard snatches of distant music every time the kitchen door swung open and it was like an old friend beckoning her closer, inviting her into an enchanted world whose existence she had never suspected. Ignored by everyone, she crept down the chilly corridor and hid behind the curtained doorway to listen, so lost in the music that she didn't see Monsieur till he stood directly before her, his monocle flashing with anger.

The kitchen seemed miles off, and fright kept her rooted to the spot. She stammered out words of apology, but they stuck in her throat, and to her everlasting mortification she threw up chunks of marzipan on the floor. She hung her head in shame as he looked her up and down with distaste, then turned on his heel and shut the door.

That humiliation rose in her throat again as she pushed open the great wooden portal of Maison Chenizot and walked through the first courtyard to one that lay beyond, and hesitated in front of a door with a plaque that read: *Docteur Julien Dalsace*. What could he possibly have to say to her now, what explanation could he offer for her abrupt dismissal?

Waiting for her to come in, I cautioned myself not to put too great a stock in happiness.

I knew storms did not threaten a blighted field, thieves kept away from a burgled house, and I'd imagined myself safe from further misfortune after what happened to me during my youth in Alsace. I had raced my schoolfellows up the hill to their fortified church, where they pushed open the wooden door and swarmed inside while I followed them warily past the colorful frescoes of St. Hune and the old organ where the schoolmaster played for both Catholics and Protestants at their separate services, always the music of Bach, which he said belonged to no denomination but to all the world. I read the German inscription chiseled into the great bell: When you, O Christian, hear me ring, To this church yourself do bring. *I had never seen the bell up close but would recognize its sound anywhere, as much a part of the landscape as the ruined châteaux.*

Once we were outside again, my schoolmates vaulted over the cemetery wall dividing the Catholic and Protestant dead while I gazed down at the peaceful scene of the village with its half-timbered houses. Then I felt the first blow. I spun around in shock to see them rushing at me, they had planned it all along and I had suspected nothing, certainly not this concerted assault. I heard their ragged breaths as they punched me, saw their familiar countenances transformed into something unrecognizable. A boy kicked me hard in the back, another picked up a rock, and then I no longer heard their hoarse cries, no longer saw their hateful faces, blood filled my eyes and stopped my ears.

But my scarred and sightless eye was a price I would gladly have paid to keep Clara safe; bitter irony that my parents had moved the family to Paris for safety, only to expose her to greater danger. Alas, security is always an illusion, often imperiled, easily shattered. As with my marriage: "safe as houses" until it was struck by lightning. My love for Sylvie was a sudden bolt out of a clear blue sky, a coup de foudre *that lit up my life while cleaving it in two.*

I had moved from the house at rue de Bièvre across the river to quai d'Anjou, no great distance but a decisive step all the same. It allowed me to take the same path along the river for my work at the Salpêtrière Hospital, and to return through the Jardin des Plantes with its long allée *of chestnut trees to Île Saint-Louis and my private practice at Maison Chenizot, where I waited that evening with a strange hopefulness.*

I had meant to prepare the ground, to feel Sylvie out. But when I saw her, the words came out without preamble: "I've left Isabelle."

She stared at me. What had possessed me to take such a step, to walk away from the house at rue de Bièvre? "Everything was so perfect," she said, "like a picture."

I smiled at that. A fair description of my life with Isabelle, it was picture-perfect. But the picture was une nature morte, *a still life, with every beauty except breath. And then by chance Sylvie was seated beside me one night and now my happiness depended on her being there always.*

The color fled from her cheeks as she understood my meaning. "How they must hate me," she burst out. "All three of them. And one day you'll regret it and you'll hate me, too."

I did not say "never," I knew the word was not to be found in the vocabulary of human emotions. Regret was unavoidable in any case, whether I left or whether I stayed.

Sylvie thought how impossible it would be to compensate me for what I had left behind. Didn't I realize we came from different spheres?

I said I did not see that as an obstacle, if my age was not.

But she shook her head, she knew better; even as a child she had sensed the unbridgeable chasm between our worlds. Looking at her earnest, troubled face, I thought it might be kinder to let her go, with time her love for me would fade like a pressed flower, to be taken out and sighed over occasionally.

But I could not let her leave. Yet how could I ask her to stay, she was not a woman of the world like Isabelle or Odile, but a girl of bourgeois upbringing, so very young, and of course, her shyness complicated the case. I smiled ironically at the word "case," the professional in me not entirely displaced by the lover.

"Could you do me a favor? Help me choose a piano for the children. I want them to continue their lessons on the days they're with me."

"Of course," she said, "of course." She saw it as a means of making amends, however pitiful, to the children, to Isabelle.

We visited various piano makers together and I watched closely as Sylvie rejected the Bösendorfer ("too unctuous!") and recoiled from the Schimmel's stentorian clarity, but was immediately taken with the discreet charms of the Pleyel. While she listened to the tones and voices of the instruments, I listened only to her. All this time, I made no attempt to touch her, parting with a brief handshake, and if I invited her for a cup of coffee or a drink afterward, I did not bother with commonplaces about the weather or

*the latest headlines in the papers. Since conversation was such an
ordeal for her, let it at least be worth her while.*

*I told Sylvie about a patient I was seeing, a four-year-old boy
who insisted he had been born to different parents in another town,
that his real papa was rich and let him play with coins of gold. My
colleagues dismissed it as a common case of wishful thinking, but
something had struck me as unusual, and based on the specifics of
the boy's story, I had tracked down Madame Virely in Grenoble,
asking her to verify a few particulars. She had written back,
confirming that her husband was a goldsmith but he had passed
away several years ago; sadly, they had never had children.*

*"I must admit it's baffling, but the boy refuses to give up his
delusion."*

*"Maybe he feels you're taking away the one thing that makes
him singular. My parents always wanted me to be more like the
other children, as if I needed to be 'cured' of being different. Only
Madame Wanda understood, she noticed how I hid behind the
door to listen and one day she called me into the salon to ask me
what kind of music I liked. I didn't know any of the names, so I
just said, 'The music that sounds like water.' She smiled. 'Chopin,
naturally. Did you know he was like you, half French, half Polish?
My husband always lays claim to Chopin and points out his tomb
at Père-Lachaise, but though Chopin's body lies in Paris, his heart,
ah, his heart is buried in Warsaw.' And then Madame Wanda
started paying for piano lessons for me, and all of a sudden I
discovered a world where my shyness wasn't an affliction but a gift."*

Well, *I thought,* well! *But given my field, it wasn't her
confidences that surprised me, it was the way she succeeded in
drawing me out. Sylvie was interested in my work, listening with
sympathy, with understanding, her quick intelligence making up for*

the gaps in her education. And when I mentioned the directorship, she said, "You were right to refuse if it means giving up your patients, that's your passion."

How different her response was from Isabelle's, but that was hardly surprising, they were opposites in every way. Isabelle was an excellent woman but not given to laughter, another reason she was easy to admire but hard to love. I told her Freud's favorite joke once, about a husband who says to his wife, "If one of us dies, I shall move to Paris." Isabelle looked at me blankly and said, "How absurd, we're already in Paris." But when I repeated the joke to Sylvie, her eyes lit up with laughter.

I took her face between my hands. "Chère amie," I said, and kissed her.

For days afterward, Sylvie replayed that thrilling moment to herself and couldn't decide which moved her more, the ardent kiss or the caressing words: *dear friend*.

Fabienne was incredulous when Sylvie told her. "You mean you haven't made love yet? What in the world do you do?"

"We talk, mostly."

"Talk? You?"

Sylvie smiled at her friend's scandalized tone. "I know it's hard to believe."

"I suppose he wants to hear all about your childhood first, *en psychologue.*"

"You're wrong, it's not *my* childhood we discuss." It suddenly struck her that after all, he *had* drawn her to speak of her own childhood, without her even being aware of it.

"Listen, sleep with him or not, just as you please, but don't skip any more rehearsals, the St. Éphrem concert is only two weeks away. And how long does it take to choose a piano for the brats, anyway, it's not as if you're picking out a Stradivarius."

"They're not brats," Sylvie protested, but she did not admit that she had known almost from the first that the piano was less about the children than about herself. And she had already made her choice.

When the Pleyel was delivered, the staircase leading to the upper floors proved too narrow and the movers had to hoist it up on a platform from the outside. Sylvie watched nervously as the piano glided over the treetops in its stately, surreal ascent, and as it came higher and higher, she thought, *If a rope should break now! If a pulley should slip!* But her fears were groundless, the movers knew what they were doing.

They brought in the instrument through the balcony and Sylvie watched impatiently as they fitted the pedals, screwed the legs back on, turned it upright. The front door had barely shut behind them when she lifted the lid and ran her fingers along the keys, the sound pure and intimate, perfectly suited to the works of Chopin. She was tongue-tied with words, but music was a language in which she could be eloquent.

As the first notes of the barcarolle filled the room, I listened intently, trying to make out something hidden behind that rippling veil of music. Only when Sylvie played the final fortissimo chords did I let out a deep breath. For the rest of my life I would remember those last notes, how they had asked "Do you?" and the answer came firm and clear, "I do."

That was us then.

And this is us now.

She plays alone in a lighted room, as I stand in the shadows below and listen to the notes drift down into the courtyard. What an affliction it is, this strange double vision.

When I lay in a hospital bed at the Salpêtrière, where I had spent much of my working life, I remarked the progression of my disease both with a scientist's detached expertise and a patient's painful helplessness. And now I consider my new state with a similar doubleness, observing how, as I am slowly being absorbed into the past, the past is also being absorbed into me.

The particularities of my life are gradually dissolving into a general undifferentiated flow like the mingled waters of tributaries and distributaries, time a river no lock-tender can sluice as it floods its banks, blurring the lines between then *and* now *into a continuous present, its swirls and eddies buffeting me into other times, other lives.*

But sometimes the water flings up an object from the depths which snags itself on a rock to arrest the ceaseless flow, and I cling fiercely to that rock, which tethers me still to this life, this world: a quest cut short but not abandoned, and a yearning for Sylvie that is quickened to life by the music.

Ever since he heard her play, Will has been gripped by a strange fascination with Sylvie. He studies her surreptitiously, casting an eye over her letters as he brings up the mail. Every time he hears Sylvie's door open, he steps out on some pretext or other and sees how she squares her shoulders before going downstairs, as if it's a daily struggle to face the world.

Observing her so constantly, he feels he knows Sylvie better than he actually does, which is why when he casually mentions his work to her one day, it all comes tumbling out, how he must finish the revisions to his manuscript this summer, as incoming department chair he'll be swamped in the fall, and then there's all the paperwork for the adoption, after ten years of trying to conceive, they're finally ready to adopt. Will stops, feeling foolish for having confided his disjointed anxieties at great length to a stranger, but Sylvie doesn't seem to find it odd as she listens to him with such sympathy, such understanding.

"It'll change our lives forever and maybe I'm too old for this transition."

To his dismay, Sylvie's eyes fill with tears and he feels like kicking himself for his thoughtlessness, his concerns so trivial in the face of her great transition. But before he can stammer out his apologies, she excuses herself abruptly and shuts the door.

Ridiculous, Sylvie thinks, to let it affect her, the American meant no harm. She was naïve to assume that having people next door would be a safeguard against self-harm, nothing more. But the presence of someone in the abstract is entirely different from coming face-to-face with people, dealing with their questions, their curiosity. How can they understand anything of her life if they don't know what Julien had been to her? She can't begin to tell them, her eloquence lies in music, not in words.

Too old, Will had said, and he not yet forty! Thankfully, Julien had never felt that way; at forty-eight, he had taken a leap into the unknown to start a new life with her. Sylvie had never once thought him too old, not then, not thirty years later. Only when she saw the X-ray of his lungs did she become suddenly aware that Julien was seventy-seven years old, would not live to be seventy-eight.

Thirty years. How short in retrospect, though more than twice as long as he had been with Isabelle, and yet Sylvie still thought of her as the rightful wife. Which she was, of course, she had never agreed to a divorce, and even when enough years had passed that Julien no longer needed her consent, it was Sylvie who had said, *"Let it be, let it be."* Let Isabelle have the artifacts of the failed marriage, Sylvie had the man himself. And the children . . . she had often said she loved Julien's children as if they were her own, it was the same thing. But now she wonders, is it the same, does it even come close? Every time they visit her, she knows they will also cross the bridge to rue de Bièvre, where Isabelle will be waiting for *her* children, while Sylvie can never say the words *"my children,"* or even *"my husband's children,"* or even *"my husband."*

But she is grateful, at least, that during Julien's great illness she found the words to tell him what he was to her, the sun, dazzling her with his light, warming her with his warmth, that without him every morning of her life would be filled with bleakness, she could not bear it, and it broke her heart when he put his arms around her and said gently, "One survives, somehow." And now she realizes why Will's remarks have cut her to the quick: She's going through the dreary motions of existence with no idea how to make it a life worth living.

Of all her empty days, Sundays are the worst, knowing that in other homes children gather at their parents' table for the ritual *dimanche en famille*. Music had always created an exalted space where her spirit found solace, but it no longer seems enough; now she seeks comfort in the nearby church, destroyed by lightning and tempests and fire but rebuilt time and again as a bulwark against despair. As the sun slants through the stained-glass windows, Sylvie's eyes remain fixed on the Hebrew letters spelling out the name of God: I AM.

I follow her gaze, but the words offer no consolation to my spirit.
When I was alive, I stubbornly refused to bow my head before
man or God, and death has not muted my quarrel with authority.
I feel a now familiar eddy and swirl of memories not my own, but
which have taken up residence in me through the osmosis of death.
I see a king pacing this strip of land which one day will bear his
name and I recognize that ascetic face, that emaciated frame.
Louis IX is wearing a hairshirt and clutching his breviary, proud
of his reputation for piety, consumed with his hatred of infidels.
He rides to the Crusades abroad, he roots out unbelievers at home,
and decrees that Jews must wear a yellow insignia which will make
it easier to find them and expel them once and for all. But it's not
enough that France should be a Christian nation, the French must
be true Christians.

It amazes me that the same king who built the exquisite
Sainte-Chapelle to house a crown of thorns and a fragment of the
true cross should welcome the Inquisition into France. I would have
thought these hallowed relics arguments against torture, not for it.
But what I view as stunning hypocrisy, the Holy See regarded quite
differently; for his relentless piety Louis IX was awarded an honor
higher than his earthly throne: In 1297, he became the only French
king canonized by Rome.

That's what the world calls him now: Louis the Saint.

For whom this church is named. Where Sylvie kneels,
contemplating the words: I AM.

The answer to a prayer, if one is a believer.

Which I am not.

But I do believe in an enduring and intertwined life greater than the little lives we lead, so small, so separate. Like the island I love, once a spit of land fit only for grazing cows and fighting duels. A bridge is all it took to create this storied isle, where moneyed Rothschilds opened their doors, where penniless writers wrote their books, where Marie Curie worked on the radiation that saved countless lives but claimed her own. On this isle, Chopin played and Wagner composed, Baudelaire and Gautier and Voltaire wrote, Daubigny, Corot, and Chagall painted, Camille Claudel chiseled her way to madness, and thousands of ordinary people lived and loved and died, their names obliterated by time. All on one small island in but one city. How much more the world.

Alice runs with a long, easy stride around the island, glad that this early in the morning there are few cars about, except for the streetsweeper's truck spraying torrents of water to wash away the dog droppings from the previous day. Mist rises off the river, the poplars rustle in the breeze, and the perspiration dries on her skin as soon as it forms. Even in the heart of Paris, one can almost imagine oneself in the country, especially at the weekly markets with their mounds of earthy vegetables, the pig snouts garnished with parsley, the wild strawberries that perfume the air. Her favorite is the covered Marché des Enfants Rouges, but when she asks who were the red children, no one seems to know.

Returning from the market one Sunday, Will and Alice find the courtyard filled with birdsong, Ana Carvalho has brought out her birdcages now that the weather is fine. She would let the birds fly about in the courtyard, she tells them, but a raptor carried off one of her darlings once, so now she is more careful. Have they seen the kestrels nesting at Notre Dame? Now, *that's* a sight worth the airfare to Paris.

She removes a singing finch from its cage and holds it in her hand. Will smiles as Ana croons to the bird and it responds with ecstatic cheeps. This was what he had hoped for—real people living real lives, scenes they would never have witnessed if they stayed at a hotel. He had just passed lines of tourists queuing up at Berthillon's for ice cream and he could not help thinking that on previous trips he and Alice had been like them, clutching

Michelin maps and museum guides, perennial onlookers rather than participants. But on this balmy Sunday, Will feels he is finally penetrating the polished surface of the city. He hopes to go deeper still, to be invited inside a home, though Fabienne says it's rare for an outsider to cross the threshold.

Sylvie returns from church dreading the long afternoon ahead. She sees Will and Alice in the courtyard and thinks of asking them over for lunch, a simple *fortune du pot*, whatever is on hand. But just then the judge and his wife drive in, and Sylvie loses her nerve and hurries upstairs.

After thirty years, the Cheroiseys still make her feel like an impostor, smuggled into this aristocratic enclave under false pretenses, unremarkable in every way and unworthy of their acquaintance.

Nonsense, Julien said, she was remarkably fine, remarkably brave.

Brave? Surely Julien was making fun of her—everyone knew how she shrank from the world.

But he was perfectly serious. *"Coeur de lion,"* he said.

It seemed meager comfort whenever she came across the haughty couple who looked her up and down with such disdain. Once Madame de Cheroisey had knocked on their door to ask if Docteur Dalsace would speak to the concierge about her birds; the courtyard was white with droppings and the smell was *"très nasty."* She liked to sprinkle English words into her conversation like parsley on potatoes. Julien said that certainly Sylvie would have a word with Ana Carvalho. Léonie de Cheroisey recoiled. "Yes," she said sourly, "one can see they're *très* chummy." And indeed Sylvie felt more at ease with Ana Carvalho than she did with the patrician inhabitants of the building. She had often stopped by for coffee in the concierge's *loge*, but after all these years, she had never entered the Cheroisey apartment and had spoken to them only on the stairs or in the courtyard.

Now, rinsing some *mâche* leaves for a salad, Sylvie glances down into the courtyard where the Americans are chatting with the Cheroiseys, who ration their smiles as if they'll run out of them if they aren't careful, while the Taylors laugh with their usual happy exuberance. But perhaps she is romanticizing the Taylors' marriage as she once romanticized Isabelle and Julien's. With a sigh, she turns back to her lunch, but the *mâche*, still squeezed tight in her hands, is bruised and discolored.

Abruptly, Sylvie pushes away her plate and goes to Julien's desk. She slides open the secret drawer and pulls out the sealed envelope, uncertainly turning it over in her hand as she remembers Isabelle's strange summons right after Julien's death. Sylvie had hurried across the bridge, Coco trotting at her heels as she turned onto the familiar street, patrolled by *gendarmes* now that one of its inhabitants, François Mitterrand, had become president. But when she reached Isabelle's house, she remembered they were supposed to meet in the public garden next door. As soon as he saw the NO DOGS sign that barred him from all the city's most inviting patches of grass, Coco heaved a deep sigh and flopped down on the pavement outside as Sylvie went in through the gate.

Isabelle was already seated on a bench, reading a magazine. She still cut a handsome figure, though the pitiless sunlight revealed her thinning hair, her papery skin. Unaccountably, Sylvie felt a lump come into her throat. They shook hands formally, and Isabelle's distinctive perfume lingered on Sylvie's hand.

The hortensia bushes were in full bloom, and their white

lacecaps nodded in the breeze. It was so quiet that they could hear bees buzzing in the vine that clambered over the garden walls.

"I imagine the last few months have been difficult," Isabelle said. At least her voice was still the same, clear and carrying.

Sylvie nodded. Seeing Julien suffer was unbearable, she would gladly have driven them both off the embankment into the freezing waters of the Seine. But they had sold the car, and Julien was hooked up to machines at Salpêtrière, and all she could do was sit there and keep watch, so that at first it had seemed like a relief when the doctor led her out into the courtyard shaded by sycamores and said it wouldn't be long now. She had nodded, thinking anything would be better than this prolonged and final leave-taking. But when the moment came, she found herself utterly unprepared.

"At least he's no longer in pain," said Isabelle. Her face was impassive, but she clasped and unclasped her hands in her lap. Seeing her agitation, Sylvie reached out to touch her arm, but Isabelle's stiffness rebuffed any acknowledgment of sympathy.

They both looked up as a young man pushed a perambulator into the park. Coco slipped in behind him, his tail wagging in triumph as he sniffed the forbidden bushes and settled himself at their feet. The three of them watched the man as he circled the park, oblivious of their presence, looking in the dustbin, running his hand along the walls and benches. Despite the warm weather, he was wearing a hat and overcoat, and his wrists sticking out from the sleeves betrayed his desperate thinness. He picked up a cigarette butt from the ground and tossed it into the carriage. In sudden panic, Sylvie looked at the pram, but thankfully it showed no signs of a baby's presence, only the shaming detritus of an adult life. Without once meeting their eyes, the man pushed open the gate and walked out again.

"They're everywhere now," said Isabelle, "the homeless."

Sylvie nodded, waiting for her to reveal the reason for their meeting.

"It's not easy, what I wanted to discuss."

Alarmed by her tone, Sylvie said, "The children . . . Is something wrong?"

"No, no, they're fine. But it does concern them, after all." Isabelle paused, her hands twisting nervously again. "I must confess I've been worrying about the will."

"But why? You know all the provisions, your lawyer approved them."

"Yes, but that was at Alexandra's wedding, there might be a later one."

"No, absolutely not, it's the same bequests." Sylvie could not understand Isabelle's sudden concern about money. Julien had been more than fair, and in addition to everything else, his pension would go to Isabelle as the "official" widow.

Isabelle was looking at her closely. "You're sure?"

"Yes."

She gestured down the street. "The house . . ."

"It belongs to you and the children, of course."

Isabelle's hands were suddenly still. "And the apartment?"

Sylvie was taken aback. What did the apartment on quai d'Anjou have to do with Isabelle? "Charles and Alexandra will inherit it, but for now it's unquestionably mine."

"What about the painting?"

"Painting?" Sylvie stared at her in bewilderment. Isabelle

must know Julien couldn't bear to look at paintings, not since his sister died. "He mentioned a valuable painting, but that's already yours, isn't it?"

"The Daubigny," said Isabelle, smiling. "Yes, that's mine, evidently. A wedding gift from my father." She rose to her feet. Whatever she had come in pursuit of, she seemed satisfied and ready to leave.

Despite herself, Sylvie felt the old yearning. As if reading something in her eyes, Isabelle's own face softened. "Poor Sylvie," she said.

And Sylvie wept. This was all she had wanted from Isabelle, the faintest hint of forgiveness.

"Poor child," Isabelle said, putting her arm around Sylvie's shoulder, and Sylvie leaned into the older woman's embrace. "Are you disappointed you didn't get it all? Everyone always said you were with him only for his money. Odile was sure you would become pregnant so that he could pay you off, as one does. But I knew even then that wouldn't be enough, you wanted it all, didn't you, my poor Sylvie?"

Sylvie gasped with shock and tried to block her ears. But it was too late, the poisonous words spoken so pleasantly had already penetrated her bloodstream, and they coursed through her veins, insidious, corrosive.

Half asleep in the sun, Coco pricked up his ears at the signals of distress emanating from Sylvie. But from whom was he to protect her? The malodorous man had already left, so he drew the only possible conclusion. Quick as a flash, he sprang to his feet and bit her attacker on the leg.

"Coco!" Sylvie swatted him with the magazine and he fell back, yelping in surprise.

"It's nothing, the merest scratch," said Isabelle, waving away Sylvie's apologies as she dabbed the wound with a handkerchief.

After their hasty exit, Sylvie scolded Coco. "No biting. *Jamais.*"

He tucked his tail between his legs, his eyes liquid with hurt. She knelt down to pat him, but he crept away. "I'm sorry," she said. All the way home, he walked on the opposite pavement, refusing to acknowledge her apologies. But once they were home, he came up and licked her hand with the perfect forgiveness to which humans can only aspire.

Still turning the envelope over in her hands, Sylvie wonders why Isabelle had asked about a painting if it already belongs to her. Is there another one that belongs to Julien? Or is Isabelle's probing about testaments and bequests only a distraction, the real contest between them for the right to Julien's remains? Not his bones, of course, which rest peacefully at the Cimetière de Passy, no, not the body, this is not a Greek tragedy after all, there has been no blood. Yet Sylvie cannot shake the fear that a great reckoning is still to come, that Isabelle is resolved on dispossessing her, as she had once felt herself dispossessed. Legally Isabelle cannot evict her, that much is certain. Then why is she filled with dread?

Sylvie draws a deep breath, opens the folder, and flips through the checkbook register, which shows a regular sum withdrawn every month. She wouldn't have given it a second thought if it weren't for Isabelle. But now those constant payments over the course of decades seem suspicious. And if there was an innocent explanation, why hadn't Julien told her?

She stares at the initial *M* on the sealed envelope and, struck by an idea, picks up the phone. It rings for a long time, but there is no answer, and Sylvie hangs up, a little ashamed that it has taken her own concerns for her to call the Gouffroys. They have enough to bear these days, she should have inquired after Max sooner. *M*, she thinks, *M for Max*. Again she dials the number of Julien's old colleague, and this time Sabine Gouffroy answers. She was just feeding Max, she says, it's a daily struggle, the only way she can lure him to the table is by playing opera, and then he becomes engrossed in the singing and eats docilely enough. "After all these years with him, I've picked up a smattering of psychology myself," Sabine says. "And how have you been, my dear?" She listens to Sylvie's story of the envelope and then says slowly, "Julien was the first one to notice Max's troubles, he knew my husband couldn't connect two thoughts anymore, let alone two words, so he definitely wouldn't leave a letter for him. But it might not be *for* anyone at all, maybe it's only a keepsake. Why don't you just look inside?"

"I suppose I could."

"Don't take this amiss, but you're lucky Julien went the way he did, all his wits about him. Not like my poor Max. The funny thing is, he still looks the same, but I know it's not Max at all, I'm living with a hollow man, a mere shell."

After they hang up, Sylvie stares unseeingly before her, trying to imagine what it would be like to have Julien still by her side, *a mere shell*, emptied out of everything except the faint murmur of the sea.

With a sudden movement, she rips open the sealed envelope and draws out a photograph of a young girl, her eyes shining, her lips parted. A stranger, yet uncannily familiar. The dark hair, the eyes so much like Julien's. Clara, killed in the gas chambers at Auschwitz, and exhumed now by the merest chance.

Sylvie glances briefly at the other papers in the envelope, a card with two lines of poetry, addressing Julien as *cher ami* and signed simply *Marie*; a scrap of Julien's stationery scribbled with a street name—rue Elzévir—but with the number torn off; and on a blank sheet of paper the single word "Belleville." The sight of his handwriting sends a shock through her, and she is deceived into believing that he is still somewhere in the apartment, in his study perhaps. *"Julien!"* she cries. Coco comes bounding into the room. She drops the papers and buries her face in his coat, his heart beating against hers in mute sympathy.

Then her eyes fall again on Clara's photograph lying at her feet. A sudden current of air lifts the deckled edge, and from that angle it looks as if her parted lips are about to speak. Sylvie feels the hair rise on the back of her neck. A strange trick of the light has brought out a resemblance which escaped her earlier: with the shadows partly obscuring her face, the dark-haired girl could be mistaken for Sylvie herself.

I see a look on Sylvie's face that terrifies me. In the aftermath of my death, she would lean out of the window or stare down at the river with the same look and I felt a desperate clutch of fear, fleeing from these streets in order to safeguard her from myself.

But where could I hide in a city where sooner or later you cross paths unexpectedly with everyone you know? For me, the only safe distance is not spatial at all but temporal. In the distant past, I am rendered harmless; all who lived then are now on the same side of the great gulf and free from mortal danger. I can slip into and out of those lives with impunity, their ending already a fait accompli. If in the past other spirits have unwittingly harmed those they love, I shall remain entirely blameless, a mute witness, nothing more; it is only in the present that my apparition poses a threat to the living.

Every time I saw Sylvie at Pont Marie gazing fixedly at the water, my threat to her seemed frighteningly real. A strong current of agitation swept me into another century as Sylvie's features deliquesced into Delphine's, leaning over the same bridge staring at her reflection in the river.

Delphine! She has been dead for a hundred years, yet I see her face clearly, the inquisitive gleam in her eye, the knowing smile on her lips. Delphine often gets her ear twisted for listening at doors, for riffling through the patronne's *papers, but she is incorrigible. In the courtyard behind the laundry, washerwomen string their clotheslines from the chestnut trees; the day is fine and the sheets will dry faster outside than by the stove. Delphine pesters them for* stories about the washerwomen's ball, asks who will be crowned this year's laundress queen. They laugh and gossip, glad to rest their aching backs and their chapped hands for a moment.

The mutilated veteran leans out of his window to ogle the girls with their skirts lifted and tucked around their waists to keep them dry. Life is sweet now, he thinks, looking at their plump limbs, not like it was barely twenty years ago, the city under siege by the Prussians and everyone starving, the poor people eating rats and cats, the rich their beloved racehorses, even the elephants from the zoo weren't spared, what were their names again, oh, yes, Castor and Pollux, well, his memory is still sharp, even though he's only half a man now, the rest blown away by a Prussian rifle, for all the good it did, Bismarck snatched Alsace-Lorraine all the same, and five billion francs' indemnity on top! The veteran goes to the Place de la Concorde every year with a wreath for the statue of Strasbourg still covered in black crêpe, but you can't go on mourning forever, and by God, look at those girls, with bottoms round and sweet as melons.

One of the girls starts singing "Plaisir d'amour," and the others join in the chorus. The patronne seated behind her cash box shakes her head, amour, amour, that's all these girls think about, but she goes back to counting her receipts and lets them stay out in the courtyard a little longer.

The widow Cornu's establishment is reminiscent of the laundries of yesteryear, a true lavanderie, redolent of lavender. Modern lavoirs have sprung up all over the city now that the floating bateaux-lavoirs are being phased out, but the fine ladies of the quarter fear what all the steam and chemicals will do to their heirlooms and send their monogrammed linen and lace to Madame Cornu's, where laundresses still wash the old-fashioned way, their arms up to the elbows in suds, using only the best soap from Marseilles and a special paste of Madame's own devising instead of the corrosive eau de javel *to bleach out stains. The widow's reputation is impeccable, and you can be certain Madame Cornu's girls don't wear their customers' dresses, or worse yet, rent them out. Their laundry comes back immaculate, the clothes scented with lavender, the linen with orris root.*

From six in the morning to eight in the evening, Delphine is wanted everywhere at once, by Clémence at the washboard, Henriette at the ironing table, Madame Cornu at the caisse, *and she flies around the laundry, adding wood to the stove, measuring out soap for the tub, scraping beeswax into the starch so the iron glides smoothly over the men's shirts and ladies' muslins. She can total the accounts quicker than the* patronne, *and it is Delphine who suggests they should charge extra for* garniture. *Madame nods approvingly, hers is a* laverie de luxe, *after all, not a wash house for men with only one shirt who have to wait on the premises while it's washed and dried. Delphine is right, from tomorrow she will charge an additional thirty centimes for frills and lace, it's a small return for the charity she has shown the foundling left on her doorstep. Clémence winks at Henriette, some charity, feeding her on scraps and letting her sleep in the laundry. But what can you expect, the* patronne *cast off her own daughter, and people say Delphine is the love child of that disgraced girl whom nobody has heard from since.*

On mild days, the old soldier limps into the courtyard, and Madame rises from behind the caisse *as a mark of respect to the veteran with his mutilated limbs and scarred face. She offers him a glass of wine and they discuss General Boulanger's prospects for the presidency, agreeing he's the only one with the guts to wrest*

Lorraine and Alsace back from Bismarck's filthy hands. They look up as the postman comes into the courtyard and before the mutilé can ask, he shakes his head, no letter for the soldier.

After the laundry closes for the night, Delphine sweeps the soap scum from the gutter and gathers up the newspapers. Boulanger, Boulanger, his name is on every lip, he's stoking people up with his talk of revenge, trying to ride that popular wave right into the Élysée Palace, especially now that the decorations scandal has forced President Grévy to resign, though he swears up and down he had no idea his son-in-law was selling the Legion of Honor for cash. That makes her laugh, but still she is awed by the power of public revelations, how they can bring down the president of the republic, might yet hustle the nation back to war. She throws the journals into the stove, but the warmth lasts only an instant, it's paper after all, not wood. As she shivers under her thin blanket, she thinks of poor old scarface waiting hopefully for a letter, when everyone knows his son won't waste a stamp on him.

But one day a letter does come. The postman, the washerwomen, and Madame herself wait expectantly in the courtyard as the veteran hobbles in with his shirt undone, rips open the envelope, and kisses the letter, wetting it with tears. Delphine observes his scarred features and feels a flare of intuition. She picks up the crumpled envelope and blurts out, "But, Monsieur, your son is in Marseille and this was posted in Paris." And everyone recoils at the words, but it is from Delphine they turn away, not the pathetic old father who writes to himself to cover up for his son's neglect.

The other girls are uneasy now in Delphine's presence; there's something sinister in her ability to ferret out secrets. Not just the ordinary secrets of the lavanderie, mind you, where people's dirty linen is aired in public: a christening gown that follows too soon after a bridal veil; the viscount's embroidered handkerchiefs sent in by a lady other than his wife. The girls recall certain indiscretions of their own—an affair, an abortion, a disease of a private nature—for which Madame would dismiss them on the spot, look what she did to her own daughter. To avoid those moments of unguarded friendship when secrets are bound to slip out, Henriette no longer curls Delphine's hair, Clémence no longer brightens her drab gown with ribbons, Véronique and Mado stop taking her to admire the window displays at Au Bon Marché, or to mock Monsieur Eiffel's monstrous tower going up for the exposition next year.

Left out by the other girls, Delphine retreats into grandiose fantasies. She has heard the rumors about her birth, and she dreams of a deathbed reconciliation between Madame and the cast-off daughter, of being restored to her rightful place, of sitting at the caisse *like the* patronne. She redoubles her attentions to Madame, anticipating her wishes even before the words are out of her mouth, a tisane when she is feeling poorly, a glass of mulled wine when she has a cold. But perhaps Delphine's too-lively interest in the widow's health alarms her, for one day Madame's niece and her husband show up with their young son. The husband looks over the premises and the laundresses' charms with a proprietary air. His dissipated face is handsome still, and staring at it, Delphine feels the old flare of intuition. This is the man who seduced Madame's daughter right under her nose, and it's amazing that others don't notice what is so evident to Delphine, the resemblance to herself in the high forehead, in the large brown eyes, in the curve of his lips. The son sees her sitting by herself in a corner, and wants to know who she is. Oh, the foundling, his father says indifferently, she's nobody.

This time, Delphine hugs her new secret close to her chest.

Lying on her cot at night, she wonders what will happen if she drops a word in Madame's ear about her niece's precious husband. But will she believe the nobody? She falls asleep and dreams that her mother has come back to claim her inheritance. "Delphine," she whispers, "Delphine," and Delphine reaches out her arms. She is somebody now, and everywhere she goes people whisper her name. Then she wakes to find herself alone, with only rats scurrying across the floor, attracted to the bucket of starch.

The next day I see Delphine strolling across the bridge and feel a pang of uneasiness. What is she doing out during working hours, has the patronne dismissed her? I draw closer as she stops to study her reflection in the river, the water wrinkling her smooth face which time will wrinkle all too soon. Ah, life is pleasant and youth is sweet, I think benevolently, dance at the laundresses' ball, ma petite, dance while you can. Lulled by the late-autumn sunlight and my own goodwill, I suspect nothing, not even when she glances mischievously over her shoulder and clambers up on the parapet. And then, to my horror, she disappears from view. I reach out to save her, a gesture both reflexive and futile. But she is playing a dangerous game, only crouching in a niche below. She cries out in triumph as a reflection appears beside hers, like a carp swimming up from the murk.

"Don't look," I want to plead, "don't look." But it is too late, she gazes longingly at the face she sees, a face so like her own. The world spins slowly on its axis, the sun slants into the river, the water flows toward the sea, but for one long moment she freezes into immobility as she looks into the reflected visage, searching the depths for secrets not meant for the living.

When was it she first sensed her mother's presence? During those long winter nights in the laundry when a draft fanned the dying *coals into flame? On still summer days in the courtyard when a sudden breeze lifted her hair? How cleverly she has flushed her out! But only those about to join our ranks can see us; and once they have, there is no retracing one's steps.*

Delphine holds on to the coping and pulls herself back. Wrapped in her thoughts, she stands there as the sun sinks into darkness, streetlamps cast their pools of light, and windows glow with the warmth that attracts all wanderers home. But she is homeless and alone, with only her mother's ghost for company.

Her face is pale as plaster in the lamplight and her mother bends to kiss her forehead, the first caress that lonely girl has known. Delphine turns back toward the river, her countenance transfigured by a smile of such beauty that I could weep. Then she climbs up on the parapet, closes her eyes, and leaps into the water, breaking the surface once, twice, thrice, before the undertow carries her away, leaving behind only the aftershock of ripples. And then the water is smooth again.

She has the same smile on her face when she is displayed on a slab at the morgue. Curious spectators jostle one another before her corpse, and a buzz of speculation fills the air. "They gaffed her at quai de Louvre, drowned recently I reckon, see that smooth skin, it would have peeled right off if she soaked too long." But the voices fall silent as they look at her peaceful face. They say even the mortician, hardened to such cases, wept when he saw the unknown woman fished out from the Seine.

No one comes forward to claim the body. She is buried in a pauper's grave, abandoned in death as she was in birth. But her death mask sells briskly. Everywhere I turn I'm confronted by a thousand Delphines, she has become a rumor dispersed around the city. No one knows her name; they call her L'Inconnue de la Seine.

It becomes the fashion for young girls to copy her appearance, for young men to write sonnets to the unknown beauty. I cannot dispel the last sight of Delphine's face, the sound of her body hitting the water, and yet the river flows as it has always done, undisturbed by one body more or less when so many thousands have been cast into its depths.

I have learned from the mistakes of the past: Sylvie must not see me. I forced myself to hide from her in uncongenial corners of the city, in obscure patches of history, condemning myself to the long ache of exile. I missed the sight of her dear face, the sound of Schubert from her window. Yet I resolved to keep away from those peaceful quays until it was safe to be in her company again.

What an effort it had cost me then to banish myself from Sylvie's presence till the waves of madness receded; only when the danger had passed did I return to this stretch of quay. But now I wonder if I have underestimated her fragility, if I have come back too soon. I had felt a deep ambivalence about burdening Sylvie with the sorrows of my past, about drawing her into the obsessive and futile quest that my death had brought to an end. With her accidental discovery of the folder, fate had taken the decision out of my hands.

But when I see the bleakness on Sylvie's face, I fear that finding the envelope might tip the scales of a mind still precariously balanced between life and death. Must I leave here again, so that if by chance she turns her head . . . but she does not.

Sylvie crosses the bridge to the Left Bank without lingering by the river, without feeling its pull. She enters the Jardin des Plantes, hurries down the *allée* of chestnuts, and stops at the entrance to the Hôpital Pitié-Salpêtrière, where a wave of grief so strong washes over her that she feels unable to move. She knows that reminders of her loss lurk everywhere, triggered sometimes by a memory, sometimes by nothing at all. Grief still ambushes her every morning when she reaches for Julien, and each time the realization hits her afresh. Never again will she wake to find Julien by her side. *Never again.* Never again will he walk home by that path from the hospital where he had been a doctor for so long and a patient before his death. *Never again.* In the immediate aftermath of her loss, those words had led her to the brink of madness, and she wondered how many women locked up howling at the Salpêtrière in a different time were only mad with grief, how many women even now in the modern hospital on the grounds of the old insane asylum were only mad like her, being treated in the psychiatric ward by someone like Julien.

But it was Isabelle's words that had pushed her over the brink: *with him only for his money.* How patiently Isabelle had waited to exact her revenge, how unerringly she had struck when Sylvie was most vulnerable. For Sylvie the house on rue de Bièvre had always existed on a different plane, a vision seen through a window, and she had yearned to be part of that world; but Julien's leaving had destroyed that vision, had broken that world into fragments. People might wonder what he saw in Sylvie that compelled him to wreck his marriage, but no one could doubt what she saw in him, no one could wonder why *she* had fallen in love. And now Isabelle had made a mockery of that love, turned it into something shabby, something sordid. Surely Isabelle was wrong, surely people hadn't thought that of her. Julien hadn't. But never again could she ask him, never again would he reassure her. *Never again.* The words were like a ceaseless chord in the silent apartment, turning it into a deafening bedlam from which death offered refuge, like the bitter comfort of cyanide to captured *résistants*. Looking down from the balcony at the iron spikes below, she would gather herself to fly through the air. Or she would stare at the river, swift and dark. One graceful leap, and then sudden, blessed silence.

And then, after weeks of such torment, Sylvie had heard a sound, a bar of music, separate and distinct from the din in her mind. A shimmering phrase that hovered tantalizingly in the air, just beyond her reach. It was drowned out again, but she knew that it existed now, on the other side of madness.

Some months later, a passing car stopped on the quay and she heard it again on the radio, that achingly lovely phrase, then the one that followed, then the one after that, and nine wistful bars later, the cello gliding into the conversation, both voices mingling in a liquid stream that drew her beyond tumult and sorrow to a consoling expanse of calm. Many years ago she and Fabienne had played that Schubert sonata at St. Éphrem for an audience made up of pensioners from the nearby *maison de retraite*, who listened as if the music could restore to them all that had been robbed by age and infirmity. That memory recalled her to her senses. Reluctantly she had turned her face from the river, from the iron spikes, from the temptation to leap. She shuttered her windows and contemplated the long years ahead.

Fabienne's remedy was perpetual motion, and indeed dividing up the apartment had kept Sylvie occupied for weeks, but the mindless activity tired her without engaging her interest. Fabienne called frequently, and sent her postcards filled with brief imperatives—*don't mope, keep busy, start teaching*. Sylvie knew she should resume the piano lessons she had given up during Julien's illness, but she didn't feel ready, not yet, the music still too closely tied to him. But when the folder came to light, she had felt the first stirrings of curiosity.

No, she thinks now, it was much more than curiosity, it was the beginning of a quest. Making sense of its contents might help her reclaim Julien, might stifle the sound of Isabelle's words. But most of all, the photograph of Clara made Sylvie feel she might finally be able to do something *for* Julien, and she realizes what she has lacked since his death is a sense of purpose.

Sylvie turns away from the entrance to the hospital, and walks quickly down a side street, looking for the name of a bank. She enters the glass door, hands Julien's card to the receptionist, and asks for the manager. In a few minutes she is ushered into Monsieur Billey's office and she places Julien's checkbook before him. He looks through the register, at the regular sum taken out every month. There is still money in the account, not a fortune but a substantial amount, as if Julien had envisaged the payments would continue for several years.

"Yes, we had standing instructions from Docteur Dalsace for a monthly remittance to be made from this account. Every year, he reauthorized us to continue with the deposits. But we did not receive authorization last year, and the account has gone dormant."

"He passed away in the fall."

"My condolences."

Sylvie wonders if he can tell her into whose account the money was deposited.

Monsieur Billey spreads out his hands; although refusals issue from his lips all day, he takes great care to avoid actually saying the word *non*. "*Désolé*, that information is confidential."

Sylvie asks if it is possible to reactivate the account and continue the payments.

"*Dommage*, it's not a joint account."

Sylvie thinks for a moment. "Well, could I withdraw the funds?"

"Possibly. You have a notarized copy of the will?"

Sylvie has come prepared with all the necessary paperwork. Monsieur Billey glances through the will.

"And the death certificate?"

As she hands it over, she thinks sadly, it's all that is left of a man's life in the end, dates on paper scanned indifferently by a stranger's eyes.

"And the marriage certificate?"

Sylvie hesitates. "I'm afraid I don't have it."

"In that case, *je regrette*, Madame . . ."

Sylvie gathers all the papers and puts them back in her folder as she considers the best course of action. Perhaps they can sort things out when Julien's son comes to Paris in the fall, Charles is a banker himself, he will know what to do.

Monsieur Billey repeats that he is *désolé* he cannot help her further. "It is not I who makes the rules, you understand, but I have to follow them, evidently."

Evidently. An image flashes into Sylvie's mind, Isabelle brandishing the marriage certificate at the bank manager. *That's mine, evidently,* she says, and dormant accounts come to life like seeds waiting for rain, vault doors open wide to reveal their secrets and disgorge their contents into Isabelle's waiting hands. Sylvie sighs and rises to her feet. But the thought of being powerless to do something for Julien awakens a fierce streak of resistance. Whoever the recipient, whatever the reason, Julien thought it important enough that he hadn't missed a single payment for more than forty years.

Sylvie takes a deep breath and says, "I would like to open my own account here." She signs all the forms and writes out a clear set of instructions: the amount remitted from Julien's account is to go now from *her* account to the same recipient. "I suppose you cannot tell me even now who that is?"

"*Désolé* . . ."

But if the person wants to contact Sylvie, can the bank manger put them in touch?

"Yes," he says. "Yes, you can be sure of that."

It might turn out to be nothing, she thinks. Someone Julien was helping out, repayment of an old debt, completely innocuous remittances. But the seed of suspicion that Isabelle had so skillfully planted has borne its toxic fruit. Sylvie can still hear the terrifyingly casual tone in which Isabelle had talked about paying off a servant in the family way, *as one does.* Had Julien had a child outside his marriage? Were these payments over decades intended to maintain that child? To support a former mistress? She may never find out. Is she even sure she wants to know? She's afraid of what it might say about Julien, about their life together, that he could keep something so momentous from her. Was there a side to his character that she'd never suspected, something that would diminish him in her eyes, would take the edge off the fineness she had always admired? She can't bear to look back on the life they lived through this prism of doubt.

But it's done now, she has sent out a flare into the darkness. Leaving the bank, Sylvie thinks it's unlikely Julien's wife will ever discover what she has done. If she knew, perhaps Isabelle would take back those ugly words: *with him only for his money.* She shakes her head and thinks wryly that it's ridiculous how much time she spends brooding about Isabelle, when it's doubtful Isabelle has ever given her a second thought.

But seeing Sylvie after all this time had shaken Isabelle much more than she had imagined. All the old bitterness had risen to the surface, like frogs hiding in mud till the ice thawed. She remembered as if it were yesterday the moment she realized Julien was never coming back.

At first she was confident the affair would blow over, even though she simply couldn't understand how Julien had lost his head over a woman in every way inferior to herself. Isabelle's family and friends had warned her that Julien was "not their kind," but she had defied them to marry him, and indeed she was right, things had turned out well, Julien's work, their children, their home, no one ever declined an invitation to dine *chez* Dalsace. And Julien had walked out on it all.

Was it worth it, she wanted to ask him, was it worth it to lose everything they had together merely for the devil in the flesh that could never be appeased? At the thought of him with Sylvie, she felt an emotion that was both primitive and powerful. Surely it was not jealousy, it was inconceivable that she should be jealous of such a woman. But the emotion spread through her like loosestrife, its invasive roots choking out all thought until she felt herself drowning in that vast purple sea.

A year after he left, Isabelle still believed Julien would return to rue de Bièvre, though fewer and fewer traces of his presence remained. The fragrance of his tobacco no longer swirled into the air when the drapes were pulled back, his desk was cleared of papers. Isabelle had taken to working in his study, her tapestries and silk threads laid out on his table.

Odile often joined her there for tea in the afternoon. Berthe brought in the tea tray and poured Lapsang souchong into cups of porcelain so fine it was translucent. Helping herself to one of Berthe's *macarons*, Odile said, "These are divine, better than Ladurée."

Troublemaker, thought Berthe scornfully, everything always *divine* or *heavenly*, but the first one to carry tales, why when Monsieur left, it wasn't five minutes before she had spread the news all over the city. As for herself, she missed Monsieur Julien, a kind word for everyone, she wondered how he was getting on, could that young girl even roast a chicken, never mind anything else.

Odile questioned Isabelle about the terms of the separation, oblivious of Berthe's presence; to her, servants did not count as an audience. Isabelle did not say anything at first, one discussed finances only with one's banker. But then she said briefly that money was not an issue, Julien had been more than generous.

"Take a trip, then, get away for a bit."

Isabelle said she might go south for a couple of weeks in the fall, the children would be with Julien then.

"Don't bother with the Côte d'Azur, it's ruined. Go to Greece, find a young lover."

Berthe pursed her lips and left the room, and Isabelle said coolly that it was much too soon to think of love.

"Love, what does that have to do with women our age?" Odile twiddled Isabelle's silk threads, irritated by her friend's composure. Not that she wanted her to have hysterics, but surely it was acceptable to show a little emotion under the circumstances. A pity, Odile thought, that Isabelle hardly entertained anymore.

Understandable, but a pity all the same. Those wonderful dinners. Since Julien had left her for that creature, Lucie or Sophie or whatever her name was, Isabelle had withdrawn from society, and the sooner she started circulating again, the better. Too long a retreat, and the world finds it can get along without you.

Even after Odile had left, her remark continued to rankle Isabelle. *Women our age*. Odile had an elastic notion of age considering she was a good twenty years older. Isabelle picked through the skeins of silk she had steeped in infusions of olive leaves and weak tea to match the faded greens and browns of the old tapestry, not an original *verdure* by Oudry, but valuable all the same. Deftly she repaired the depredation of moths, sunlight glinting on the needle as it darted in and out. A stroke of luck that the museum had offered her this employment, it had made the last few months bearable. And of course it suited her perfectly to work from home. She looked at her surroundings with satisfaction, her eyes resting on the Daubigny she had recently moved into the study.

How soothing it was to look upon that sunlit rill; like the tapestries she worked on, an immutable landscape, a changeless France. Perhaps that's what had attracted so many to *pétainisme*, the promised return to an idyllic past. Isabelle shrugged, Julien was the analyst, not she. So brilliant at penetrating people's minds, but unable to see what was going on right under his nose, completely taken in by that sly girl.

Julien wouldn't look at paintings, he claimed that after the horrors of the war, art seemed an indulgence. Isabelle had argued he was inconsistent, he loved music, didn't he? But still, she had respected his sentiments, had left the walls of his study bare. Even now, the Daubigny rested on an easel, she hesitated to hang it in case he returned. But the silence of the house struck her suddenly and she realized she was deluding herself; Julien would not return. A sob rose in her chest and burst out into the stillness, then another, then another, grating harshly in her own ears.

When the outburst was over, her first thought was relief that Odile had not witnessed her weakness. Pathetic! But no more pathetic than the fact that she sometimes trailed the children to Île Saint-Louis and watched from a distance as they entered the iron gate with its ornate peacocks. Julien had chosen the apartment for practical reasons—close enough to rue de Bièvre that the children could walk there alone—but looking at Le Vau's legendary mansions on either side, she felt it a second betrayal that he had installed his mistress at such a desirable address.

Isabelle sat with the tapestry forgotten in her lap until Berthe came in, surprised to find her sitting in the dark. Isabelle tugged at the lamp cord, but turned her head away from the light. She did not wish the maid to notice her reddened eyelids, her tear-streaked face. With an effort she collected herself; she would not succumb to panic. That's where the danger lay, just look at Odile, fearful and foolish, with expensive young lovers who mocked her behind her back. She had no intention of turning into Odile, she had too much pride for that.

And all these years she'd handled herself *comme il faut*. But seeing Sylvie in the park, the old bitterness had come flooding back. Thirty years later, Isabelle still could not accept that Julien had turned his back on her, on the life they had built together, what a waste, what a terrible waste. And just as if he could still hear her, the reproachful words burst out: *How could you? How could you?*

*Ah, Isabelle, forgive me. I am grateful for all that you gave me,
as much as it was in your power to give. But it wasn't enough; only
when Sylvie came unsought into my life did I realize that gratitude
is not love. And it turned out that love was what I wanted. I did try,
for your sake, for the children, to continue as we were. But in the
end what drove us apart was stronger than what kept us together. It
can't have been easy for you, either, living with a man hollowed out
by grief, the horror of what happened to my sister, to her family,
casting a dark shadow on what you tried so hard to make a picture-
perfect life.*

*Sometimes, when I saw your head bent over your needlework,
the lamplight reflecting off your golden hair, I thought maybe we
had made it through, that your certitude would carry me along.
You wanted to protect the children from the past and we agreed on
a pact of silence. But the silence reverberated deafeningly within
me. I never stopped looking for answers, even though there could be
no answer, no excuse, no justification for what happened. Arsène
tried to rationalize it, but Sylvie stared him in the face and gave no
quarter. I think that's when I first noticed her, really straightened up
and took notice.*

*Why does one fall in love with one person and not another?
You might as well ask why this piece of music strikes a chord and
not that one. Desire is a mystery the dead fathom no more than the
living.*

I still see your perplexed face when I joked: "If one of us dies,

I shall move to Paris." And, after all, the joke is on me. I'm the one who died, only to find myself still in a city of light where I walk always in darkness, a shadow among shadows.

Blinding spotlights recall me to the present as a bateau-mouche *drones past, its polyglot commentary garbled by the wind, and I cannot distinguish which is the unreal vision, the flesh-and-blood life I once lived or this twilight inhabitation into which the outside world noisily intrudes.*

The lights from the boats sweep through the concierge's lodge and the false dawn sets the caged birds chirping. "Hush, my angels," says Ana Carvalho, as she looks at the invitation hand-delivered for Sylvie. Another recital, just the kind of thing Sylvie loves, but Ana knows she will not go, not alone. She would offer to go with Sylvie, but that kind of gloomy music depresses her, frankly; a *bal musette* now, that's something else, she likes a bit of dancing as much as the next person. She wonders if the Americans would care to accompany Sylvie, but maybe they only like the mournful cowboy songs one hears on the radio.

Instead of taking the invitation upstairs right away, Ana waits until Sylvie and the Taylors are both in the courtyard. Handing Sylvie the card, Ana Carvalho says, "Perhaps *les Américains* would like to accompany you?" Sylvie smiles. Could her prompting be any more transparent? But she holds out the invitation to Will and Alice and asks if they're free to join her for the recital.

"We'd love to," says Alice. "Oh, wait, it says Tuesday. Sorry, I can't, I'll be on a conference call with my department."

Meetings at night, thinks Ana Carvalho, who's all for working hard, but that's carrying things too far. Then she remembers the time difference, and realizes of course it will be afternoon there, Alice's colleagues will be working through lunch. That seems a bit excessive, too, but what can you expect from Americans, they are not reposeful people, their shops are open day and night, their television channels never shut down, no wonder they're all rolling in money, just like the show *Dallas*, she's completely hooked on it, never misses an episode.

Sylvie says, "Another time, then." She puts the invitation in her purse, thinking she must call Félix, come up with some excuse.

But Alice turns to Will and says, "You'd like to go, though, wouldn't you?"

"Absolutely."

So that's settled, then, thinks Ana Carvalho, as she goes back to watering the clivia.

Will has been looking forward to the concert, a chance to study Sylvie at close quarters for an entire evening. She seems as enigmatic to him as the city, which holds its true nature in reserve, revealing itself in secret glimpses through gates that open only to the initiated. Will's impression is confirmed when at the end of the street Sylvie turns left into an unmarked entrance. He must have walked by a hundred times without suspecting the existence of this neighborhood theater, an intimate space with three or four dozen seats at the most, too minuscule for a sloping floor, so each row of chairs has legs sawn to different heights, a solution that seems endearingly French.

A young man sees them enter and hurries toward Sylvie, his bow tie askew. *"Mademoiselle,"* Félix says, *"I'm so grateful you came."* He leads them to the first row, and as they take their seats Sylvie is thankful to have Will by her side. The first time she attended a concert with Julien, she had looked around apprehensively as if she might see Isabelle sitting by herself, and Julien, with his instinctive courtesy, would go and sit beside her. *"Illogique,"* he pointed out, because then he would leave *Sylvie* alone. Yet, after all, they never saw her; they did not go to the opera on opening night, when Isabelle was sure to be there, drawn more by the spectacle—the décor, the costumes—than the music. *And* Isabelle preferred Puccini to Mozart. One thing, at least, in which Sylvie could claim better taste.

All thanks to Madame Wanda, of course, who had taken

Sylvie's musical education in hand. For her tenth birthday, Madame had invited her to a concert as a special treat. To this day, more than forty years later, Sylvie remembers the ride in Madame's chauffeured car, the glorious view of the Eiffel Tower from the Palais de Chaillot, and once inside the packed hall the excitement that gripped her when Madame Wanda whispered, "Tonight we have a direct line to Beethoven. We're going to hear Schnabel, who studied with Leschetizky, who studied with Czerny, who studied with the master himself."

Some years later her mother's employer had arranged an audition with the legendary Nadia Boulanger. Sylvie felt her heart quail as the exacting teacher put her through her paces, then decisively shook her head. "The wrong temperament," she said. Madame Wanda looked even more dejected than Sylvie, but Nadia Boulanger was right, the strain of performing before strangers would have made Sylvie ill, she was better suited to teaching and particularly adept with children. Parents started recommending her to their friends, and that's how she came to the notice of Isabelle. But naturally, the piano lessons for Charles and Alexandra had come to an abrupt end.

As the lights dim in the little theater, there is a last-minute flurry of people taking their seats, exhaling the final puffs of the cigarettes they've thrown away outside, filling the hall with the sudden reek of smoke. Félix takes the stage and the audience, made up largely of friends and relatives, gives him an enthusiastic round of applause.

"Thank you." Félix bobs his head like a bird pecking seeds, "thank you all very much." He clears his throat and says, "I'm very honored, and, as you can imagine, very nervous, that my teacher is here tonight. She has taught me all that I know about music, and much that I know about myself. *Je vous remercie, mademoiselle.*"

Sylvie blushes at the applause and shrinks back against Will. But when Félix begins playing the barcarolle at breakneck speed, she leans forward intently. *Too fast,* she thinks, *doucement, doucement,* and as if he has heard her, he relaxes into the piece, and Sylvie nods, *Better, yes,* and she smiles approvingly at him when he brings his hands down in the final octaves.

Hearing the rhythmic applause peculiar to Paris audiences, Félix gives another of his awkward bows and says, "When Robert Schumann heard the music of Chopin, he said *Hats off, gentlemen, a genius.* And Schumann was no stranger to genius himself, as you'll hear in his Fantasy, Opus 17, inspired by the love of his life, Clara Wieck."

From the first notes, Sylvie is absorbed in the music, both a passionate declaration of love for Clara and a wrenching lament at their separation. Even when the piece ends, she sits there dazed, unable to join in the applause. She remains silent and pensive as she and Will walk back to the apartment, recalling the music's epigraph: *Sounding softly through all creation is an undying note for the secret listener.* She feels a physical ache for Julien; that's what he was to her, the pervasive note, the beloved listener.

Sylvie crosses the street and looks down at the river flowing swiftly below, as Schumann must have looked at another river in another time, another place. In the grip of madness, Schumann had thrown himself into the Rhine, and when a boatman fished him out, he defiantly flung his wedding ring into the water. From the asylum where they took him, he wrote to his wife that she should do the same; at least there in the depths they would never be parted. Sylvie still wishes that during her own spell of madness she had taken the leap, had joined Julien in death. But the time for that is past, her days of unreason over. With an effort she turns to Will. "Did you enjoy the evening?"

"I did, very much. Your pupil does you credit, but I wished it was *you* up on stage."

"Oh, no, the very thought makes me faint. Fabienne and I sometimes gave recitals together, and my bouts of stage fright before every performance drove her mad."

"Well, *she* certainly loves the limelight."

"Yes, she lives for it, the audience, the applause. But for me, the music itself is enough." As they turn into the wrought-iron gate, Sylvie puts her hand on Will's arm. "I've been thinking about what you said the other day, about the fear of transitions, do you remember? It suddenly occurred to me that in music, at least, a transition isn't like closing a door but crossing a bridge; you remain connected to what has gone before even as you move into what is to come. If that makes any sense."

"Yes," says Will, "it does, it makes perfect sense."

Hearing voices in the courtyard, Ana Carvalho parts the lace curtain at her window to look out and is gratified by the sight of Sylvie's animated face, a long way to go yet, but at least there's a glimmer of her old self.

Back in her apartment, Sylvie finds a message on the answering machine from Charles, dear boy, checking up on her. He and his sister are both so attentive, so regular with their calls and visits. Alexandra had come in early May to help set up the apartment for the Taylors. Such a pity she left before the desk was moved and the folder came to light.

It's too late to call Charles back, but she knows he will be happy to hear of her "outing"; the children worry she is turning into a recluse. They take turns to come so that there isn't too long a gap between visits, but she often wishes they would come together, it would be like old times.

Sylvie still shudders when she recalls the awkwardness of the children's first visit to quai d'Anjou, eleven-year-old Charles grave and polite, but his younger sister determined to fight Sylvie tooth and nail. And that day, of all days, Julien was held up at work and called to say he would be home late. Sylvie relayed the message to the children, and even as she said *désolée*, she knew she was apologizing not for his lateness but for something else entirely. Alexandra said furiously, "This isn't *home*." Sylvie didn't blame her for her hostility. She asked if they would like to try out the new piano, but Alexandra glared and said no, nobody gave a fig for her stupid piano.

Without a word, Sylvie put away the Clementi she'd placed on the music stand. Before their next visit, she went out and bought them a gramophone. From then on, she would hear them singing along with a favorite record as she came up the stairs—*"on prend le café au lait au lit"*—but as soon as she entered the apartment, they fell silent. Charles answered her questions politely enough, but Alexandra would respond in sullen monosyllables.

Once Sylvie overheard Alexandra complaining to Julien, her voice shrill with indignation, "I don't have to listen to her, she's not my mother."

"At least make an effort. It's hard for Charles, too, but he tries to be civil."

"We don't have to love her just because you do."

"No," he said, "you don't. I know you're angry, but don't take it out on her, take it out on me, *I* was the one who left."

Sylvie had thought of staying behind for the Toussaint holidays so that Julien and the children could go on a trip by themselves, but Fabienne shook her head in exasperation. "Can't you see that's what the little beast wants, to get her father back from you?"

"Don't be so hard on her, she's only eight."

"Old enough to know what she's doing."

"She needs time alone with him."

"What she needs," said Fabienne, "is a good slap."

Sylvie racked her brains for a way to reach Alexandra. She borrowed a couple of birdcages from Ana Carvalho and put them on the balcony. The children kept looking at the boldly colored finches, but when Sylvie asked if they wanted to feed them, Alexandra said no, nobody gave a fig for her stupid birds. Charles looked embarrassed by his sister's rudeness and asked what they liked to eat.

"Seeds and grains, mostly, but sometimes they like cuttlefish bones to grind down their food—they don't have teeth, you know."

Charles held out some seed to the finches, and Alexandra scowled at his betrayal. All of a sudden she turned to Sylvie and said, "Don't you have any birds that like to raid the nests of others?"

Sylvie stood there in stunned silence. Before her brother could stop her, Alexandra wrenched a birdcage open and the finches streaked out, fluttering around the balcony. Sylvie managed to coax them back into the cage, all but one, which flew down to the judge's window. It perched there, cheeping loudly for several minutes, and then sailed off toward the river.

Alexandra said wildly, "There, you can tell Papa, I don't care."

Seeing her tear-streaked face, Sylvie suddenly realized the girl's fierce opposition was fueled not by anger but by fear. She took a deep breath and said firmly, "Stop it, Alexandra, it's not a contest, your father loves you, he'll always love you, but you should know that every time you lash out at me, you end up hurting Julien."

Both children looked at Sylvie in astonishment, and in truth she was somewhat surprised herself. But she did not want to draw Julien into these skirmishes, she must remedy the situation alone. She rearranged her schedule so that when their father was at work, she was free to accompany the children to the book stalls by the river, or to the cinema for the latest Jacques Tati film. At the end of the day, she and the children would stroll down the island's main street to watch the fire-eaters and tumblers on the footbridge, and on the way back they would push open the wooden door of Maison Chenizot to wait for Julien in the courtyard.

In front of their father the children continued to address Sylvie as *"vous,"* but when they were by themselves, they used the less formal *"tu."* One day Alexandra said that she would be home late, and then bit her lip as she realized she had called quai d'Anjou *home*. Their transformation into a family was so gradual that Sylvie could hardly say when things changed. But one winter night with Alexandra curled up beside her father and Charles playing a duet with her on the piano, Sylvie had the strange sensation that someone was staring into the lighted window yearning, as she had once yearned, to be part of that brightness.

And now that brief enchantment was over, Julien gone, Charles and Alexandra far away, with children older than they had been when they first came to quai d'Anjou. Sylvie did not expect to see either of them till September. They always spent August in Vandenesse with their mother. She had often thought of them in Isabelle's family home, imagining the soft green hills, the golden light of the Côte-d'Or.

One summer, when the children were still young and away at Vandenesse, Sylvie had sighed that the apartment seemed so quiet without them, so empty. Julien looked up from his work, put it aside.

"*Chérie*, do you want children?"

"I have Charles and Alexandra."

"A child of your own."

She hesitated, considering the possibility of that great metamorphosis in her life. Would it shatter the fragile peace she had achieved with Alexandra, with Charles? "It's the same thing," she said, "they *are* my own."

"I love you *even* more than I thought. Much, much more."

And so I do.

Even *more than I can tell her now.*

She brought me such happiness. In the autumn of my life.

"Not autumn," she would correct me. "It's only midsummer yet."

Yes. Well.

And yet she never estimated herself at her true worth. Just because she didn't have a concert career like Fabienne or wasn't as well known in her field as I was in mine, does not make her any less extraordinary. Never in all the years we were together did I see her do an unkind thing or say an ungenerous one. Her shyness often made her tongue-tied, but she never stayed silent when it was important to speak up. And she was gifted with an exquisite, instinctive tactfulness. Tact, I've found, is an underrated virtue, helping to lubricate the cranky machinery of human interactions.

I watched her mount a long and patient campaign to win the children's trust. Especially Alexandra, what a wildcat she was then, flying fur and extended claws. But Sylvie never gave up on her. It was only when Alexandra asked impulsively if Sylvie could come with them to Vandenesse that I took the full measure of Sylvie's success. But then Alexandra quickly realized how unthinkable it was and flushed bright red. "Never mind," she said, "she'd probably rather stay here with you anyway."

And I wonder if I should not have been so quick to let the matter drop when Sylvie said she didn't want a child of her own. Does she regret it now? I certainly regret not asking her again.

Now that she is alone, Sylvie is gripped by the bizarre notion that Isabelle will finally invite her to join the family at Vandenesse, to play for them, perhaps, reinstated in that circle. She shakes her head to dispel the absurd fancy, it's clear Isabelle will never forgive her, and what does it matter anyway, it won't alter anything between them.

Sylvie wishes she had not wasted precious time on such profitless rivalry. She can't help recalling the disastrous evening with the Gouffroys soon after she moved in with Julien. Returning from a conference in Zurich, he had bumped into Max and Sabine at the station and invited them over for *fortune du pot*, but when the three of them showed up, it was to find paint cans everywhere, the roasted chicken tough as leather, and Sylvie in tears at the thought of that memorable dinner at rue de Bièvre. But Julien only smiled and shrugged. *That's why it's called potluck, sometimes the pot is lucky, sometimes it's not*, he said, as he whipped up an omelet.

All through dinner, Sylvie toyed with her food and kept looking anxiously at Julien. She knew he had noticed the changes to the apartment, but he hadn't said a word. While he was at the conference, Sylvie had tried her hand at decorating and Madame de Cheroisey referred her to an upholsterer who was *très* smart. After the Gouffroys left, she asked eagerly if he liked the transformation. He stared at the imitation tapestry on the wall, the chairs covered in celadon silk, then remarked ironically, "You forgot the mirror."

Sylvie's eyes filled with tears. How humiliating that he should recognize it for what it was, yet another attempt to imitate Isabelle, like the bottle of her signature perfume L'Heure Bleue hidden in the armoire, or Sylvie's newly precise way of speaking, so that a color was not simply green or blue but, like the Turkish stone, *turquoise*. How naïve to think that she could learn what was proper merely by copying someone who was raised *comme il faut*.

Without saying a word, Sylvie left the apartment and walked for hours, crossing and re-crossing the river by one bridge or another, until, hardly aware of what she was doing, she turned down rue de Bièvre, overcome by an impulse to knock on Isabelle's door and ask for her advice. But as she approached that familiar doorway, she realized her folly and hurried past with her head down, turning on Boulevard St. Germain, glad to be caught up and carried along by crowds of people going about their business.

It was dark when she returned to the island, and still she lingered in the street, looking up at the lighted casements. Most people had already drawn their curtains, but a few windows remained unshaded. In one room, a nurse fed an elderly woman, dabbing up her spills with a napkin; in another, chic young people danced to music Sylvie could not hear. Eventually even those lights were extinguished. The partygoers stumbled out to the street where a purring Bentley awaited, and the chauffeur drove them away in a plume of exhaust.

A chill wind off the water reminded Sylvie that it was late, it was cold. She had barely eaten all day, and now the shops and res-

taurants were closed, the quay deserted. Time to go home. Her
pale face glimmered in a darkened storefront, and she stopped to
stare at the reflection. *You forgot the mirror.* She suddenly realized
she had misunderstood, Julien hadn't meant to mock her at all but
to reassure her; no need to turn herself into a second-rate imitation of Isabelle, he loved her as she was. And then it struck her
that there would come a time when she would look back on the
day's squandered hours with regret. She walked faster and faster
back toward him, breaking into a run when she saw the wrought-
iron gates, aware that being separated for even an instant longer
now would lengthen the long separation yet to come.

Julien was pacing back and forth in the courtyard, waiting
for her. Even before opening the gate, he reached through the
bars to grip her. "Don't leave," he said.

"Never," she said, "never."

But they both knew that he was the one who would leave,
who had a history of leaving.

When Julien was alive, Sylvie slept through everything, even the loud stuttering of jackhammers as old buildings were renovated up and down the quay. Now she wakes at the slightest sound, thunder in the distance, rain on the roof tiles, a sudden silence after the storm. She cannot go back to sleep, troubled by a strange dissonance, a dissonance that in life, as in music, seeks resolution.

She gets up and crosses the room noiselessly in her cloth slippers. Coco is instantly alert. His tail thumps on the floor as he considers the delightful prospect of an unexpected walk. But Sylvie does not put on her shoes, and Coco sighs and lowers his head again.

Convinced she has overlooked something significant, Sylvie goes to Julien's desk, pulls out Marie's card from the envelope, and studies the two lines of poetry that she had only skimmed before. Rereading them now, she is struck by their beauty, the palpable yearning for a dear friend whose mere remembrance assuages all grief. But it is the unremarkable words *cher ami* that she dwells on with a pang of jealousy.

More than ever she is certain that the contents of the envelope are not random but meaningfully linked. Perhaps Marie, if she is still alive, can provide the link. But how in the world will she find her?

Sylvie draws back the curtains and looks out. The rain has stopped, the puddles in the street reflect the first streaks of dawn.

She makes herself some coffee, then calls to Coco, who bounds ahead, down the stairs and out to the pavement.

Sylvie crosses the street and leans over the stone wall to look at the river. The water has risen after the rain, the island seems like a boat floating on the waves. Nowhere else in Paris does the city's coat of arms feel more apt: a ship with the motto FLUCTUAT NEC MERGITUR: *floundering but not submerged*. The same is true of her, she thinks, here she is, shaken, but still standing.

Alice Taylor calls out *"Bonjour,"* smiling at the sight of Sylvie wearing pearls just to walk the dog. Coco wags his stumpy tail as Alice jogs past, lolloping beside her for a few yards before stopping to look over his shoulder. The dilemma is clearly written on his face. But then, without being called, he turns and trots back to his mistress. Loyal, thinks Alice, but surely the dog needs more exercise than he gets, cooped up in that apartment all day, he should be out running with her.

Alice's shoes squelch softly on the wet pavement and she feels the familiar exhilaration of hitting her stride. On quai de Béthune, she glances up at a third-floor apartment. It still gives her a thrill to imagine Marie Curie at the window. As she rounds the corner into quai d'Anjou, Alice's face is dripping with perspiration, and she wonders how Frenchwomen never seem to sweat. Walking into the courtyard, she finds the main door ajar and Ana Carvalho beckoning her into the stairwell.

"Regardez." She points out a plant flourishing in the dim light.

"Very nice."

"Il faut regarder," Ana Carvalho insists.

Alice looks closer and sees a tightly curled bud. "In the dark? That's impossible!"

Ana Carvalho waves a reproving finger. "Remember what Napoleon said, nothing is *impossible* for the French."

Alice smiles. She's always thought of the "can-do" spirit as typically American, while the French veer more toward the "can-can" spirit, bright and sparkling like their champagne, or like their croissants, airy and light.

I'm amused at how Alice puts us in our place. This is what the glories of French civilization are reduced to, feathered costumes, flaky confections. And the cream of the jest is the croissant isn't even French. It comes from Vienna, famous for the pastries we still call viennoiseries. *According to legend, a seventeenth-century Viennese baker—up before dawn, like all bakers—heard enemy troops tunneling underground and sounded the alarm. The Ottoman invasion was crushed and the enterprising baker created a pastry shaped like the vanquished crescent.* Voilà, *our croissant.*

As for our "can-can" spirit, tourists who flock to Moulin Rouge to see an authentic example of la gaieté parisienne *might be surprised to discover it's just borrowed feathers: Offenbach was born in Germany, the son of a Jewish cantor, and the risqué dance now inseparable from his music came originally from Algeria.*

In omnivorous Paris, foreignness is absorbed into Frenchness like gravy into bread. Even my dear Ana Carvalho, born in Lisbon, feels as much a Parisienne *as the judge's wife, quoting Napoleon with such assurance to Alice Taylor.*

But, of course, Napoleon wasn't French, either.

*Given our penchant for assimilation, I'm also amused at how we always say, quite without irony, "*Vive la différence!" *I wish I could share these reflections with Sylvie, to watch her eyes brim again with laughter on my account instead of with tears.*

Sylvie overhears Alice and Ana Carvalho discussing the clivia in the stairwell. "Discussing" is perhaps too strong a word, the concierge is talking volubly while Alice just listens and nods. Walking upstairs, Sylvie encounters Madame de Cheroisey on the landing and calls Coco to heel, she knows the older woman doesn't like the dog coming too close. Not that Coco has shown any desire to frisk around either the judge or his wife; in his own way he is quite as snobbish as they are.

"Ah, *bonjour*, and how are you managing with our Americans?" Madame de Cheroisey inquires, as if the Taylors are a shared tribulation.

So the judge's wife now thinks they are on the same side of the divide? Sylvie smiles and replies that frankly she finds them a breath of fresh air.

"It doesn't derange you, having them so close?"

"Not at all, it's a great comfort."

"*Très* cozy, no doubt," Madame de Cheroisey sniffs as she goes back inside.

Sylvie is amused by this reminder of one of the unspoken rules of *les riches*: Being exclusive always entails having *someone* to exclude. She grew up hearing about *les riches*; her mother observed them as an anthropologist might some reclusive tribe. Returning from work at Madame Wanda's, Ewa would say, "*Les riches* are nervous people, very anxious about their fine things but they hate to admit it. If a guest spills red wine on a rug they shrug as if they have hundreds of Aubussons rolled up in the attic, but the maid knows they'll make her scrub the stain for hours. Food makes them anxious as well, they think soup is vulgar, because you can see bits of meat and vegetables, so they order *potage*, with everything pureed, or even better, *consommé* clear enough to see the pattern inside their Limoges bowls."

"Why do you fill the child's head with rubbish?" asked her husband, lowering his newspaper. "Is she likely to dine with a duchess?"

"I'm sure *Hrabina* Wanda will come through for her."

"I'll thank her not to do us any favors." No more cast-off clothes, no more chipped dishes. As if they would make up for the incessant ringing of Madame's silver bell to summon Ewa, and when she came running, Madame would ask her for a thimble or a piece of lace that she could have reached herself by stretching her hand. Madame Wanda needed her services and paid for them and that was that, no reason for Ewa to curtsy and carry on about her precious countess. He would never truckle, would rather take to the barricades to fight, he was a Frenchman through and through.

Sylvie glanced at the veins bulging in her father's forehead, at her mother's pinched lips, and thought, *Please, God, please don't let* Maman *bring up Father Tadeusz right now.* But of course she did, and her father crumpled the pages of *L'Humanité* and threw them on the floor. His wife refused to understand that the church was in cahoots with the rich, they told the poor they would inherit the earth so they wouldn't rise up and claim what was due to them now.

Sylvie bent her head over her copybook, trying to fit each letter neatly into its own square, but then she started coloring in the squares and noticed that each color made a particular sound, and she arranged the colors so that they made a pleasing melody, and then the melody filled her with such happiness that she forgot the quarrels that filled the kitchen and remembered only the times when her parents would dance to songs on the radio.

How often had I pictured that scene to myself: Sylvie as a child, the same age as Clara's twins, in the same city, at the same time. A time of terrible darkness, when children vanished from an occupied city, leaving no trace behind. Beset by troubling visions of girls her age—not more than six—fallen in the river, picked up by the Germans, lured into a brothel, I imagined the worst not because I have a particularly lurid imagination, but because in my work and in my life I have witnessed the worst impulses of human nature overcome the basic decency of people. But the idea of Sylvie was comforting in its very ordinariness: a child with both her parents beside her, doing her homework secure in the knowledge that there is dinner on the stove and school the next day. An ordinary scene, and it was only the extraordinary times in which it was set that rendered it as luminous as a stained-glass window, before which I lingered while around me darkness gathered with visions so terrible that they threatened to engulf all light.

I closed my eyes to dispel those visions, and when I opened them again but a moment later, my life with Sylvie had just begun.

And then, in the blink of an eye, it was over.

When Sylvie told her parents she was moving in with Julien, they were silent at first with disbelief. They knew she was "different" and could not think how to talk her out of her decision; shy she might be, but she was also unshakeable. After the initial shock had subsided, her mother thought it was a shame that if Julien *had* to be old, why he couldn't be a widower as well; the way things were, his wife would keep the name, the house, everything. A pity, it would be nice for Sylvie to marry "up," but of course Ewa couldn't say that to Didier, he would erupt that they were as good as any toff. She hoped he would at least be civil to Julien for Sylvie's sake.

Julien had invited them to dinner at a nearby restaurant, and over apéritifs the waiter's advice was sought and given at great length. Drinking her kir royale, Ewa regarded Julien appraisingly. She could see why her daughter was head-over-heels in love, such a serious girl, not like herself at that age. Although Ewa herself would have held out for marriage, there was no doubt that Julien would make Sylvie happy, and she raised her glass to his health.

Didier, too, thawed in Julien's presence, reassured his politics were not those of *les riches*, he was an intellectual, with leftist sympathies no doubt, maybe even a socialist like himself, now that he had resigned from the Communist Party after the Soviet tanks rolled into Budapest. Julien said he needed a bit of advice and Didier looked at him suspiciously. Was the doctor making fun of him? What the hell kind of advice could he give, he was not an educated man, a plasterer and proud of it, if it weren't for working stiffs like him *les riches* would rot to death. But Julien was serious, the paint had started peeling off his walls, and he had no idea why. Didier explained that effervescence was a sure sign of leaks, he wouldn't worry about the walls so much as the roof.

Sylvie was happy her parents had enjoyed the evening and had not openly, at least, shown any signs of hostility. Hard to believe they had made it through the entire dinner without a single mention of *les riches*. And her truculent father, always on the lookout for slights, had not perceived anything to make him bristle. On the contrary, Julien had listened respectfully as Didier showed his skill in his *métier* rather than holding forth about his own work. But when they were walking home, she looked back on the evening that had put them all at ease and it slowly dawned on her that without saying a word about his work, Julien had amply demonstrated his expertise.

She stopped suddenly in the middle of the street and flung her arms around him. He kissed her passionately and a passing *bateau-mouche* caught their clasped silhouettes in its net of light. At that most Parisian of sights, a cheer went up from the boat. Then the searchlights moved on, releasing them to the sudden dark.

Le grand amour! *Late in my life I discovered the kind of love which comes once in a lifetime, if at all. Sylvie could not make my life whole again, but she did make it complete. Yet the grandest of passions must fall prey to devouring Time. An old story, and no matter where it begins or how it is told, the ending is always the same.*

A deluge of emotion washes over me and I'm swept into a strange marriage ceremony, the tying of an indissoluble knot, not between a man and a woman but a king and the city he loved more than the woman he married to get it, loved more than his soul even. A lifelong Protestant, Henri of Navarre turned Catholic for the sake of Paris.

Strange nuptials in which the Huguenot groom plays no part, kneeling outside Notre Dame while the Catholic ceremony is conducted within. Their union is meant to end the wars of religion tearing the country apart, and Henri knows that his marriage to Margot is strictly business; for pleasure he must look to his mistresses. Evergreen gallant, people call him, and nudge one another as Margot emerges from the cathedral, dousing her handkerchief with a perfume specially blended for her by Renato the Florentine before she embraces le vert galant, *who smells like the goats from his native Navarre. With the knot safely tied between the "heretic" prince and his Catholic bride, all Paris dances in the street. Peace, at last!*

But in less than a week the old hatreds erupt again, and on

St. Barthélemy's Day the Seine runs sluggish with blood, bodies stack up like firewood in the streets. Huguenot or Catholic, they decompose at the same swift rate under the merciless August sun, and not all the perfumes Renato the Florentine has brought with him can disguise that stench.

Everyone knows of course how the bridegroom escapes and returns years later as a newly Catholic king: "Paris is worth a mass," he says, and people laugh at his flippancy, but he is in deadly earnest. He is hell-bent on ending the religious persecution which threatens to destroy France. It is not the only bargain Henri IV makes for his kingdom; he annuls his marriage to childless Margot to wed a clinking purse of a woman, Marie of the Medicis, who obligingly disburses several legitimate heirs to secure the Bourbon line. And as for his many bastards, Henri laughs, he is only a king, not a saint.

Forever in love with some woman or the other, the only thing that excites Henri more than flesh and blood is mortar and stones. This island captured his heart when it was just a set of architectural drawings presented for his approval. No monarch loved building more; under Henri, all Paris is scaffolded, the dust barely settles in one quarter before it rises in another. I see him prepare to leap across an unfinished span of the Pont Neuf. Some boatmen below call out a warning, but he shrugs it off. "I might flounder but will not sink," he says, and they laugh, delighted that His Majesty knows the motto of their guild, fluctuat nec mergitur.

That is the state of things when a shabby man hurries past, muttering to himself. People turn and stare, thinking him mad, but it is not madness but treason. He makes his way purposefully toward the king. An overturned hay cart blocks the royal carriage on rue de la Ferronnerie, and while people struggle to clear the path, the king tugs at his earring, filled with strange presentiments. But why? He leads a charmed life, his heirs are healthy, his mistress comely, and his city flourishing. No one can deny his edicts have brought peace, peace has brought prosperity. A sudden gust of wind ripples his cloak and he turns and sees a specter visible only to him, his brother-in-law, Margot's brother, who unexpectedly gained the throne as Henri III, and just as unexpectedly lost it when he was killed by an assassin's dagger. Henri IV's eyes widen as he realizes what his predecessor is trying to tell him: Regicide! But before he can form the word, the shabby man jumps on the wheel, his knife glinting in the sun and Henri falls back, no longer a king but only a bloodied and silent corpse.

But the lives of cities do not end with the lives of men. The island finally rises like a mirage from the water, and when I look at what Henri did not live to see, his grand vision turned from parchment to stone, how strange it seems that this island should be named not for Henri IV, but like all Henri's descendants to wear the crown, for his distant ancestor, Louis the Saint.

I hold no brief for kings, but how much greater he seems to me, the far-from-saintly Henri, when I compare him to his sainted ancestor. One tried to bind up the raveling threads of the country with his edict on religious tolerance, the other broke "heretics" on an inquisitor's wheel. Louis IX had a dream that all Jews would be branded with yellow badges and cast out of the land; Henri IV had a vision of a France held together by bonds whose harmony neither man nor God could disrupt. Though the island is called Île Saint-Louis, there's no question whose vision it embodies.

And it's equally strange how stubbornly the vision has resisted time's transformations. Today this exclusive quarter is desirable not for what it offers but for what it lacks: no metro, no cinema, *no fine museums, no grand monuments, not even a* bureau de poste—*people used to deposit their letters at the ironmonger's till a post office opened recently on the street connecting the isle to the mainland and to modernity. Even now, when I leave the bustling main streets with their restaurants and boutiques for the slumbering quays where stone and water do not change with the times, I feel I have stepped back several centuries. That is the appeal of this place, so close to everything and yet so far from it all.*

It was certainly exclusive enough for the Cheroiseys when they installed themselves there in the postwar years. Though the judge grumbles that now the place is being taken over by Arab sheiks and movie stars—not the sort of people whose company one frequented—it's still the best address in town. And Sylvie's renters might not be *fréquentables,* either, but he enjoys engaging them in conversation, the young man's French is quite passable and he speaks of French wines with the reverence they deserve. Feeling expansive after one of their discussions in the courtyard, the judge invites Will down to his *cave* to see some remarkable vintages he has laid down. Léonie de Cheroisey says, another day, *nounours,* you can see they're going out. The endearment *teddy bear* draws a fierce scowl from her husband.

Will is flattered by the judge's invitation, even though it's only to the wine cellar, but Alice takes his arm. "Another time," she says. "We're headed to the bistro across the bridge."

The judge shrugs. "Passable, quite passable, but not the grand cuisine of France."

"Georges-Henri is from Normandy," his wife says, as if that explains everything. "Me, I find the bistro perfectly fine, but not *le top,* obviously."

At the word "top," Will glances at Sylvie's window. He thought he had seen her looking down at them but he can't be sure, and he wishes he had asked her to join them for dinner, instead of eating by herself.

The Taylors cross over to the Right Bank and find the bistro abuzz with conversations, all in French. A good sign, no tourists. But the room is thick with smoke, so they seat themselves on the *terrasse*, which is nothing fancier than a couple of tables set up on the sidewalk. A busy waitress, her hands full of dishes, calls out from the doorway, *"J'arrive."* There are no menus, the day's offerings scrawled on a blackboard: a main course of guinea hen and cherry clafoutis for dessert. Will orders a bottle of Sancerre, and the waitress looks surprised, Americans drink *un coca* even with dinner, *n'est-ce pas?* Will replies with feigned meekness that indeed some people consider Coke *le vin américain*, and Alice, who has just heard him speak knowingly of vintages with the judge, turns away to hide her amusement.

The dinner is simple but delicious, they must remember to report back to Ana Carvalho. Alice and Will stroll back toward the island, but the evening is fine, and instead of taking Pont Louis-Philippe, they continue to the next bridge, where they pause to look at the imposing Hôtel de Ville behind them, Île de la Cité ahead. A *bateau-mouche* comes down the river with couples dancing on deck, and the music floats up to the bridge, then fades away as the boat chugs toward Pont Notre Dame. They walk toward the familiar silhouette of the cathedral, the open square in front packed with tourists and the motley band of those who make a living off them, jugglers, musicians, fire-eaters blowing flames of kerosene into the sky.

Curious about the crowd streaming into Notre Dame, Will pulls Alice into the crush and they are swept inside to press against other latecomers, the church filled to capacity for a concert of sacred music by Vivaldi. A heavily perfumed woman next to them fans herself with a program, dispersing the scent of violets into the air. The low murmur of voices around them rises to the vaulted ceiling like a swarm of bees. Behind the altar a simple unadorned cross is illuminated with such skill that its substance seems not wood or stone but pure light; before it, the orchestra is already in place, and an expectant hush descends as the soloists and chorus enter in their flowing robes.

Alice enjoys the bright opening with strings and trumpet, but when the choir starts the *Gloria*, her attention flags. The air in the cathedral is stuffy and the wine from dinner is making her drowsy, but sandwiched as they are, there's no hope of escape until the concert is over. Her gaze wanders over the chandeliers casting a golden glow, the gleaming pipes of the organ, the black and white flagstones that innumerable believers have worn smooth with their footsteps.

A man across the aisle ogles her openly, and Alice turns away. It takes getting used to, the admiring stares, the hand-kissing, the fulsome compliments which strike her as hypocritical, clearly the French are as prejudiced as anyone else. She can't get over the fact that not a single woman is buried at the Panthéon, not even Marie Curie. It's more than an academic question for Alice, she's had her share of being patronized as a scientist, a researcher, a professor up for tenure. But at least in America attitudes are starting to change, there's a woman on the Supreme Court, finally. A chance to compete on level ground, it doesn't seem too much to ask, not as if women are demanding to be put on a pedestal. And it's funny that the Statue of Liberty, the *one* woman Americans willingly placed on a pedestal, was a gift from France!

Stifling a yawn, Alice looks at her watch. The *Gloria* ends to a burst of sustained applause, and the audience disperses, still under the spell of the music. Out in the open, Alice's head clears, and she breathes the night air gratefully as they cross the footbridge to the Île Saint-Louis.

Though headed in the same direction, I linger by the ancient willow at the island's tip, strangely disturbed. "As prejudiced as anyone else." How I long to contradict Alice, to point out, as any Frenchman would, the three glorious words—Liberté, Égalité, Fraternité—*carved in stone all around the city.*

But even as I mouth the words, the memory of Clara's reproachful eyes stops me in my tracks, and I think of what Voltaire said, "To the living we owe respect, but to the dead only the truth." Very well, then, here's the truth: Men hungry for power will sell their souls to get it, and do even worse to keep it. There's the rub. Equality is too grand an idea to entrust to little men with a lot to lose.

Ashamed that I have tried to defend the indefensible, I say the words that come hard to French lips: "I am sorry." For those like Clara sent to their deaths because we betrayed our own ideals, how meager seems the apology, but I say it again: "Désolé."

A lone skater zigzags on the deserted bridge as I gaze at the willow weeping into the river, where reflections of the illuminated city shimmer in the dark like so many will-o'-the-wisps, those capricious lights we call feux follets.

Lying awake in bed, Sylvie struggles to make sense of the contents of the envelope. She has done what she can about the mysterious bank account, but what of the rest? A photograph, a note, the names of a nearby street and a far-flung neighborhood. If she had found them separately, she would have lingered over Clara's photograph, wept at Julien's handwriting, thrown away the unknown card. But they've been placed together in an envelope, surely they are somehow connected. Julien was not a sentimental man, he had no use for keepsakes. So why hoard these particular things? And why hide them away?

Belleville is too large, too overwhelming, she would have no idea what to look for, or where to begin. In any case, she is convinced the road to the mystery runs through rue Elzévir. She pores through the street listings in *l'Indispensable* until she finds what she is looking for: Éluard, Élysée, Elzévir. She'll go there in the morning, not out of idle curiosity, but because it's what Julien would have wanted. *Isn't that so, mon amour?*

Julien does not reassure her and Sylvie feels she has lost him a second time, not just to death, but to silence.

Instead of continuing with my habitual round, I remain by the willow, overcome by painful memories as green as the park before which I stand. Its locked gates do not deter me, and slowly I descend the steep, narrow stairway into another world. Instead of a city of light, I find myself in a triangular well of darkness.

This site once housed the morgue, where bodies were laid out on display behind curtains and glass, a titillating spectacle of corpses—dragged pregnant from the river, perhaps, or found hanging from a balcony, or frozen in the unforgiving streets— attracting sightseers from far and wide. But it is long gone, the morgue where Parisians came to identify and claim their dead. In its place is a cenotaph for those whose bodies can never be claimed.

Other memorials soar to the sky; this one sinks into the earth. A low portcullis bars the water; jagged sculptures lacerate the sky. No exit, say these iron spikes; no hope, say these concrete walls.

Through tomblike portals, I enter a crypt. Encrusted with two hundred thousand beads of light, a narrow corridor leads to the tomb of the unknown deportee, a single unadorned tomb to keep alive the memory of the two hundred thousand French who were forcibly deported during the Occupation, "lost in the night and fog, exterminated in Nazi camps." Those glowing lights are like the unwinking gaze of history, before which I lower my eyes, ashamed that so many of my countrymen thought a moral reckoning with our own culpability would tear us apart and chose amnesia instead. But some resisted, working tirelessly to unearth from "the night and fog" the individual names of the disappeared, to provide evidence of their collective fate through films and books and archives which would make it impossible to deny knowledge, to disclaim responsibility, to whitewash this stain on our history.

At my feet a bronze circle is chiseled with the words: "They went to the end of the earth and they did not return." It is too dark to decipher an inscription on the wall, written by one who did not return. Yet I would not wish it any brighter, for I know his words by heart: "For me all that remains is to be a shadow among shadows." By the time I leave this pantheon of shades and turn toward quai d'Anjou, it is almost dawn and Sylvie's window, like all the rest, is dark.

The lowering sky at dawn provides Sylvie with an excuse to put off her expedition. She knows it's not the threatening clouds that give her pause, it's her ambivalence about finding *Marie*, whose note Julien kept hidden in a sealed envelope for so long. But now that she has resolved to take action, the hesitations and uncertainty of the last few weeks have fallen away. Moving with a sudden sureness, she hastily swallows her coffee and gathers her belongings: an umbrella, a leash, and the envelope. She hears Ana Carvalho enter the apartment below and hurries down the stairs to avoid her. If she were to tell the concierge she is off to look for an unknown woman at an unnumbered address, Ana Carvalho might think it a recurrence of Sylvie's old madness.

As she walks down the narrow streets of the Marais with Coco sniffing the unfamiliar gutters, Sylvie notices how much the area has gentrified in the last few years, home now to trendy restaurants and shops selling ethnic textiles and exotic foods. Only the streets surrounding the Jewish Quarter still look the same, with men going about their business soberly dressed in their black garb and long sidelocks. The fried smell of falafel lingers in the air, reminding Sylvie she should have eaten a decent breakfast before leaving.

She turns into rue Elzévir, glad it's only two blocks long; just one street over is rue Vieille du Temple, which seems to go on forever. She mentally eliminates certain buildings, the redbrick school, the stark courtyard of the Hôtel de Donon and the Swedish cultural center next door. No point searching the storefronts displaying cookware and furniture, or the offices into which workers are making their purposeful way, which leaves only a few apartment buildings worth canvassing. As she loiters at the entrance to the closest one, the gate opens and a concierge steps into the street. She eyes Sylvie suspiciously, but evidently something about her appearance—the pearls, the umbrella—reassures her and she wishes her good morning in a civil enough tone.

Sylvie hesitates, unsure of what to say. She should have planned it in advance. "I'm looking for someone," she says, and unclasps her purse to pull out the envelope.

The concierge stares at it, her face bright with avidity. When Sylvie hands her the scrap of paper, she looks disappointed. Barely glancing at it, she says, "Yes, this is the street, all right. What name did you say?"

"Marie. That's all I know."

"*Oh là là*, that's quite a challenge. This friend of yours . . . has she come into money?"

Sylvie hesitates, then nods.

Now the concierge warms to the task. "The only Marie I have here is Madame Willemin's daughter, and she's in school."

"No, no, the woman I'm looking for is quite a bit older."

"Well, good luck." The concierge turns away abruptly, wheeling her trash cans back into the courtyard.

At the next building, Sylvie bends down to study the names on the digicode, none with the initial *M*, although it's possible

Marie lives with her husband. A car horn beeps irascibly, and she moves out of the way as an elderly gentleman drives in, grumbling about the imbecility of pedestrians.

Through the open gate, Sylvie glimpses a house with ivy-covered walls. In the front courtyard, an old woman is deadheading flowers, her arthritic fingers moving slowly and painfully among the stone pots. "Em," he calls out, "Em." Sylvie stops. Em? *M* for Marie? She waits for the man to get out, to say something more. He moves toward the woman and reaches for her hands, streaked with dirt. "Ah, Emmeline," he says, kissing her gnarled fingers, "why won't you wear gloves?"

As the gate shuts on them, Sylvie feels a sudden pang of grief. She walks on to the adjoining building, with its front door ajar. Pushing it open, Sylvie calls out *"Bonjour, bonjour."* A clicking bead curtain is drawn aside and a woman peers out of the concierge's lodge, holding a squirming little dog in her arms. Seeing the open door, the bichon frisé slips out of the woman's grip and streaks toward the street, barking at Coco, who turns his head from these antics and yawns.

"Stop, stop, you little rascal," the woman shrieks.

Sylvie scoops up the dog before he can escape. "A mind of his own," the concierge says proudly, holding out her arms for the dog. "You wanted something, Madame?"

Sylvie has thought of a ruse. She holds out the scrap of Julien's stationery and says, "Is there someone here called Marie? I've come from Docteur Dalsace."

The word "doctor" works like a charm. "Come in, come in," says the concierge, "that must be for Madame Charbon." She shouts up the stairwell, "Madame Charbon, someone from the doctor's."

"Tell him to mount," a man's voice yells back.

"It's a woman."

"Well, tell *her* to mount."

A thickset man waits for Sylvie two floors up, his arms crossed forbiddingly across his chest. "Marie-Louise," he calls over his shoulder, and a woman comes to the door, her face anxious. "I thought the tests were normal."

"I didn't mean to worry you, I just wondered if you knew Docteur Dalsace."

The woman shakes her head and the man says, "We don't know him and we don't want trouble."

"If it's important, you can wait for the postman . . ."

"That's enough, Marie-Louise." He shuts the door.

For the rest of the morning, Sylvie wanders up and down the street knocking on doors, wondering if hidden eyes are watching her. A face behind a curtain, an eye at the peephole. There are fewer and fewer concierges in the city nowadays, but they seem to be here in full force. Will they call the police? Her presence might prove difficult to explain, though she's done nothing wrong. *"Coucou,"* Madame Charbon calls out from her window and points to the end of the street. At last, *la poste.*

Sylvie hurries to catch up with the postman. She hands him the note and explains her quest. He examines the paper with minute attention, then slowly puffs his cheeks. Sylvie prepares herself for the words she has heard all morning, *"aucune idée."*

But instead of shrugging it off, he says thoughtfully, "It's very, very old, this note—see how the black ink has faded to gray? Written after the war, no doubt. During occupation, every scrap as thick as this would have been used to sole shoes or line clothing. And she's obviously French, this Marie of yours, which means we can eliminate all foreigners right away, the Marias and Marys and so forth. So let's assume that if she ever lived on this street, she lives here still."

The mailman strokes his beard and recites the lines, like a connoisseur savoring rare wine:

"Mais si pendant ce temps je pense à toi, cher ami,
toutes mes pertes sont réparées et tous mes chagrins finis."

To Sylvie's surprise, he knows the words by heart. "Evidently a cultured woman," he says, "to have chosen the Victor Hugo translation. The only person I can imagine writing this note is Marie Dubonnet at the end of the street. But she died a few months ago."

Sylvie sighs. Brought up short by death, where all trails run cold. Seeing her disappointment, the postman says, "Perhaps it's Marie Forrestier, in that building with the blue door. I doubt she wrote this, poor woman, but who can say?"

No one had answered when Sylvie tried the blue door earlier, and she wonders if she should return another day rather than wait around. No, better to put this quixotic impulse to rest once and for all. She walks to the end of the street, turns on rue du Parc Royal and enters the little park, looking for an empty bench to sit and rest her aching feet. But the sun is out now, and all the benches are taken. As she is leaving the park, a snub-nosed child brushes past her, pushing a pram and resisting all help from his parents. *"Moi, moi, moi,"* he says. A baby sleeps peacefully in the pram and Sylvie smiles at the mother, who smiles back at her. *"Moi, moi, moi"* says the whole world, look how sweet life is on this summer's day, how beautiful the foxgloves nodding in the breeze, the butterflies fossicking in the grass.

The corner café is empty, the lunch rush over. She sits at an outdoor table and orders coffee and a roll. The waiter hovers over her, disposed for pleasantries. He remarks on the weather, fills a water bowl for Coco, then leaves to attend to the Japanese tourists clustered at the entrance.

Sylvie stirs her coffee. What a vast world it is, close to her doorstep. Tunneling for so long into her own sorrow, her vision has suddenly turned outward, taken note of other lives. The anxious woman with her bully of a husband, the concierge doting on her dog, the loving couple in the sunset of their years. And the erudite postman who had greeted those lines of poetry like an old friend chanced upon after years; Sylvie had been too embarrassed to admit they were unfamiliar to her, that she had not realized it was a quotation. And she had been so intent on finding Marie that it's only now something else strikes her. *The Victor Hugo translation*, he'd said; but then who wrote the original? Julien would have known and she feels she has somehow let him down.

Over the years Julien had guided her to his favorites, the Greeks for drama, the Russians for fiction, the English for poetry; but it was French novels she had devoured, Balzac, Hugo, Colette, Dumas. She regrets now she never took to the poetry Julien loved, her attention wandered as she read. But when the postman recited the lines, their music had penetrated her ear. If only she had asked Julien to read aloud to her, what a treasure she would have laid by, to take out and exult over like one of Balzac's misers. But surely it's not too late, she can still listen to poetry, there must be recordings. And this winter she will go somewhere warm, if not Florida, then Italy, perhaps. Yes, it is a vast world.

But instead of comforting her, the realization brings despair.

A vast world in which she feels utterly alone. Her transformation into a "cultured" woman who travels to Florence, who quotes poetry, will be invisible to the only eyes that matter.

Even when Julien floated between this world and the next, hooked to life by the machinery of modern science, his eyes remained fixed on her, though at times his gaze turned inward as the morphine did its work. Once he whispered urgently, *"Belle vie."* Tears sprang to her eyes that he could say that now. She laid her cheek against his. *"Oui, chéri, la vie est belle."* But he shook his head and repeated the words with increasing agitation, *"belle vie, belle vie."* Another time he had asked, *"It's late, have they come yet?"* His words were slurred and she thought he said *"les cigognes."* Surely he meant the children when he spoke of storks? She dipped her finger in a glass of water and gently stroked his cracked lips. "Yes," she said soothingly, "yes, the storks are here."

In the bluish hospital light, his face was translucent, as if his skin had lost all memory of the sun. Overcome with fear, she clutched his hand and whispered, *"Don't leave me."*

Julien's eyes flew open and his gaze focused on her, a sudden shaft of lucidity piercing the fog of morphine. He struggled to raise his head, his lips moving. Her heart leapt. There was life in him yet. But as he sank back she realized it was only a spark from dying embers.

Sylvie, let me go.

She read the message clearly in his eyes. They both knew it was not the tubes and wires that kept him tethered to the world of the living, it was love of her. But she could not snap that filament. Not yet, not yet. Not when it meant a separation that would last forever, and the long years stretched ahead, years in which she would be alone in this uncaring world, without the shelter of his love, her head bared to the elements. Even if her life were to suddenly fill with people or crowd with incident, she would be absolutely, entirely alone. But as Julien's body gave a shudder and a long, heaving sigh, she released her tight grip on his hand, raised it gently to her lips.

Sleep, my darling.

His breaths grew slower and slower, and even as his hand relaxed in her own, she knew she was already alone.

Sylvie finishes her coffee, cold now and tasteless. Coco stretches out on the pavement, tucks his nose between his paws, and waits for Madame to come to her senses and head back home. His eyes wink back and forth between the passersby and Sylvie, until the afternoon shadows lengthen and his lids lie heavier and heavier on his eyes. A street musician materializes, sees the tourists, puts out his hat. On his old-fashioned accordion, the kind with typewriter keys, he spins out the *bal musette* melodies popular with both visitors and locals.

Hearing the familiar strains of "Valse Midinette," an old woman picks up her skirts and dances by herself. She has a string bag in her hand, like thousands of women returning from market all over the city, but unlike them, she seems unconcerned about her appearance. Everything about her is awry, crooked seams, mismatched stockings, a gaily striped skirt sagging at the hem, and her face, too, is like a cubist painting, nothing quite lines up, her smile especially crooked but infectious all the same.

The snub-nosed boy pushes his pram past her, with the baby awake now and squalling. The old woman's face lights up, and she bends over the pram. In a voice high and sweet she sings the familiar, tender song that has lulled so many fretful children to sleep. Recognizing the lullaby, the accordionist changes from the swirling dance to a rocking cradle without missing a beat. The scene carves out a silence on the bustling street as people turn their heads to look. Recognizing a moment of spontaneous enchantment, they stop whatever they are doing to listen to this chance duet in the street.

Sylvie feels tears spring to her eyes as the Schubert lullaby comes to a close. She dashes them away impatiently. Foolish. More than foolish, ignoble, to come all the way here only to pick a bone with the dead.

*I have often thought how little it would take . . . a nudge, a whisper,
a well-timed warning . . . to change the course of events. To turn
the very tide of history, even. But that little is denied to the restless
dead.*

*Across the barrier of time, this is what we have in common:
doomed to witness catastrophe, not prevent it. It's the iron law of our
twilight existence, against which there is no appeal. Yet it does not
lessen our burden, the guilt of the word not spoken, the gesture not
made.*

*Once on a day filled with rain, Pierre Curie, his mind teeming
with great discoveries, looked across the street and thought he saw
his old teacher Jean-Gustave Bourbuze.* "Cher maître," *he called
out, and stepped eagerly off the sidewalk, paying no heed to the
sound of hooves. A heavily laden cart with its runaway horses
thundered into the intersection and it would have been the work of
an instant to grab his sleeve, to pull him to safety. But his mentor's
ghost could not do it, could only gaze in horror at what happened
next. The cart rolled right over his brilliant student, the front wheel
missing him by millimeters. And then the back wheel crushed his
skull.*

*When they took the body in to his young widow, all she could
think was that her husband was dead, but the wildflowers he had
picked for her the day before were still alive. From that day on,
Marie Curie's pale face turned away from the sun, finding comfort*

*only in the gray skies that had covered Paris the day Pierre Curie
was killed.*

*The endless tragedy of her life. And if we were capable of
acting, we could have prevented it—the endless tragedy of ours.*

*I turn away as Sylvie pushes back her chair, gathers her
belongings. Suddenly there is a commotion. As the musician
squeezes out the final bars of the melody, Coco solemnly rises on his
hind legs and dances round and round. And he does what I cannot,
he changes the course of events.*

Clapping with delight, the boy lets go of the baby carriage and runs toward Coco. Some distance away, his parents call out *"Attention, Paul, attention!"* as the perambulator rolls toward the curb. The old woman in her harlequin clothes leaps to intercept it and the baby suffers no greater harm than a rude jolt which sets it squalling again. The mother runs toward the pram, the woman wanders away, and reports of the incident grow more and more exaggerated as they pass from mouth to mouth. An old lady hurled herself between a child and a rabid dog, the dog bit her, they've carried her off to the hospital, perhaps she is dead.

Gradually the excitement subsides, and the crowd thins out. The tourists go back to their *apéritifs,* and the waiter mutters under his breath that he still hates to hear German in the streets of Paris, even if it's only a song. Sylvie bends to fasten Coco's leash. Time to admit defeat and go home.

I had failed in my quest, but Sylvie's defeat strikes me harder. How bravely, how stubbornly she has pursued each unpromising lead. To give up now when she is getting so close! If only I could point her in the right direction, nudge her toward a certain door. If I could do something. Anything. But there's nothing I can do.

Except . . . except . . . except . . . just one thing. Very, very carefully I balance myself on the razor's edge between two worlds.

Sylvie feels a sudden gust of wind and turns to look down the street. Everything is still, except for a piece of paper flapping on the sidewalk. And then she sees the old woman's net bag with its meager contents spilled out: a morsel of cheese, some sugared almonds, a chop wrapped in butcher's paper. She gathers them up and hurries around the corner to rue Elzévir. There is no sign of the woman, but farther down the street, the blue door is open. She slips into the building, tells Coco to wait, and starts up the staircase.

She is taken aback to find the old woman peering down at her from the landing. "It's you," she says excitedly, "I knew you would come. But what took you so long?" Sylvie's bewilderment grows at the woman's strange behavior. Instead of remaining barricaded behind the door like a true Parisienne, she hurries toward Sylvie, takes hold of her hand and draws her into the apartment.

The shutters are pulled against the sun and as Sylvie's eyes adjust to the gloom, she notices the frayed and worn furnishings, the plain wooden furniture. But everything is immaculate, the wood polished to a gleam, the mantelpiece crowded with framed photographs freshly dusted. A large bookshelf displays beautifully bound books, their leather spines and gold lettering strangely opulent in the dim surroundings.

But like the woman herself, there is something askew about the room. Though the windows are lofty, their effect is marred by the low ceiling which presses down upon them. The woman waves Sylvie to a chair and whispers, "The grandmother eats our bonbons."

Sylvie stares at the face beaming down at her. *"Pardon?"*

"But Marie says it's a secret."

"Marie?" Sylvie falters. "Are you Marie?"

The woman laughs merrily. "My, how you get things mixed up, you silly girl, *I'm* not Marie, I'm Mathilde."

Sylvie can't make sense of what the old woman is saying, she's talking in riddles. And then Sylvie realizes she's speaking to a child in a body that has grown old without her awareness. In any event, she won't get any sense out of her. Sylvie tries to get up, but Mathilde pushes her back with surprising strength and stands before the door.

Nervous now, Sylvie glances around the room, looking for a means of escape. Inscrutable faces stare back at her from the mantel. Her gaze is arrested by one in particular, a face she recognizes. No possibility of a mistake, she has seen it all too recently.

Clara.

Sylvie's head swims and everything goes dark.

When she comes to, she is alone. Her legs are unsteady as she tries to stand, and she realizes she is faint from hunger. She feels around the chair and notices that her purse is gone. Nothing of great value taken, but she finds it disquieting all the same. Suddenly Coco bounds in through the open door, barking in triumph.

Mathilde bursts into the room behind him, brandishing a stick to chase him away. Holding on to Coco, Sylvie gapes at the transformation in the woman, now in a neat and sober dress. Her expression is different, too, no longer welcoming and friendly like a door flung open, but shuttered with mistrust. She stops dead at the sight of Sylvie. To her amazement, the old woman says, "How did you get in?"

Sylvie struggles to her feet. "I'm just leaving."

"Who are you? Are you alone?"

"Yes, I'm by myself." Then she thinks the words unwise and adds, "I must leave, they're waiting for me at home."

"Answer me. Who are you? What do you want?" The woman's tone is aggressive as she takes a step toward Sylvie and Coco growls, *No closer.*

"I must go, Mathilde."

"Mathilde?" Her surprise is unmistakable.

Mathilde comes in behind her and says reprovingly, "Wrong again, silly, I told you *I'm* Mathilde, she's Marie, we're ex-act-ly the same."

Marie turns to her sister and says despairingly, "Don't let

people in like that, we'll be robbed and murdered in our beds one day."

"How *can* she rob us when I already took away her purse?" She brandishes it, proud of her cleverness. "Here it is. Oh look, a dog, he'll protect us, won't you, good dog?"

Coco pricks up his ears hopefully. *Good dog.* Those words always mean some treat is forthcoming. He follows Mathilde to the kitchen, smells the chop on the counter, and waits for it to slide providentially to the floor.

Alone with Sylvie, Marie pulls open the shutters. The rays of the late-afternoon sun flash into the room and Marie draws a deep breath. "Yes, I see it now, the resemblance. Of course Clara would be much older than you now, but that wouldn't occur to Mathilde, she's been *expecting* her all this time."

"Forgive me, I didn't mean to disturb you."

"Who *are* you? Why did you come?"

Sylvie pulls the note from her purse and holds it out. Marie squints at it, then her face sags. "Julien," she says.

One word, that is all. Sylvie feels the blood pounding in her ears. A large wave crests in the distance, racing toward shore. "Do you know he is . . . ?"

"Yes, Isabelle told me."

Isabelle. The wave breaks over Sylvie and she discovers how powerfully the past can engulf the present. Once again she is a child hiding behind the door while her mother serves Madame Wanda's guests, the men with ribbons pinned to their chest, the women sparkling with diamonds, and now, as then, she feels herself an outsider.

Sylvie sits there overwhelmed at where her quest has led her, to these elderly twins, one sister eaten up with suspicion to safeguard against the dangerous innocence of the other. With an effort she struggles to her feet, but Mathilde rushes out from the kitchen to stop her once again. She pulls Sylvie to a table, unknots a burlap parcel, and the rolled-up canvases within spring open after their long confinement.

Sylvie looks through a series of landscapes, of vineyards, hills, and ruins. There are also familiar city views, the rooftops of Paris, a courtyard full of pigeons, a street crisscrossed with tricolored flags. Yet the technique is the same, the brushstrokes skillfully blurred to give the impression of things seen long ago and far away; only the window framing each scene has the hard edges of contemporary life. Sylvie cannot explain why these romantic landscapes should seem so menacing. She examines each painting more attentively and realizes the focus is not the prospect at all, but the window, its insistent lines placing the artist inside and the world outside: landscapes meant not for living, but for reliving.

Abruptly Sylvie pushes away the paintings and makes for the door. Mathilde tries to detain her, but Marie says, "Let her go."

"She must take her things," Mathilde protests. "The jewel box." She darts to the window and tugs a cord hidden behind the curtains. A trapdoor yawns open and hangs down from the ceiling to reveal the space which has cunningly robbed the room of its harmonious proportions. Sylvie's breath sticks in her throat as she sees a windowless room within a room, just high enough for a small child or a crouched adult. Her eyes turn instinctively to the photographs of Clara and her girls. "Is that where . . ." she whispers, and Marie nods grimly.

"That's where they found them, *ce jour-là*."

That day. To Marie it can mean only one day, although close to half a century has elapsed since then. Her heart had jumped into her mouth every time she heard a sound. She realized she was still waiting for Bernard, though there had been no sign of him for several days. There was a soft tapping at the door, and she and Clara both jumped up to answer it. Marie shook her head and waited till Clara and the girls were safely hidden. No point taking chances. Opening the door a crack, she was surprised to see Madame Grzybyk, the fat little confectioner from around the corner, with her heavily accented French and her pastries certified *cacher* by the rabbi's seal. Whenever they passed her shop, Mathilde would run in for some bonbons from "Madame Cacher."

Marie had not seen her since the day her shop was vandalized, like so many others now forced to display the yellow sign: *entreprise juive*. The windows were smashed, glass crystals frosted the pastries, and a group of men stood at the street corner, smoking nonchalantly. Members of the Croix de Feu, no doubt, stirring up trouble as usual. A few passersby cast sympathetic glances at the shopkeeper sweeping up the broken glass, but did not stop. Marie, too, lowered her head and hurried past, until Mathilde put her to shame by stopping to hug Madame Cacher.

Why had she showed up at their door? Eyeing her suspiciously, Marie saw that the woman was laden down with various odd-shaped bundles, and, of all things, her samovar. Mathilde beckoned Mrs. Grzybyk in, but Marie refused to open the door any wider.

The woman whispered, *"Cacher."*

Whatever did she mean, Marie wondered, and in case anyone was listening, she said loudly that Clara and her children had left for the Free Zone, no point looking for them here. Mrs. Grzybyk continued to repeat the word, *"cacher, cacher,"* and when Marie tried to shut the door in her face, she pleaded urgently, *"Les juifs . . . il faut s'cacher."*

Marie realized she had been misled by the woman's accent, she was talking about concealment, not confectionery. Abruptly she pulled Mrs. Grzybyk into the apartment. How much did she know? Who had told her? The carpenter? The concierge? That was the trouble these days, you couldn't trust anyone.

Mrs. Grzybyk said a friend had telephoned from the prefecture of police, warning her to hide. *"Il faut s'cacher,"* he said, but where could she go that night?

"Here," said Mathilde, pointing under her bed.

"Bless you, my dear, I could no more crawl under there than I could fly," said Mrs. Grzybyk.

"If you could fly," said Mathilde, "there's room up there." She pointed to the ceiling and hurried behind the curtain to pull the cord. *"Voilà!"* she said with a self-important air as the trapdoor swung open.

Mrs. Grzybyk stared in wonder at Clara looking down at her. "Can you squeeze in one more, my dear?"

"Of course," said Clara, "of course." But after all it was the rope ladder that decided the issue. No matter how much they tried, they could not hoist her up. She would have to look elsewhere, said Mrs. Grzybyk, she hoped it was not too late.

Too late? It was still light outside, Marie thought, but then remembered the curfew began several hours earlier for Jews. Anyway, the woman couldn't go around encumbered like that, she had best leave some things behind. Clara and the girls came down and repacked her parcels, while Marie boiled water for coffee, if you could call it that, nothing but a teaspoon of burnt barley.

Mrs. Grzybyk reluctantly left behind a painting, a gift from an artist whom she had fed when he hadn't money enough to buy a crust of bread. Clara said the lighting was exquisite, like a Rembrandt, but Marie stared at the hideous canvas, two plucked chickens on a plate, and wondered how it could even be called art.

The confectioner's visit had shaken Marie, and the words "too late" sounded like a knell in her ears, but she wasn't thinking of Mrs. Grzybyk, she was thinking of Bernard, how fiercely they had argued the last time she saw him.

"They'll never hand over women and children," she had insisted, "it's unthinkable."

"Unthinkable! And Jews wearing badges, did you think *that* would ever happen?"

Since the decree, his wife and daughters couldn't leave the house without the yellow star of David sewn to their clothes, and Bernard had wasted their precious textile coupons to buy one for himself, had insisted on fastening it to his coat.

Marie argued that it was foolhardy, the authorities didn't look kindly on *amis des juifs*, either, best to be prudent.

Her nephew said sharply, "Can't you see that's what they count on, our being *prudent?*"

Someone pushed open the bindery door, and hearing the jingle of the bell, they fell silent. A young man placed a tattered book on the counter, and Bernard murmured, *"Morocco leather and fine Florentine endpapers, of course."* He opened a drawer and pulled out the last scrap of gilded paper, the likes of which Marie did not know if she would ever see again. Along with the receipt, Bernard slipped a handwritten list to the customer, who pocketed it without a word as Bernard said the book would be ready next week.

Marie pressed her lips together. Next week it would be some-one else who came with the receipt to pick up the book and drop off another list. Dangerous business, but he would not listen to her, he despised her *prudence*, when all she was trying to do was get through the war, what use were futile gestures of resistance?

How often since that day she had regretted every contentious word that passed between them, she would recall each one if she could. But it was too late.

She had come into the bindery late the next morning, it was Bernard's day for opening up. But Bernard was gone, the shop in a state of chaos, with drawers pulled out and rummaged through, papers scattered everywhere, books flung to the floor with their spines broken beyond repair. She had felt something sticky underfoot and looked down in horror, but it was only glue from the upturned bottle. Next to the cash drawer, an awl glinted in the light. She picked it up and saw the congealed red liquid on the blade. *Ink,* she told herself, as she backed away. She looked at the book press, but her mind refused to register what she saw. How proud Bernard had been when they bought the book press, capable of exerting a thousand kilograms of pressure on a book so that it would lie neat and flat. Despite herself, she looked again at the press, screwed down firmly, but with no paper on the wooden stand, only a fragment of fingernail surrounded by jagged flesh.

She had staggered out and vomited in the gutter. The green-grocer across the street brought her water and whispered they had taken Bernard away. *"Tell me who,"* she begged, *"tell me where,"* but he looked fearfully over his shoulder and hurried back to his heads of lettuce, his basket of crimson radishes.

Had they taken him to rue de Saussaies? Where the neighbors complained they could not sleep at night because of the screams. Where they had a bathtub in which they drowned prisoners, resuscitated them, drowned them over and over again. Where bodies were recovered with fingers mutilated from scraping the limestone walls of the interrogation room.

Ten hours, Bernard had said, twelve at the most, before the prisoner sang. Just time enough for the cell to disband and go into hiding, his own refuge in the ceiling ready for that eventuality. But Bernard was the one picked up first. Had he made it that long under interrogation? There was no one she could ask. No one would come to the bindery anymore.

Distraught, Marie had run everywhere she could think of, the *commissariat*, the *préfecture*, the *mairie*, and had spent the day being handed off from one official to another. Although they dutifully noted the information, she could see from their shrugs that one missing person in these times was not a pressing matter. Marie forced herself to go back into the bindery, to put away the familiar tools she handled at work every day, pick up the books from the floor and glue and stitch their broken spines as best she could, her fingers working mechanically while her mind raced.

By the end of the day, she could finally see her way clear. Returning to the apartment, she smelled the lingering odor of turpentine in the stairwell. Clara at her painting again, now that she wasn't allowed to work anymore, all Jews shut out of their professions, even teaching art considered subversive these days. Marie climbed the staircase slowly and paused at the door, trying to compose herself before she had to face Clara.

Inside, everything was as it had been when she left, the children busy with their coloring books, Mathilde singing lullabies to her doll. All of a sudden the day's events assumed the unreal dimensions of a nightmare. Marie had the strangest feeling that if she turned around and went back to the bindery right now, she would find it as it had always been, Bernard bent over an old book, looking up as the bell jingled. But she shook her head, she could not afford these foolish fancies, not now. She took Clara aside and whispered that Bernard had gone underground, it would be best if she and the children were also to "disappear."

Wordlessly Clara turned to open a window. She gripped the railing to steady herself and took several deep breaths. Marie was overcome with pity. How much had been taken from this young woman already, little daily diminishments, her livelihood gone, her bicycle confiscated, and in any case where was there to go, public places like museums and cinemas out of bounds, though Clara would hardly want to see filth like *The Jewish Menace*, or enter *cafés* with signs that said NO DOGS AND JEWS.

Clara turned back to face Marie, her features pale and set. She knew that this, too, was being taken away from her, the open window, but it seemed a small thing she could do to help Bernard in his work. It was clear from the way Clara said "work" that she imagined him hiding in subterranean tunnels, dodging the Gestapo, sabotaging their plans. And Marie was satisfied that her deliberate use of "underground" had led Clara to think that. But everything now depended on Marie, Mathilde no more help than the children. Less, in fact.

The next morning, Marie took Mathilde to a convent on the other side of town, wondering how her sister would fare without her. But it would certainly make things easier at home; she could use Mathilde's ration card as well as her own, no one could tell them apart, but she would shop in a different neighborhood just to be sure. Of course, they could no longer use Clara's card, but that didn't get them much anyway, Jews were only allowed to line up at the food shops late in the afternoon when the shelves were already empty.

Left by herself with the nuns, Mathilde wailed for her sister, for Clara, for the twins. *"Gigi,"* she kept calling, *"Lilou, where are you?"* The mother superior would willingly have taken Clara's girls as well, she had hidden many Jewish children in the past, but the Germans were searching even the Catholic schools now. She wished the Holy Father would openly denounce the persecution of the Israelites, instead of talking vaguely of charity and justice. But if she had to choose between being a good Catholic and being a good Christian, well, for her, the choice was clear. She was bound by conscience to follow the words of Christ rather than the silence of his church.

Within a day Mathilde ran away from the convent and inexplicably found her way home, beaming at her own cleverness. Marie wondered where to take her next, but Clara begged her to let Mathilde stay, to teach her how to open the trapdoor in case of emergency. What if Marie was out and there was a fire, how would Clara and the girls escape? But when Marie tried to explain the situation, Mathilde laughed and said *"cache-cache,"* as if it was a game of hide-and-seek.

"It's not a game," said Clara, taking Mathilde in her arms, "Listen to me carefully, you're a big girl now and you have an important job, you have to pull the cord if you hear someone knock like this: *Tap-tap-tap. Tap-tap.* It means *Open up, Mathilde.* Do you understand?"

Mathilde nodded. Yes, she understood, per-fect-ly.

But Marie continued to worry. Mathilde did not realize how dangerous the situation was, look how she had revealed the hiding place to Madame Grzybyk. After the confectioner had left that night, Marie remained keyed up and anxious. Even when the lights had been turned off in all the neighboring windows, she sat up in the kitchen, looking out at the street. She thought she heard a cock crowing in the distance and wondered if she was dreaming, surely there was not a single rooster left uneaten in the city. Marie rose and checked on her sister, sleeping soundly, and couldn't recall the last time she herself had drawn such carefree breaths. In the next room, she heard Gigi coughing and went in to find Clara worn out with worry, listening for the telltale whoop of pertussis. Marie told her to sleep, she would keep watch. She sat in a chair by the window, her eyes burning in the dark.

She must have dozed off, dreaming of Bernard as a little boy. They were all in her brother's kitchen, with *le petit* Bernard hiding under the table. Suddenly he started kicking the table legs, and all the adults peered under the cloth to see what Bernard was up to. He was hammering nails into the floor, and Marie said, "*Attention*, you'll hurt yourself," but she was too late, he had already smashed his finger. Marie woke up shuddering, her face cold with perspiration despite the oppressive heat. She heard the hammering start up again, but now she knew it wasn't a dream, someone was pounding at the door downstairs. At first she thought Mrs.

Grzybyk had returned, but realized at once it was not the knock of a fugitive, it was too loud, too peremptory, too official.

"*Ouvrez, police!*"

Silently Marie shook Clara's shoulder. Gigi started to cough again, and Clara pressed a handkerchief to her mouth, as she and the girls, still half asleep, disappeared into the ceiling.

Marie heard the concierge's shrill voice in the stairwell and fear clutched at her heart. Would she betray them? But Madame Fichot's son had been sent to join the labor force in Germany and she was busy airing her own grievances. Why didn't they go and fight the Boche, she berated the police, instead of terrorizing innocent women and children asleep in their beds like god-fearing Christians. Her tactics delayed the men only for an instant. Marie heard their footsteps climbing the stairs and looked at the ceiling to make sure the trapdoor was shut.

"*Ouvrez, police!*"

She slowly drew a shawl around her shoulders and waited. They knocked again and she threw open the door to confront the policemen, French, after all, not German, but doing their dirty work for them in any case. She glared at the two men, one in uniform, the other in civilian clothes. "Listen, *messieurs*, if you're here for my nephew, I don't know what he was mixed up in and I don't want to know. He's gone, and so have his wife and kids, and good riddance to them all."

The uniformed man muttered, "Flown the coop."

His older colleague, fiddling with his pipe, asked if they could take a look around.

"Well, be quick about it. And whatever you do, don't wake my sister," she answered irascibly.

He poked his head into the bedroom where Mathilde was sleeping. Then he looked into the other room, the unmade bed. "Forgive us for disturbing you," he said. As he was leaving, he stooped to pick up a doll from the floor. "Whose?"

"My sister's. Mathilde is . . ." Marie tapped her forehead softly.

Sleeping through all the commotion, Mathilde was woken by the sound of her own name. She came into the living room, rubbing her eyes. Her sister looked at her warningly. Mathilde nodded, she understood. Per-fect-ly. Then she saw the policemen and scolded them, "Haven't you found Bernard yet?" That's what the police were supposed to do, find people who were lost, things that were missing.

"We're still looking," said the older one, smiling kindly at her. He had a child who was "simple" in much the same way. She'd lost a doll, perhaps? "It's an important job, and we take it seriously." About to leave, he tapped his pipe absently against the mantelpiece, *Tap-tap-tap. Tap-tap.*

Mathilde heard the signal, *Open up, Mathilde,* and nodded to show him that she was a big girl with her own important job, which she took as seriously as he did. She ran over to the curtain and pulled the cord. The trapdoor yawned open and Marie struck her as hard as she could. Mathilde fell howling to the floor, why was her sister angry, she had done ex-act-ly what they told her to do, but Marie refused to look at her and only when they were left by themselves again did she kneel beside Mathilde and join in her anguished wails.

Even I, who have long known every detail of what happened that day almost fifty years ago, find myself shaken, and I can only imagine Sylvie's distress when I see her deathly pallor. She wrenches the door open to flee the site of a tragedy whose sleeping ghosts she has willfully disturbed, her mind in turmoil at having unearthed a shard of the city's secret history—no, not secret, it was out in plain sight—but its silent history, repressed by guilt, driven underground.

Uncanny! It's the first word that springs to my mind at the sight of the trapdoor swinging open, just as it sprang to Sylvie's when the unmarked folder first fell from my desk to the floor. How right Freud was about that eerie sensation we feel when "something that was meant to remain hidden comes to light."

His insights about the unconscious had influenced my own work and I came to regard the conscious mind as a vaunted château, its dazzling brilliance blinding us to the dungeons equipped with their refinements of torture: the spokes of a bone-crushing wheel, the crippling pulleys of the estrapade, or a diadem of spikes encrusted with blood. Most horrifying of all, the oubliette, a pit into which people were thrown and lost forever to the world. They died of starvation, of madness, occasionally of drowning as the water rose from below, nothing left of them but bones gleaming in the dust.

No wonder we call them oubliettes, these sites of forgetting. But in time these eloquent bones do come to light, these repressed memories return with a vengeance. Only then can we make a reckoning with the past, a reckoning that offers consolations for the present, cautions for the future.

Sylvie has just peered into the oubliette and come face-to-face with its horrors. She now has a personal stake in the story: it is my story, Clara's story, and the story of her daughters. The Shoah is larger than any one person, or city, or country, yet how strange is the reckoning of tragedies, where single numbers are easier to understand than the incomprehensible number: six million.

Yet even as I long to comfort Sylvie, I cannot help feeling a renewed flicker of hope. Will she finish the quest I had begun? I hope, but cannot be certain; all I can do is wait. Despite the innumerable stories that have taken up residence in me, I lay no claim to omniscience: My terrain is not the future, but the past.

Overwhelmed by the events of the day, Sylvie pushes open the gate, crosses the courtyard, and drags herself upstairs. But instead of turning the key in her own lock, she taps on the neighboring door.

The Americans don't answer at first, and Sylvie hesitates. It is late, but she can't wait till morning, she needs the answer now, and surely Will must know. She knocks again. Will opens the door and takes a step back at the sight of her troubled face.

"Come in, come in," he says, and Coco makes a beeline for Alice, wagging his stumpy tail for all he is worth.

Sylvie apologizes for disturbing them in the middle of dinner.

"We've just finished," Alice says. "Can I get you something? A cup of coffee?"

Sylvie shakes her head, disoriented by the normalcy of the scene, a world away from what she has just discovered. "Just a quick question," she says, pulling out the card and handing it to Will. "Do you know these lines?"

"*Do* I? Do I ever!" He reads them aloud:

> *"Mais si pendant ce temps je pense à toi, cher ami,*
> *toutes mes pertes sont réparées et tous mes chagrins finis.*

"Quite fine as far as it goes, but it doesn't do justice to the original, although what translation can? Listen to the difference:

"But if the while I think on thee, dear friend,
All losses are restored and sorrows end."

Hearing his "classroom" voice, Alice thinks, Shakespeare.

"Shakespeare," says Will. "The thirtieth sonnet, a long reckoning of heartbreak and then this final couplet, compensation for all that is lost."

Alice notices Sylvie's stricken look and shoots her husband a warning glance, but he is already launched on his lecture, "That's where the English title for Proust comes from, you know, the opening lines of this sonnet: *I summon up remembrance of things past.*"

Sylvie thinks, Proust, *that* at least she has read, but then the words penetrate and a wave of emotion washes over her, leaving her light-headed. She sways on her feet and the Taylors rush toward her, hold her steady. Sylvie leans against them gratefully. Earlier today, the disturbing thought had crossed her mind that despite what she said to Marie, no one waited for her at home, no one would miss her right away, no one would track her down. Suddenly she feels that of all the people she knows, Will and Alice might be the easiest to confide in, they aren't French, the story has nothing directly to do with them.

"I've had some bad news," she says, and doesn't know how to proceed. Can the horrifying revelations of the afternoon even be called *news?* It all happened so long ago, but the shock is still fresh, still immediate. Haltingly she tells them what she has discovered, and they listen in silence. Her voice trails away as she describes the paintings, and Will feels humbled by her trust in them, strangers from across the sea who have come into her life by chance.

Alice asks if there is anything they can do to help, anything at all. And Sylvie clasps her hand and says, "You don't know how much you've helped just by being here."

Alice accompanies her across the landing. "Are you sure you're all right?"

Sylvie nods, but when Alice is about to leave, she stops her. "Could you do me a favor? Could you take Coco down in the morning?"

"You bet." Alice promptly takes the leash Sylvie holds out to her. She returns to their apartment and goes back to addressing a stack of postcards in thoughtful silence. How pale Sylvie had looked, how shaken. *Why don't her children come?* thinks Alice, and is surprised at the sudden wave of emotion that washes over her. Sticking on the new bicentenary stamps, she notices that Will has scribbled a P.S. on the postcard to Fabienne: *Worried about Sylvie, call her kids.*

Still racked by shudders, Sylvie sits down at Julien's desk and writes a brief note. She addresses the envelope to Marie Forrestier at rue Elzévir, the number clearly marked for the postman.

Forcing herself to swallow some soup, she changes into her slippers and notices that blisters have formed on her feet. With a sigh she slides between linen sheets, cool against her skin after the heat of the afternoon. What good has it done her to track down Marie, to learn the full magnitude of Julien's loss much too late to offer him solace?

Sylvie wonders if she should have taken the other course and returned the envelope unopened to its hiding place in Julien's desk. Then she falls asleep and dreams that she has cast the envelope into the fire, and the photograph of Clara curls and blackens in the flames, the face slowly eaten away, the dark hair lightened into smoke, until all that is left is a scattering of ash.

Alice hesitates in front of Sylvie's apartment, unsure whether to call out. The door is ajar, but there is no light, no sound. Is Sylvie ill? Should she ring the concierge? But it's early yet, perhaps Sylvie is still sleeping, she looked worn-out last night. Hearing the jingle of the leash, Coco noses his way out and runs down the stairs in conspiratorial silence. Down in the courtyard he lets out an excited bark. Ana Carvalho sees them go through the gate and thinks the scamp has taken up with the American now, has he?

She remembers the day Coco had crept half drowned and shivering into the courtyard. He hid behind the dustbins, and no one could coax him out, but when Monsieur Julien approached, the dog came right up and licked his hand. The man knew just how to deal with animals, and people, too, for that matter. Such a pity he is gone, things aren't the same without him.

The concierge turns away from the window and settles into her rocking chair, crooning softly to her birds. They respond with whistles and cheeps, fluttering about the room as their feathers waft to the floor, noiseless as dandelion fluff. A budgie, bolder than the others, hops down her arm to peck at the seeds she holds out in her palm. After a while, Ana Carvalho rises to her feet with an effort. Her ankles are swollen, and for the first time she thinks about retiring to her brother's place in Hossegor. It's getting harder to climb the stairs to attend to the judge and his wife, to look in on Madame Sylvie, to run errands for the young man on the second floor, wasting away with a disease they do not name.

Most of the old occupants have already died, and the new ones moving in barely have time to say *bonjour*, always in a rush. The island, too, has changed over the years, the main street constantly sticky underfoot, how many ice-cream shops do they need, why not put in something useful, like a dry cleaner.

The concierge goes about her work, checking the *minuteries* on the lights, watering the clivia in the stairwell, delivering mail to the housebound man on the second floor who trembles at every knock, more afraid of eviction than death. She hums softly under her breath, *Quand on s'promène, au bord de l'eau.* In a few weeks, she will be off for her holidays. It will be good to put up her feet and watch the high waves roll in from the Atlantic. But she knows that by the time September comes around, she will be longing for her *rentrée* to the city.

More than halfway through their trip, Will's unfulfilled desire to *know* the city has acquired a feverish urgency. Or is the fever a sign he's coming down with something? No point mentioning it to Alice, she'll insist all he needs is fresh air and exercise, that's what she prescribes for everyone, look at how she's taken Coco in hand. His wife gives a new meaning to the concept of *rude health*, nothing but contempt for "coddlers." Will waits till Alice is at her lesson before going to the neighborhood pharmacy and browsing its shelves crammed with tisanes and creams for every ailment, including that dreaded French malady, *cellulite*.

Behind the counter, a white-coated pharmacist is listening courteously to an elderly man's recital of his daily aches and pains. Will has a sudden impulse to join the three women who are waiting their turn to unburden themselves to a sympathetic listener. The French take coddling seriously, no one here would scold him for being a *malade imaginaire*.

He buys some propolis lozenges and saunters down the island's main street, crowded as usual with tourists. Two young women stop to admire their reflection in shop windows, and Will recognizes them as Americans just by their leisurely stride, so different from the neat, hurried steps of Parisians. He picks his way carefully through the next stretch of pavement, beloved of dogs. A man wheels his bicycle through the wooden portal of Maison Chenizot, and Will slips in after him, curious what lies behind the building's imposing façade.

Crossing a large courtyard with mossy cobblestones, Will wanders through an archway into a second courtyard, feeling he is penetrating into the very heart of the city. In one of the apartments, someone is practicing the harp, arpeggios drifting down like snowflakes. Balanced on a scaffold, a workman stops his painting to light a cigarette. A giant sundial chiseled into the wall marks the noon hour, and little girls in ballet slippers run out from class, their childish trebles echoing in the courtyard. In secret corners such as this, away from the cameras and curiosity of tourists, real Parisians attend to their daily concerns. Even though he has accidentally entered this self-contained world, Will realizes he will never be an insider, no matter how long he lives here, no matter how hard he tries. The city will keep all its secrets, and he will leave behind lives he can only imagine, names he will never know.

His wandering gaze is arrested by a plaque set discreetly into the wall, and with a slight shock he realizes that he *does* know the name, he sees it every day by the front door to the apartment: *Docteur Julien Dalsace.* Peering past the FOR RENT sign, Will sees a waiting room leading to another room behind a curtained doorway, and thinks what an apt setting it provides for the work of psychoanalysis: a room within a room, in a courtyard within a courtyard, on an island within a city.

Perhaps Sylvie was once a patient? He can see her as a young woman perched on one of the stone posts flanking the portal, remnants of the days when they protected the walls from damage by carriage wheels. He walks back through the great wooden door and out into the street, and as if his thoughts have summoned her, he sees Sylvie sitting alone in a tea shop window, looking up expectantly every time the door opens.

I watch Will walk down the street and turn the corner toward the école maternelle, where the joyous shouts of children fill the air like brightly colored balloons. But when I look back at Sylvie, I am startled by a face at once familiar and unfamiliar.

Even when I realize it's my own reflection in the window, the uncanny sensation lingers. Invisibility is so much a part of me, it no longer seems second nature but my true self. As if I have never been a man of substance, have always been only a shadow. I feel a prickling at the back of my neck, a physical sensation as puzzling as a vestigial bone in a skeleton. Hastily I step back. Is it a warning that I am getting too close to events, revealing too much of myself?

Nonsense!

Reassured, I look again, and my reflection has vanished, leaving only Sylvie and Marie seated across from each other. The steam from their cups of cocoa clouds the window, like breath on glass, which in the end is all that separates the living from the dead.

Sylvie wasn't sure if Marie would ignore her note, but she has come. Without a word of greeting, the old woman thrusts a wooden box and the rolled-up canvases into Sylvie's hands. "Here, take these. Isabelle didn't want them, but maybe you can pass them on to Julien's children."

Sylvie fingers the carved cedar before opening it, and the only treasures in the "jewel case" are a few round pebbles, a square of black lace, and a folded letter. She can hardly bear to look at the meager contents, all that is left of Clara's life.

"Julien told me so little about her."

"What was there to say?"

Marie's brusque response shames Sylvie. What right does she have to force anyone to break that long silence? "Perhaps you are right," she says humbly, "perhaps it's better to forget."

"How *can* I forget, living with Mathilde. And yet *she* remembers nothing." Marie's face twists into a painful grimace. Her eyes wander around the shop, lingering on the copper chocolate molds in the shape of rabbits and lambs and roosters. "Sometimes I wish I was the one born with the defect. What must it be like, never having to worry about how we will live, what will become of us. I've always had to take care of her, and no one can imagine what it cost me, I'm not speaking of money, we have our troubles but I manage, I've never asked anyone for anything. But it's not easy for her, either. She looks at me with a puzzled expression sometimes, trying to understand what makes us different. And when Clara's twins came, she kept asking anxiously, *'Are they the same, exactly the same?'*"

Marie stirs her cocoa furiously, spilling some in the saucer. "When they were taken away, she couldn't understand it, she kept calling, *'Where are you, where are you?'* as if they were playing *cache-cache*. Then one day she told me, I know where they're hiding, and pointed to the radio. She would always listen intently to the broadcasts from London, as if those messages were meant only for us."

"The blue horse is on the horizon," says Sylvie, surprised that the words have stayed with her for, what, forty years now, forty-five? She remembers crouching in her parents' kitchen with the drapes drawn and a towel stuffed under the door while her father tried to tune in to Radio London. Over the static of the Germans trying to jam the transmission, they heard the thrilling four-beat signature: *Da-da-da-daaaa*. Morse code for *V*, her father said, *V* for Victory, but Sylvie recognized the opening bars of Beethoven's Fifth Symphony. And then they heard the words *Ici Londres*, reminding them that across the Channel people were still fighting to free France.

"The violins of autumn wound my heart," replies Marie, her face relaxing its habitual grimness as she recalls the message that signaled the final push for liberation.

Sylvie thinks at last a human connection had been made between them, if only for a moment, through a shared memory. Then she remembers another of the coded messages—*the grandmother eats our bonbons*—which Mathilde had parroted back to her. "Maybe she thought that's where they were, with Julien in London?"

Marie shrugs. "I don't know what she thought. After the war

was over, we were told those who survived the camps would be taken to the Hotel Lutetia, and we all crowded behind the barricades to wait for the Red Cross buses. Some people had brought flowers, but when they saw the faces of the survivors, no one had the heart to offer them. A woman dropped her bouquet of lilacs to the ground, and their scent filled the air as we trampled them in our rush." She could still feel the surge of the crowd as it accosted the returnees, clutching their arms, clamoring, *"Have you seen my husband? My wife? My child?"* But the men in striped clothes and the women with hollow eyes shrank back from the loud voices and looked around vacantly. It was as if they did not see the desperate faces, did not hear the desperate voices, as if they were still among the missing.

Marie stares into the cup, where cocoa has congealed at the bottom. She tells Sylvie she had never set foot inside that grand hotel before, but in the old days, every time she got off the metro at Sèvres-Babylone, she would see elegant women whisked inside by the revolving doors. She imagined them settling down to dainty tea sandwiches for *le four-o'clock*, or newlyweds gazing at each other over the rims of champagne glasses before retiring discreetly upstairs. To think that this hotel—where de Gaulle had spent his honeymoon before the war, and the German Abwehr had spent the Occupation—was now sheltering survivors from the concentration camps! The idea of their sleeping on the same expensive sheets, eating the same tempting delicacies, struck her as a macabre irony.

When Marie finally entered the lobby with its sparkling chandelier, instead of the whiff of expensive perfumes, there was the overpowering smell of DDT as the survivors were fumigated for lice and disease. Along the walls, invalids too weak to stand lay motionless on stretchers; others sat patiently in chairs, their gaze turned inward. Everyone was waiting for something. For a doctor, for an identity card, a government allowance. They clutched anything that was given to them—a piece of paper, a roll of bread—close to their chests as if afraid it would be snatched away. Despite the swirl of activity, the doctors and volunteers spoke in low voices, while the perfectly trained hotel staff went about their tasks in silence. Suddenly there was a crash from the dining room as a tray was knocked over, and everyone turned to stare. But the returnees instinctively raised their arms to protect themselves, revealing the tattooed numbers they had tried to conceal.

Everywhere one looked, there were photographs of *les absents* pinned to the walls. So many of them, photographed in happier circumstances, in family portraits taken at the beach, at a wedding, smiling into the camera, unaware of what was to come. Now their happy countenances seemed unbearably poignant, three generations wiped out at once.

"My photographs of Clara and the girls were there as well, and that's how I met Julien. He was only a couple of years younger than I was at the time, and somehow I had imagined Clara's brother looking quite different, I don't know why, but there was no mistaking the resemblance, the same blue eyes, the same way of carrying himself. When I introduced myself, all I could think was that Julien had left Paris when peace still seemed possible. To return to this!"

Julien and she went to the Lutetia every day, except Saturdays, of course, when the registry closed for the Jewish Sabbath. At first they still had hope. It was spring, the chestnut trees were in bloom, and the dark years were finally behind them. But as May turned to June, and the stream of survivors slowed to a trickle, the people crowded behind the barricades became weary, discouraged. Something about Julien drew others to him, among them a woman who looked like she could have been a habitué of the hotel in happier days, but who was now there for the same sad reason as everyone else. She pestered people to look at the picture of her daughter, a beautiful young woman posing with her hand on her hip, defiantly flaunting the star of David on her coat. *"Belle, comme elle était belle,"* Mrs. Stein sobbed, *"what have they done with her, who will make them pay?"*

Julien replied that he wanted something more terrible than vengeance. Marie wondered what could be more terrible, but just then a woman broke away from the line of people filing into the hotel and staggered toward them. Mrs. Stein thrust the photograph at her and cried, *"Have you seen her, have you seen my daughter?"* She shook her head and gazed at the photograph with sorrowful eyes. Mrs. Stein stared at this specter robbed of all defiance, all youth, all beauty, then she embraced her, weeping, *"Ma belle, oh, ma belle,"* and Marie thought that this is one thing at least that we've been spared.

"Julien and I continued to wait all through the summer, until finally the Ministry sent out an official memo that repatriation was terminated." It was September, and the chestnut trees were starting to turn color. They turned away from the Lutetia, knowing they would never willingly walk past its grand façade again.

But Julien refused to give up. He pursued every lead, however slight, and yet all he could discover was that Clara had entered the Vel d'Hiv with her twin daughters and had left from there alone. At the police headquarters, a couple of *gendarmes* recalled the little girl who had berated a German officer; at the Red Cross, a nurse remembered the twins, one had died of a raging fever, she wasn't sure about the other. Marie told him the twins were inseparable, if Gigi was dead, Lilou must be presumed dead. But *presumed dead* is not the same as dead, and Julien kept hoping for a miracle. Marie no longer believed in miracles, but still she had held on to Clara's letter inscribed *to my daughters*.

Immersed in scenes of the past, Marie is unaware of time in the present, paying scant heed to the hour, to the street outside the tea shop crowded with people walking home with loaves of bread, others hurrying toward the *boulangerie* before it closes for lunch. She says in a low voice, "I never told Julien about Mathilde's role in all this, I was afraid he wouldn't forgive her. There was a lot I didn't tell him."

"You loved Julien?"

"Yes." She bites her lip, and then the bottled-up words come out in a rush of bitterness. "Yes, I was in love with him. But by then he had met Isabelle. So beautiful, so *comme il faut*. What man in his right mind would choose me?"

The image of Isabelle glides between them, and they both fall silent. From the first, Marie had taken a dislike to Isabelle. It was partly jealousy, of course, but something about her just rubbed her the wrong way. Isabelle had no inkling that her efforts to "correct" Mathilde might be unwelcome, or that her tips on how to keep tulips fresh in a vase might be useless; in her world, everyone could afford cut flowers. And Isabelle simply couldn't fathom that someone who was poor should be as proud as she was herself. But in the end, it was Julien who had severed the connection.

"When he told us about his new position at the hospital, Mathilde couldn't resist showing off, she had an important job, too, and then it all came tumbling out, what she did *that day*. Julien's face went white as chalk. He didn't blame her, but it was too painful to be around us after that. I never saw him again, but he continued to send me money to make life a bit easier, to make up for all the years of privation when I had to say no to Mathilde for everything. The payments stopped after his death, and then last month, they started up again. I suppose it takes time, all the formalities. But I can't tell you how thankful I am, not just for the money, but that Julien . . ." Her voice trails off.

Seeing the expression on her face, Sylvie holds her tongue. She has no desire to take credit for the restarted payments, it means more to Marie this way.

Marie sighs. "He was a fine man. But I suppose you lived with him long enough to know that. I wrote to him when he left Isabelle. He could take it however he chose, a token of friendship, a declaration of love . . . but he never replied."

"He kept your card, all the same," says Sylvie.

"All these years!" Marie cannot hide her emotion, and Sylvie tactfully looks away.

A couple of women enter the tea room, pick out a cake, wait for change. One of them greets Sylvie, and she struggles to place her before recognizing a former pupil. When she turns back, Marie has tucked the pastry into her string bag and is picking imaginary crumbs off the cloth. "Anyway," she says, "when Julien died, Isabelle came around to rue Elzévir for Clara's paintings. But when I offered her these canvases, she was no longer interested. Later

I wondered if it was the other painting she wanted, the one Mrs. Grzybyk had left with Clara."

During the Occupation, Marie had sold everything she could, including the unclaimed books in the bindery. The secondhand dealer grumbled he was only buying them out of charity and paid her a pittance for a costly set of Balzac. But when she took him another set, the complete Proust, he shook his head and said, "No Jewish writers." She hated the grasping old man, everyone knew he did a brisk business with the Germans, they were the only ones with enough money to buy books and paintings, once necessities for Parisians, now luxuries like butter and eggs for which the Boche could pay fivefold, tenfold, while she and Mathilde were always hungry. One day she had thought of Mrs. Grzybyk, and wished she had left the samovar behind instead of the painting, at least that would be worth something. In any case, she took the painting around to the old *brocante*, who looked at the signature and said, "It's a Jewish artist," and her heart sank, because she knew he would buy it cheap. He made an offer so insulting that she wrapped the painting back up. But in the end she took the money for it after all.

Marie sighs, "I was always ashamed of that. I didn't tell Julien I had sold it, and many years later I read that one of Soutine's paintings was auctioned for an extraordinary sum at the Hôtel Drouot." The newspaper article said he had gone into hiding during the Occupation, and it made Marie feel peculiar to think of him concealed somewhere, in someone else's attic, maybe, while his painting was secreted in her ceiling. In her dreams, she would see Mrs. Grzybyk holding her samovar and gazing sorrowfully at her till she would wake up in a cold sweat.

Marie clutches the tablecloth, creasing the immaculate linen.

At the sight of Sylvie's face, she recollects herself and smooths out the creases. Sylvie glances at the pastry in the string bag, and tells the waitress to add a box of chocolates to the order.

Guessing her intention, Marie recoils. "I don't need anything," she says, bristling.

"They're for Mathilde."

Marie hesitates, then says gruffly, "In that case . . ."

Sylvie sees that she is eager to leave, has said all she has to say, more than she intended, perhaps. As they part on the street, Sylvie thanks her again and wishes her *au revoir*. Marie responds with the much more final *adieu*.

They part to go their separate ways, but I stay where I am, turning over in my mind Marie's unanswered question: What is more terrible than vengeance? More terrible than the violent reprisals after liberation, when people were paraded naked through the streets, women with shaved heads and mutilated breasts, men with broken arms and crushed testicles. The last-minute résistants who switched sides when they saw which way the wind was blowing were loudest in their demands for "purification," denouncing neighbors, cudgeling black-marketers, shooting collaborators without a trial.

But is even a trial enough? I think of Pétain in the dock, flaunting the seven stars of his rank. He refused to submit to the court's jurisdiction, claiming he was answerable only to God and posterity. Impassive throughout the testimony, Pétain's blue eyes flickered only when he was charged with sending Jews to their death, as if he was looking beyond the packed courtroom to a host of phantom accusers.

Remembering these mute witnesses, I realize why the perpetrators tried to destroy all records of their crimes: More terrible than vengeance, more enduring than the verdicts of men, is the final judgment of history.

A couple of shopgirls hurry past me to their hostel on rue Poulletier. At the sight of their bright faces I shake off thoughts too morbid for this summer's day. The cobblestones radiate warmth from the afternoon sun, and down by the river a welcome breeze silvers the green leaves of the poplars. When I pass the hostel, its gates are open and its young inhabitants spill out on the pavement, craning their necks to stare at an ambulance blocking the street. I feel a familiar clutch of dread and look instinctively toward the river.

Two men from the fluvial police sprint toward us, carrying a girl on a stretcher which they place on the ground, right at my feet. One of the men kneels and breathes into her mouth, presses down on her chest. Her pale eyelids do not flutter, her pale lips do not part. But I feel the world spin around me at the sight of that face.

Delphine!

"So lovely," one of the girls whispers. "So lifelike."

An ironic stroke of fate has transformed the death mask of the laundress into the countenance of the CPR dummy; L'Inconnue de la Seine smiles her mysterious smile as the young man continues to demonstrate the kiss of life, the science of resuscitation seeking to duplicate the greatest miracle of all, the raising of the dead.

Seated at Julien's desk, Sylvie opens Clara's jewel case, releasing the dormant aroma of cedar into the air. She takes out the contents—three smooth pebbles, an Alsatian bonnet of black lace, a folded sheet of onionskin paper sealed with a drop of wax and addressed *to my daughters*—and wonders if Marie had kept the letter from Julien to spare him pain or because she hoped it might yet be claimed by the lost children. *The lost children!* If they had lived, they would be as old as Sylvie now, but the dead never age.

She pulls out Clara's photograph from the desk drawer and studies once more that young countenance. The bright eyes, the parted lips. Again she seems on the verge of speaking. But what Clara has to say is not meant for her eyes, it is addressed *to my daughters*. It's not for Sylvie to unseal the secrets of that letter; and as for the secrets of the envelope marked with the letter *M*, she has done what she can, she can do no more.

Sylvie hears a knock next door and wonders who can be calling on the Americans. She sticks her head out and finds the judge on the landing. Monsieur de Cheroisey hands her a magazine he has brought for Will. He sounds disappointed that the Taylors aren't home.

"I was just clearing out some papers and found this issue from last summer. I think the American will find it interesting."

Sylvie is surprised the judge has chosen to bring the magazine up himself instead of leaving it with Ana Carvalho. Perhaps like herself he finds it refreshing to be around the Taylors. And, of course, their impermanence makes such overtures of friendship perfectly safe; by summer's end they will be gone. "I believe they've driven down to the Loire."

"Ah, the châteaux," he says approvingly. "But one needn't go that far, the most dazzling one is only fifty kilometers from here. For true connoisseurs, Vaux-le-Vicomte outshines them all, even the palace of the Sun King. But then Le Vau was the architect, so no wonder, and we're fortunate to be surrounded by his masterpieces without even crossing the bridge."

Sylvie smiles at being included in the "we" and wonders again whether the arrival of fresh outsiders has led to this acceptance, or merely the passage of time. The judge turns to leave and Sylvie goes back inside. The cover strikes her as vaguely familiar, and she is sure she has seen it before. Flipping through the glossy pages of *La Vie Française*, she sees the article earmarked for Will, about a billionaire collector who had recently acquired some bottles from Thomas Jefferson's famed wine collection. She glances at the remaining articles, all lavishly illustrated: *Belle Époque* interiors in Paris, famous recipes from *Relais et Châteaux* hotels, an interview with Georges Simenon. About to put the magazine away, her attention is suddenly arrested.

She looks closely at the black-and-white photograph on the last page, accompanying a regular feature called "I Remember . . ." The photograph shows a scene at a railway station, nothing remarkable about it, there must be thousands of photographs like it in family albums all over the country, children leaving for a summer holiday at a *colonie de vacances* up in the mountains, waving as the train pulls out of the station. The only thing that sets it apart from those innocent family photographs is a young boy on the platform, looking up at German soldiers in uniform.

Sylvie reads the accompanying essay, no misty stroll down memory lane, no lament for *the snows of yesteryear*, but words written at white heat, burning themselves on the page:

Yes, I remember. I had just turned thirteen that summer of 1942, an age to prepare for my bar mitzvah in normal times. But these were not normal times, and nothing could prepare me for this hard coming-of-age. My father was rounded up the winter before and since then his employer, a wine merchant named Jacques Laferrière, had shown us extraordinary kindness, above and beyond what one might expect from someone linked to us neither by blood nor friendship, but simply as one human being to another.

When rumors of a great roundup reached us, no one believed it would include women and children. But Monsieur Laferrière insisted on hiding us in the wineshop, huddled in the same small room where my father had done his accounts in more "normal" times. Even after the raid was over, we could not go home, the police had sealed off our apartment. In any case, Monsieur Laferrière said it was dangerous for us to remain. He arranged false papers, bought us tickets to the unoccupied zone, and volunteered to accompany us. My little brother and I spoke faultless French, but we were afraid our mother's strong accent might give us away, so we filled her mouth with gauze and bandaged her face as if she was recovering from dental surgery.

Monsieur Laferrière instructed us to separate and act as though we did not know each other. I sat at the far end of the carriage across from my mother. Monsieur Laferrière and Benjy were near the front. The carriage was filled with children leaving for their summer holidays, some being dropped off by their parents, some accompanied by schoolteachers, and Benjy and Monsieur Laferrière looked unremarkable among them. Our papers were checked without incident, and as the whistle sounded, I let out a sigh of relief. Too soon. Three German officers boarded the train with their dogs, and all we could do was watch in horror as they took Benjy and Monsieur Laferrière off. My mother moaned and tried to tear the bandage from her mouth, and people all around commiserated with her agony. A pulled tooth, *quelle douleur!* But Benjy got down holding Monsieur Laferrière's hand, and did not cast a single glance at us as the train pulled away without him.

My mother and I made it to Nice, where we took refuge with her cousins. Monsieur Laferrière wrote to us that the Germans roughed him up and took away the boy. The wine merchant was released after six weeks in prison, but he had no further news of Benjamin. We learned my brother's fate once the war was over, that he had been sent to the death camps with a group of orphans. My mother never got over it. She had fled Russia for France, but now she could not bear to live here any longer and left for Israel, the only place she said where it was no trespass to be a Jew.

But I chose to come back to Paris and shout Monsieur Laferrière's heroism from the rooftops, as much to thank him as to shame others. He was recognized as Righteous Among the Nations, an honor Israel bestows on gentiles who helped a Jew during the dark years of the Occupation at great risk and with no thought of reward. I later married Jacques Laferrière's granddaughter, and he is truly my family now, great grandfather to my children. He is proud that when they ask what he did during the war, he can look them in the eye and say, I was among *Les Justes Parmi Les Nations*.

Thanks to him, I am alive today, no longer a boy on the verge of manhood, but a man of almost sixty. But one thing has not changed in all the intervening years: in my dreams my hand still reaches up to pull the safety chain, forcing the train to stop, to return time to that instant, so that it is I who hold my brother's hand and descend with him to the platform, and each time at the moment of waking I realize that no train and no clock on this earth can take me back, that I can only keep moving forward, relentlessly forward.

Dazed, Sylvie looks again at the old photograph, examines each face with close attention, not just the little boy, but the stocky man with him, squaring up to the soldiers, the faces looking out of the windows of the moving train with expressions of surprise, pity, indifference. She rereads the author's note, which says Ari Wolkowsky lives in Paris and is working on a documentary film for the *Centre de documentation juive contemporaine*. And then she is struck by a notion so daring that it hardly seems credible.

She rushes to Julien's desk but finds only a pile of his scientific journals, neatly stacked and freshly dusted by Ana Carvalho. In a frenzy she looks through the boxes of books and papers she and Alexandra had moved from Julien's study during the recent remodeling. Sylvie cannot explain why she feels this sense of urgency. She empties out the boxes, rummages through the papers, until at last she is ready to admit defeat. Maybe she hadn't seen it in Julien's study at all, it's not the kind of magazine he would have bought. Perhaps she had seen it at a newsstand, or at someone's house. But whose? She hasn't visited anyone since last summer, not after the quick progression of Julien's disease, from diagnosis to death in a matter of months. In any case, she had better start putting away the books and tidying up the papers, she doesn't want Ana Carvalho to see the room in such disarray.

She sighs and picks up one of Julien's books. Freud's *L'Interprétation des rêves*. She places it back in the box with as much reverence as Julien himself accorded his teacher. Though the windows are closed, a slight gust of air blows some papers across the floor, and as she bends to pick them up, she notices a folded-over periodical that had fallen behind one of the boxes. She unfolds it and smooths it out. Yes, it is the same cover, she wasn't mistaken after all.

Hardly daring to breathe, Sylvie opens it to the back page, which is dog-eared with Julien's characteristic fold. And at the bottom of the page, in his unmistakable hand, is a telephone number. Feeling she is being guided in some mysterious way, Sylvie goes to the phone and dials the number. It is indeed the CDJC.

She asks for an appointment with the documentary filmmaker. She can't explain why she has this strong impulse to connect with him, what can he tell her, after all? But in any event, she feels compelled to tell him that she has been pierced to the heart by his story, that his sorrow has helped her to understand Julien's sorrow, to grasp the scale of the Shoah, that there were six million such stories, and so few left now to remember.

She puts away the magazine, strangely impatient to meet Ari Wolkowsky, haunted by the words which continue to echo in her mind over the following days: *Each time at the moment of waking I realize that no train and no clock on this earth can take me back, that I can only keep moving forward, relentlessly forward.*

I am filled with a rush of emotions so mixed that it is impossible to peel one away from the other to examine them closely, to articulate them even to myself. All I know is that the torch has been passed to Sylvie, that she is carrying it into the darkness with the courage I have always admired. For Sylvie, as for me, that photograph has raised the same hopes, Ari Wolkowsky's words have struck the same chord.

It's true that no one living can make that return journey, those who still have the power to act must move forward, relentlessly forward, leaving us further and further behind, until we are mere undifferentiated shadows in the great procession of history. And today history itself will parade through the streets, announcing its arrival with the promise of glorious weather and resounding celebrations. When they were little, my children loved to wake up early on le quatorze juillet *though they were still sleepy from the torchlight processions of the night before. It's as if they had a personal stake in the holiday, their chests puffed up with pride and thankfulness that of all the countries in the world, it was in France they had been born, unquestionably and unquestioningly French.*

My own attitude to France is more complicated, of course. Though French to the marrow of my bones, I was made to feel like an outsider in my own country. A foretaste of my present existence . . . in the world but not of it.

Yet I find myself swept up in the celebration on this fourteenth of July which marks two hundred years of the revolution that led to

*the stunning declaration: "All men are born and live free and equal
in their rights." ALL men, without exception. Because who does
not thirst for freedom? Who does not hunger to believe his own life is
worth as much as another's?*

*Two hundred years ago, a crowd listened to Camille
Desmoulins as he balanced himself unsteadily on a makeshift
platform and recounted their long tally of grievances. Simmering
with anger because their children were hungry, the crowd's rage
boiled over at his words, transforming their hunger for bread into
a hunger for liberty. And two days later they surged toward the
Bastille, symbol of the king's absolute power, where thousands of
prisoners were rumored to languish based on nothing more than
secret letters and royal whims. But when the Bastille fell into
their hands, they discovered only half a dozen prisoners in the
fortress, seven, to be precise, and the faces of the freed men gaped
at their jailer's severed head, both wearing identical expressions of
astonishment at this shift of power from the grasp of kings into the
hands of people. What a dramatic turnaround! The very definition
of a revolution.*

*How we long to believe that revolutions will change the world!
That indeed* Liberté, Égalité, Fraternité *will remain our birthright,
and that the first line of our anthem will live up to its promise, that
we are all children of France. I think of my sister Clara putting on
her bonnet of black lace and running down to the village square
for the flag-filled ceremonies of* le quatorze juillet, *singing in her
piping little voice:* "Allons enfants de la Patrie-ee-uh."

Yes. Well.

*As always, when I am profoundly moved, I gravitate toward the
banks of the Seine. The river's arms bear Notre Dame like a chalice,
and I climb the spiraling staircase in the cathedral's north tower, its*

stone steps steep and then steeper still, narrowing like a constricted windpipe until I finally reach the doorway at the top, where the first breath of air, even to a disembodied unbeliever, feels like a prayer.

I cross over to the second tower through the grand gallery of chimeras that gaze at the city with their petrified stare, and pass by the oak belfry housing the bourdon bell named Emmanuel, its voice so rich and gleaming it seems cast not from bronze but gold when it summons the devout, celebrates the living, laments the dead. At present Emmanuel's great clapper is still, yet the bell is eloquent even in its silence.

The south tower leads me higher still, and the city lies spread out at my feet, a symphony of spires and domes and towers. Here and there, monoliths of glass and steel thrust themselves like brash adolescents into a conversation they don't quite understand. People said the same about the Eiffel Tower when it went up for the first centennial, but I admire the way its sequined lights shine like early stars in the dusk, the filigreed ironwork making it seem for all its substance to float weightlessly, an inspired emblem for the City of Light—in both senses of the word—not just luminosity but also lightness, which we prize above all, in wit, in art, in life.

It vexes me that the buildings commissioned for the second centennial are grandiloquent without being grand. I turn my gaze instead to the pleasing works of Le Vau clustered on the island behind me; the parks and gardens spread out like Aubusson rugs; the neat apartment buildings, which look like dollhouses from this height; the idiosyncratic bridges that, despite their quirks, form a harmonious ensemble; and the river on which this beauty converges and shimmers.

The throbbing beats of a thousand drummers are audible even up here, like the accelerated heartbeat of the city. My own pulse *quickens at the sound of marching footsteps, of rolling wheels, and how recent seem those dark days when such celebrations were banned, "La Marseillaise" forbidden, a giant swastika draped the Eiffel Tower, and all clocks in Paris were turned forward an hour to Berlin time, as if time itself was occupied territory. But deep time cannot be reset like clocks; it inhabits a zone impervious to chronology.*

Tonight's festivities sweep me into a crowd of other jubilant faces, other voices cheering on le quatorze juillet. *The Great War was over—no one called it the first war then, no one imagined there would be a second—and on July Fourteenth, the* mutilés de guerre *led the victory parade to the Soldiers' Chorus from Gounod's "Faust," their mutilated faces and amputated limbs evidence of the irreparable costs of war. But people's spirits lifted as the hero of Verdun rode by on his white horse, seven stars on his sleeve proclaiming Philippe Pétain the newest marshal of France, and the sight of young girls in their Alsatian bonnets of black lace reminded the crowd that we had recovered the stolen provinces of Alsace and Lorraine, her two million lost children were back in the embrace of France, the statue of Strasbourg had cast off her mourning cloak. It seemed a fitting tribute to the glorious day that the words to "La Marseillaise" were composed not in Marseilles but in Strasbourg, and with tears running down our cheeks we knew that finally* "le jour de gloire est arrivé!"

Last night those words resounded again, when a new opera house was inaugurated on the spot where the Bastille once stood, and the world's greatest opera stars joined together to sing "La Marseillaise." And tonight the spectacle is out on the street. When Marianne, symbol of the Republic, rises out of the ground like an earth goddess to sing "La Marseillaise," I'm pleased she is represented by a black American, a visible embodiment of our commitment to égalité. *The crowd falls silent at the clarion call:* "Allons enfants de la Patrie," *and while the anthem's bloodthirsty words arouse no emotion in my breast—I have seen enough blood to know that friend or enemy, we all bleed alike—the music stirs me all the same. As the singer circles the obelisk, I blot out the image of the guillotine that once stood there, glad that tonight it is only fireworks that will slice through the darkness like a thousand shining blades.*

Will and Alice feel the palpable thrill of watching the parade from the bleachers. The judge was astounded that the Americans wanted to go in person; he and his wife preferred to watch it on television, away at their country house. "This way," Madame de Cheroisey added as they were driving off for the weekend, "we will avoid the rabble." The judge stepped on the gas before Will could retort that the rabble is the very *point* of the celebration.

When the festivities begin, cheers go up from the million spectators, some of whom have camped all day along the parade's route, and they are joined by five hundred million more in front of their televisions around the world and for a few hours what Benjamin Franklin said still rings true: *Every man has two countries, his own and France.*

As the sound of drumbeats draws closer, Alice says, "We're watching history with a capital *H*."

"Hokey with a capital *H*," retorts Will. But he has to admit the parade is visually spectacular, and no wonder, it is the work of an adman after all, plenty of Kodak moments, like the women in black twirling down the street in giant motorized skirts or the pyramid made up of African drummers, all selling a "new, improved" revolution, with liberty and fraternity given their due though equality's a touch problematic seeing how leaders from the world's richest countries, gathered here for the G7 summit, are separated from the *rabble* by bulletproof glass.

The parade moves down the Champs-Élysées to the thrumming of a thousand drums, a surreal fusion of military march and folk spectacle, resembling nothing so much as a circus, which is fitting, thinks Will, the French are crazy about circuses. And about revolutions, obviously, the flavor *du jour*, spotlighting countries that can lay claim to them. France, needless to say, and its old enemy Britain, along with their former colonies, including America and India. Russia is well represented, but not China, which backed out at the last minute. Replacing the official Chinese entry is a makeshift float on which a massive Chinese drum sits silent, flanked by students wheeling bicycles, their faces painted to conceal their identity. It's little more than a month since Tiananmen Square, and the image of a lone man facing down tanks is on everyone's minds; not all revolutionary acts are in the distant past. It's unlikely, though, that anything revolutionary will happen today, the place is crawling with police. A surveillance blimp is up in the air like a giant eyeball, and a good thing, too, it's just the kind of event that's a magnet for terrorists.

A stroke of luck, Will thinks, that the weather's exceptionally balmy in Paris tonight, which gives the French yet another thing to feel superior about, since so many of the floats riff on the vile weather of foreign lands, English rain, Russian snow. The cloudless sky provides a welcome touch of nature to a pageant whose effects depend so much on fakery, there's fake snow, fake rain, a fake bear, and even, come to think of it, fake zebras; had it actually rained, their stripes would have washed off, revealing them as horses. But "artificial" is not a pejorative word for the French, they admire artifice as much as Americans admire naturalness.

He and Alice can't decide which is the parade's greatest moment; for him, it's either Jessye Norman singing "La Marseillaise" in a billowing tricolored robe that makes her look like a frigate in full sail, or the chuffing old locomotive greeted so enthusiastically by the French, they love trains the way the English love horses and Americans love cars. Alice says her favorite is the black marching band from Florida, given the honor of ending the parade to rapturous cheers, nice to see the French so wholeheartedly pro-American for once. But the image that stays with Will long after the night ends is the crowd spontaneously breaking through the barricades to rush into the street and mingle with the pageant in instinctive realization that what they are celebrating today is themselves. Then the fireworks start, a dazzling exhibition over both ends of the Champs-Élysées, the Arc de Triomphe at one end and the obelisk at the other.

I admire the fireworks filling the sky with their coruscating light.
And yet.

And yet, a niggle of unease persists. I try to trace it to its source.
Did it begin this morning, when a crowd of protesters threw six
hundred severed heads into the river? The police fished them out
before they could float away and frighten the wits out of people.
As well they might. Fake or not, severed heads are a staple of our
collective nightmares. Children are weaned on tales of Saint Denis,
bishop of the Parisii, whose head was sundered by a sword while
he preached the holy word, and he picked it up and carried it in his
hands, still exhorting the unbelievers to convert, a disembodied
voice that must have seemed an emanation from God. He was
buried where he fell, and there his basilica now stands, the final
resting place of the kings of France, including the only one who
lost his head to the guillotine. Beheaded bodies were as common as
pollarded sycamores during the revolution and its aftermath, and
surely this must be the only city with an entire cemetery just for
the décapités. *Statues of saints and kings had their marble heads*
lopped off; not even the dead were immune, as royal remains were
dug up and destroyed, and the embalmed head of Henri le vert
galant *mysteriously disappeared. And on Île Saint-Louis, you*
can still see a name chiseled into stone, the Street of the Headless
Woman. People assume the "femme sans tête" *is the headless*
statue there in an angled niche, but they are wrong, that torso is in
fact Saint Nicholas, patron of children and the wrongly accused,

guardian of those without guilt and without guile, the innocent of the world.

Headless torsos, floating heads. No wonder they awaken an old unease. And yet my perturbation started well before today. When? Was it when the Americans came to Sylvie's, as a fresh wind stirs up sediment in the water, or a log added to the fire breaks the old pattern of flames? No, it dates further back, though I cannot pinpoint when. Something trembles in me on the verge of recognition, but wayward memory does not always come when called.

As the last fireworks spangle the sky, I let my mind wander, thinking of other things, of Sylvie, of the Americans who have briefly alighted here but will soon be gone, like countless others before them. I think of Thomas Jefferson, who by a chance of history was in Paris on the day the Bastille was stormed, and then I think of the man who was ambassador to France before Jefferson, Benjamin Franklin, of whom one of my compatriots said, "The lightning shaft from heaven he snatched, and the scepter from tyrants." I am glad to have remembered those words today, given the occasion. However splendid the fireworks, they can never hope to compete with lightning in the sky, its terrible beauty flashing from darkness with the power to blind even as it illuminates.

And the image of simultaneously seeing and not seeing suddenly pinpoints that elusive disquiet; my insistence on dating its source has obscured the fact that it's caused by the date itself. This *was the day when the great raid on Jews was to have taken place in 1942, but the authorities quietly postponed* "la grande rafle" *for a couple of days when they realized that hunting down and rounding up people on a day consecrated to liberty, equality, fraternity, would be a blunder of, shall we say, historic proportions.*

Lost in my thoughts, I become aware that the festivities have finally ended, the crowds are thinning out, leaving silence on the streets, rubbish in the gutters. Under the Arc de Triomphe, the unknown soldier slumbers in his tomb undisturbed, like a hero of antiquity in the Elysian Fields, the Champs-Élysées where neither snow nor rain disturb his eternal dream. Up above the city, the wind sounds like the whips of a mighty God, or the fluttering banners of invisible hosts. I smile at my fancifulness, I who pride myself on having my feet firmly planted on the ground. But here, in the company of chimeras, it is hard not to imagine things. Shivering a little, I come down from the heights and walk along the quays.

A homeless man who habitually lies against a metro grate for warmth has quit his post to celebrate this festive night by the river. We share the bench in silence as he swigs away, brandishing his bottle in wordless toasts. When he turns his head in my direction I instinctively recoil, but the visions he sees are fueled by wine, not mortality. He tips his head back, swallows the last drops, and tosses the bottle to the ground. With no more drink to ward off the chill, he thinks of his snug grate and staggers to his feet. "Vive la France!" he shouts, "life's a whore, but vive la France! all the same."

I stay where I am, alone. The mist rising from the river nibbles at the sharp outlines of things, blurring the boundary between water and land. How dark seems the night, how profoundly dark. The revolving light atop the Eiffel Tower flashes like a beacon, and those lost in the city find their bearings by its measured scan. Against the unending march-past of history, each individual life seems but a beam from a lighthouse, a brief dazzling illumination, and then darkness once more.

By contrast to the dazzle of the night before, the day seems drab to Alice, the entire city hungover. Even the island's usually sedate quays are littered with broken glass and the streets are deserted; like the judge and his wife, many of the island's residents have fled the city to avoid the holiday crowds. She whistles for Coco, who is sniffing with interest at something unspeakable in the gutter. Every morning now Alice finds the neighboring door ajar, Coco waiting to conduct her around the island. The little terrier is perfectly amiable toward the shopkeepers sweeping their stoops and the children dawdling on their way to school, but he never passes up the opportunity to lunge ferociously at the Rottweiler outside the Hôtel de Lauzun.

It's nice to have some company when she runs, not that she expects Will to join her here, when he never has at home. The street sweepers turn into quai d'Anjou, their brooms and brushes stirring up the decidedly ripe odors on the street, and Alice changes her route. She takes the stone steps to the lower quay, whistling for Coco, who refuses to budge. She ends the tussle of wills, saying sternly *Coco, come here*, and he patters after her in a sulk.

The river's lower verge has an entirely different feel, wilder somehow, no wonder youngsters like to hang out there, smoking pot and playing music loud enough to be heard even up in the apartment. At her approach, a lizard sunning itself on a rusty mooring ring wriggles into a stony crack, and Alice thinks of the great floods that breached the wall in the past; you can still buy postcards of the island's streets transformed into Venetian canals. But the river is as sluggish as the street today, with only an occasional *bateau-mouche* to break the silence. No fishermen either, angling for the minnows they like to fry up, though she would hesitate to eat anything from the polluted waters, dirtier than usual this morning with the detritus of yesterday's celebration. A rat floats by on a raft of plastic bags, but even that fails to rouse Coco as he slinks close to the wall, his tail between his legs. He seems as scared of the water as she is.

A police launch thrums closer and closer to shore, its diesel fumes making her choke. Two policemen lean over the side, dredging the water with a net. One of them shouts *voilà*, and lifts his catch, a head wrapped in a clear plastic bag. Alice watches in horror, not the gruesome head, it is obviously a rubber mold, but the wake of the departing launch. As it washes up on the bank and the water laps at her feet, she realizes the ledge connecting two staircases is already submerged, it won't take much to engulf that narrow strip of stone. Overcome by a sudden wave of nausea, she bends over and throws up. The vomit swirls in the water now rising above her ankles, and she stands there unable to move, unable to cry out, firmly in the grip of an old nightmare.

Coco, already halfway up to the street, stops and barks sharply. But the street cleaners muffle the sound and no help comes. He shivers and whines, staring fearfully at the water lapping the steps. Then, screwing up his courage, he leaps onto the watery ledge where Alice stands as if turned to stone herself. Coco presses himself against her legs, and the feel of his wiry coat steadies her. She edges her way to the balustrade and at the touch of cold metal, her head clears, her nausea recedes.

Ana Carvalho, spraying down her birdcages in the courtyard, watches Alice crossing the street, surprised to see the American looking quite peaked, and no wonder, everyone knows *le footing* shakes up your insides, it's downright unhealthy but Coco seems to enjoy it, look at the rascal, wagging his tail for all he is worth.

The Rottweiler outside the Hôtel de Lauzun keeps a wary eye on his nemesis, but Coco does not bother to lunge at him, savoring his recent triumph over a more powerful foe.

*When the sun rises on the sixteenth of July, the sabbath sky loud
with church bells, my thoughts return to another dawn, almost half
a century ago. I was in London then, ruins and rubble all around
me from the German blitz the year before, those months of bombing
when fires engulfed the city and it seemed that the Twilight of the
Gods had descended from the sky. I spent many nights at the bomb
shelters in a strange camaraderie with people I would never have
met otherwise, and coming out of a shelter one morning I saw a
freshly painted sign on a neighborhood restaurant: Keep Calm and
Curry On. The unquenchable spirit of Londoners seemed as much a
miracle as the sight of St. Paul's Cathedral rising serenely toward
the sky from its wreath of smoke, its ring of fire. And then the
bombings stopped as Hitler set his eyes on the Eastern Front.*

    *Of course the Germans had no need to bomb Paris, which had
fallen into their hands like a ripe golden plum, a delicious* reine
claude, *and they strutted around the city with pride of ownership.
A phrase from my youth flashed into my mind:* Wie Gott in
Frankreich. *Happy as God in France.*

    *Across the Channel my thoughts returned again and again to
Paris, but blockaded as I was, I had no way of learning the truth.
Only later did I discover the sickening details: A July night in 1942.
Footsteps turning into rue des Rosiers, then up rue Elzévir. The
peremptory knock on the door. I had imagined that scene so vividly
while I lived; and now I surge on a wave of emotion to that place,
that night.*

As the sky turns from black to cobalt, the blue hour, the city seems uninhabited, no light anywhere, the curtains drawn, the shutters pulled. It's dangerous to be out during the curfew without a pass from the occupiers, but no one asks for my papers; death confers its own laissez-passer.

I am taken aback by a purposeful hum of activity and feel a shiver go through me. What is it? What great bird of prey menaces the sleeping city?

Something big is afoot, some long-planned operation. Green and white city buses idle before garages, schools, gymnasiums. The police are forming teams, some in uniform, some in plainclothes, going over lists. Areas are cordoned off, intersections barricaded, escape routes blocked: a dragnet is tightening under cover of darkness. It's something they are trying to conceal not from the enemy, but from Parisians.

There have been rumors, of course. But this time, something more concrete, fliers, phone calls, whispers: il faut s'cacher. *But where to hide in an already besieged city?*

*Mrs. Gr*ż*ybyk has found refuge with an old friend. Samuel Fenster might be a Jew, but no one will dare lay a finger on a decorated veteran. He stays up in his living room while she sleeps, smoking one of his hoarded cigarettes, though the doctors have forbidden it, bad for his lungs, or lung, to be more accurate, he has only one since the war. The last war, the Great War they call it, those who have never been in the trenches. There's nothing great about it, all war is hell.*

*He lights another cigarette and stretches out on the sofa. He can sleep anywhere, soldiers' habits, used to sleeping on straw when there was any, on soil when there wasn't. Rachel Gr*ż*ybyk was all in a panic when she arrived, poor soul, he almost didn't recognize* *her; she's lost a great deal of weight, looks like a collapsed balloon. Shame about her shop. She's fed a lot of people in her time, whether they had money or not, couldn't bear to see anyone leave hungry.*

Samy puts out the cigarette and resists the temptation to light another, feeling a tightness in his chest, his own fault, one too many cigarettes today. Rachel snores gently in the next room and it feels good to have someone in the house, he lost Flora that first winter of the Occupation, coldest winter he can remember, to think she died of pneumonia and he with his one lung still hanging on. Life's funny that way, he used to long for peace and quiet, with Flora it was always "Samy, have you done this, Samy, have you done that?" He used to tease her, saying he deserved another croix de guerre *for living with her, but now he finds the house too silent. He would turn on the wireless just to hear a human voice during the long evenings of the curfew, until they came and confiscated the radios. But one day the sodding war will be over, and then they can all get on with it.*

Oh, what the hell. He lights another cigarette. "Samy, Samy, you'll set the mattress on fire." Well he hasn't yet, and Flora's gone and here he is, still smoking. He should try to sleep, what time is it, almost four o'clock? He hears a sound quite some distance away, but noises carry on a windless night. Trouble's coming, he can sense it. He gets up to put on his jacket, no harm in being prepared. And then it comes.

A loud knock at the door and the curt order, "Ouvrez, police."

The scene plays out simultaneously in other buildings, on other streets. Boots on the stairs. Knocks at the door. "Ouvrez, police." Lights go on in darkened windows, frightened eyes peer through the door, alarmed cries ring out. Men argue, women plead, children cry, but the police are implacable. They order people to pack necessities for a couple of days, and since they have no idea where they are going or what they might need, they hastily throw into their valises, bundles, bedrolls, anything that comes to mind, a coverlet, an extra pair of reading glasses, a photo album. An old woman struggles to put in her dentures, but her hand shakes so much that they fall and shatter. A child wants to take his rocking horse, but the policeman shakes his head. "Allez, allez," he says impatiently. "Allez."

One woman runs to the window, throws open the shutters, and shrieks out a warning. Her cries are abruptly cut off, the window slammed shut. Those who hear her scurry into cellars and attics, hoping the dark city will swallow them up. But the police are not unduly concerned. They'll track them down, or someone will give them away. In any event, they won't be able to return home. The policemen seal the door with tape, move on to the next address.

"Ouvrez, police."

Some do not answer the door, like the doctor who injected his wife and children with potassium chloride before plunging the syringe into his own arm. Like the woman who leapt off a window ledge with her child, splattering blood and brains on the cobblestones. The writer who disconnected the gas pipe from the stove and put it between his lips. They, and others like them, are beyond the reach of any mortal voice.

"Ouvrez, police."

Samy opens the door without hesitation, and the first thing the police see is the croix de guerre pinned to his jacket, just above the yellow star. They speak to him respectfully, but the list in their hand trumps his medal.

Rachel Grzybyk is awakened by a policeman shaking her shoulder. Clutching her chest, she gets slowly and unsteadily to her *feet, tries to gather a few things.* "Allez, allez," *he says, and the words fall unpleasantly on Samy Fenster's ears, reminding him of the* "schnell, schnell" *of the guards when he was a prisoner of war.*

As they start down the stairs, the samovar drops from Rachel Grzybyk's hands and the clang resounds in the stairwell, echoing on and on and on. Oh, well, it will be of no use where she's going, she thinks, and sits down heavily. Her face is pale and covered with perspiration. Samy fans her with his hat. She lets out a long sigh and clutches Samy's hand. Despite the impatient exclamations from the policemen, he does not move until the cardiac arrest finally stops the beating of that large heart. Then he turns toward the men and says quietly, "We can go now, for her the war is over."

All across the Marais, the voices continue their stern commands. *"Ouvrez, police."*

In the apartment at rue Elzévir, Mathilde lies on the floor, rubbing her cheek and bawling. *"Marie hit me,"* she wails as Clara comes down the ladder. *"She hit me."* *Poor innocent,* thinks the policeman, *no idea of what she's just done, but God made her that way, she's not to blame.*

He examines Clara's identity card, with the word "Jew" stamped in red ink, and compares it against their list.

Born: September 6, 1913.

At: Hunawihr.

"In Germany?" he asks, though her nationality is marked *française*, naturalized, perhaps.

"No. Alsace."

He wavers, the word "Alsace" carries a deep resonance for men of his generation who remember too well the history of the lost province. But his younger colleague impatiently reminds him the Tulard files are impeccable. In any case, he knows his orders: no arguments, no discussion, no exceptions.

The older man rubs his hand across his eyes. He should have seen this coming when the Germans wanted a census of the Jews, why else start asking about race and religion all of a sudden? A bad business, he wants no further part of it, he'll hand in his resignation tomorrow.

Marie goes to the door and bars it, daring the men to push

her aside in her own house. "You can see how ill the child is," she says, "let the girls stay." The younger policeman shakes his head. No exceptions, not for the sick, not for the dying. But the older one asserts his authority. They can stay, he says. But Gigi starts screaming *"Maman, mamaaan,"* and, alarmed by the feverish glitter in her eyes, Clara picks her up. Gigi wraps her arms around her mother and won't let go. And if Gigi comes, there is no question of Lilou staying behind, the twins are inseparable.

The uniformed policeman is annoyed at the delay, he's hoping for a promotion out of this night's work and they are already behind schedule. Time to move on. He assures Marie if the children go with their mother, she'll be released sooner.

Grimly, Marie gathers a few provisions, a shawl for Clara, aspirin for Gigi's fever, a box of crayons to keep Lilou distracted. Mathilde hurries to pack her own things—a packet of Banania chocolate, a straw hat—as if they are going on a pleasure trip, but when Clara and the girls leave, the nice man with the pipe won't let her go with them, he hands her the doll and tells her to go back to sleep.

Out on the street, there is already a crowd of people asking, *"Where are we going? When will we be back?"* The policemen don't answer, but keep them moving toward various primary centers— garages, schools, gymnasiums. *"Allez, allez."*

Sleepy and puzzled, the young children cling to their mothers' skirts. Their parents' fear transmits itself to them and they start crying. The clamor wakes people in the neighboring buildings, and they look out of their windows to see what the commotion is about at this ungodly hour. It is not hard to draw conclusions: All the people are wearing yellow stars. Some shake their heads and go back to bed; others call out words of encouragement. A hard-faced concierge standing in a doorway says, *"Look how many they are, they breed like vermin."* One of the onlookers says tartly, *"I wouldn't gloat so loud if I were you, I hear they're coming for harpies next."*

A young nurse returning from her shift at the hospital stares at the piteous scene before her eyes. Suddenly a boy of fifteen or sixteen breaks away and runs down the street, veering off into an alley. Blowing their whistles, a couple of policemen chase him down. While everyone is distracted, a woman pushes against the nurse and before she knows what has happened, she finds a baby thrust into her arms. The nurse tucks the infant into her cloak like a black-market parcel and melts away as the policemen bring back the runaway and push him into line, blood trickling down his face. A woman takes out her handkerchief to dab at the blood, but drops it when she sees a priest hurrying past with his eyes averted. She clutches his soutane, imploring him to save her, she has three small children alone at home. He breaks free of her grip and takes to his heels, his borrowed cassock hiding the yellow star beneath.

Clara and the girls are taken to a primary center chaotic with people pushing, shouting, waving their papers, demanding answers, as if they still believe this is merely more of the bureaucratic harassment they have come to expect. An inspector looks at Clara's identity card, tells her he'll deal with her case in an hour. But when she approaches the counter again, there has been a change of shift, and the new policeman motions her to the door. *"Allez, allez,"* he says, directing people into two lines, one for those with children, another for those without, they are bound for different destinations. The crowd surges out the door and Clara and her daughters are swept into a bus whose deep rumblings vibrate through their bodies. As the bus lurches forward, a woman in a fur coat stumbles, and a factory worker extends a callused hand to steady her. They look at each other without saying a word. Despite the gulf that separates them, they both have the same stunned expression on their face. If this can happen in France, then where in the world can they be safe? The children stand with their noses pressed against the window, and the bus driver curses under his breath, this is not what he bargained for, not the children, and he hunches over the steering wheel until they pull up before the winter stadium.

At the sight of the Vélodrome d'Hiver, a loud murmur goes up. Some of them have been there before, to see bicyclists race around its circular track in the grueling contest known as the Infernal Round. But this time no innocent sport has brought them to Vel d'Hiv.

The misery and squalor resemble a natural disaster in some distant Third World country. Yet this is in the heart of Paris, and the cataclysm was manmade, meticulously planned, flawlessly executed. No detail, however trivial, was overlooked: The electricity and water were turned off in the empty apartments, pets left in the care of the concierge. But less thought was spared for their owners. Despite the zeal in rounding them up, the provision made for them is woefully inadequate. Worse than inadequate, inhumane. For all these people, there is no bedding, no food, no water. A single standpipe dispenses a trickle for which people have to queue for hours. All the toilets with windows have been barred, the remaining are clogged up, and the stench funnels outward, fetid, nauseating, unbearable. People relieve themselves against the wall or sit in their own ordure. An elderly man shields his wife with his coat as she defecates, tears of humiliation running down her face.

The *vélodrome*'s glass roof, painted blue for the air raids, is like a giant bell jar that traps the smell, the heat, the clamoring voices. In a constant relay the buses release their human cargo into this gloomy, panting darkness. By one o'clock the next day, it is over. The largest single roundup of Jews in Paris, in the works for three months under the innocent name of Opération Vent Printanier, has caught almost thirteen thousand people in its net, and of the seven thousand or so blown into the stadium by that Spring Breeze, more than half are children.

They run up and down the sloping embankment or curl up on the floor, while the adults huddle on tiers of narrow benches and retrieve from their abject bundles what meager sustenance they can, a handful of *biscottes*, perhaps, dry as dust on the tongue. In the welter of objects, their hands encounter something, a beloved memento they could not bear to leave behind, a grandmother's garnet brooch, or a wedding scroll, and for a moment it reminds them of the life they have lived, the person they used to be. But they are now part of a suffering mass, stripped of country, of home, of every trace of individuality. Wryly they think they would have done better to bring something more useful than that heirloom brooch, an ordinary tin cup perhaps, as a receptacle for water.

At first they approach their captors and loudly demand milk for their infants, medicine for an old man's seizures. But they are ordered back to their seats, sometimes politely, sometimes brutally. In any case, with indifference. Worn out by supplication, they relapse into a helpless stupor. All they can do is continue waiting, without knowing what it is they await. Suddenly in these joyless surroundings those nearby hear an unmistakable sound, a child's squeal of laughter. A boy of four blows his toy whistle and tugs at a *gendarme*'s leg. The man growls like a bear and chases him up the steps, the boy laughs, the man smiles, and for a moment it seems as if everything hangs in the balance, that the day dividing them into hunter and hunted will also turn out to be only a game. But the moment passes and things are as they were, unreal and yet all too real.

Guards are massed by the double doors into the arena, and desperate women crowd around them, pleading for a chance to run to the *épicerie* across the street to buy milk for their children or a loaf of bread, but they are rebuffed. On the other side of the doors, people who have seen the buses arriving full and leaving empty, have heard the desperate cries of the captives within, have smelled the nauseating smells escaping from the stadium, gather outside with food, water, offers of help. But the two sides are kept apart by the guards, sullen at being caught in the middle.

Several doctors volunteer their services, but only two are allowed in at a time to tend to all those in extremity, like the woman giving birth, her excruciating screams audible even to the factory workers in a neighboring building; the children suffering from measles, dysentery, impetigo, quarantined and crying in the stalls for which sporting patrons had once paid a premium; the man beating his head against the concrete floor till his skull is misshapen with welts and contusions. In the face of so much suffering, doctors and nurses offer what comfort they can, toiling heroically with little support and less equipment. But nobody can do anything about the panic that spreads through the stadium like an epidemic.

In the enveloping chaos, one couple seems set apart from the rest, something holy about them, Joseph and Mary in this strange stable without a wisp of straw where she can lay her head. They had not thought to bring candles or matches, but they observe the Sabbath together and it seems astounding that after the black Thursday they have lived through, they can still move their lips in prayer. Against her rounded belly, the little boy with the whistle sleeps the innocent sleep of childhood. The mother looks down at him with wondrous love, then gives a slight nod perceptible only to her husband's fixed and anxious gaze. He kisses the sleeping boy, then takes a pillow and presses it over his son's face. The little legs that were running a few hours before kick with all their might, and the woman whispers over and over, *"Douce-ment, doucement,"* and as if he hears her, the boy kicks slower and slower until he stops and the man finally lifts the pillow and gathers in his arms his pregnant wife, his dead son. Then he takes out a shard of glass secreted in his sleeve. Quickly, before he can change his mind, he slices his wife's wrists, cuts open his own veins. Their mingled blood spurts on the child, soaks through the pillow, drips on the people below. They look up to remonstrate, but when they see what has happened, their loud shrieks summon the guards. By the time they reach him, the man has already bled to death, but a nun scrambles up the crowded bleachers, tears her veil into strips for a tourniquet, and manages to staunch the woman's flow. Gradually her eyelids flutter open. As conscious-ness returns, she breaks into an anguished howl, and all who hear it think it would have been more merciful to let her die.

How long does this go on? Five days? Six days? An eter-nity. Those who are marked for death feel the premonitory moth wings of darkness brush their face and look around them with bitter recognition.

There is a stir among the *gendarmes* as the double doors open, and from the way they snap to attention, it's obviously a visit by an officer of the highest rank. The prisoners barely look up. Offi-cial visitors have come and gone before, bringing not the slightest improvement in their condition, nor the remotest possibility of being freed. This time it is SS Obersturmführer Röthke himself who has come to take stock of what he calls his little "birdcage."

He looks around with a proprietary air at the prisoners and guards alike, and for a moment the *gendarmes* feel a kinship with the crowd that erupts in spontaneous hissing, the sound of a pres-sure cooker releasing steam. As the wave of helpless fury builds, a young man shakes off his wife's restraining hand and jumps over the handrail to rush at the officer looking down distastefully at the dust marring his boots' mirrored shine. Before he can get close, the young man is clubbed over the head with a rifle butt and drops to his knees like a felled ox. With a superhuman effort he struggles to his feet and continues to stagger blindly forward. Röthke watches impassively as he is clubbed again till he crumples over and lies still, then gestures that the man should be attended to, and points out a few other people, a woman going into fits, an old man vomiting blood. They are carried out on stretchers, and the hush that suddenly descends on the stadium is almost palpable. What an exquisite refinement of cruelty, to leaven it with a small, unexpected touch of kindness.

But the *gendarmes* know it is not kindness but mockery. The Rothschild hospital with its barbed-wire walls is no place of refuge. They have seen it emptied of its patients, no one is spared, not the woman attached to a saline drip, nor the young boy on whose fractured leg the plaster has not yet dried. They are needed to fill the trains. Word has been going around the prefecture that the Germans are dissatisfied with the numbers. Fewer than thirteen thousand rounded up! They had budgeted for thousands more, though where would they have put them, the stadium already inadequate, and the situation not much better at Drancy. Anyway, if the Boche are upset the trains will run half empty, it means the next convoys are ready to leave. But where will the trains take them, asks one of the *gendarmes*. Another shrugs, out of France, that's all he knows.

Röthke turns to leave and a girl's voice calls after him, *"Monsieur, s'il vous plaît."* Strange as it seems, at the sound of that childish appeal he has a strong urge to justify himself. Ridiculous!

He's not on trial, why should he feel defensive? His hatred of Jews is powerful, unquestionable, yet he wants her to know it was not his idea to take the children, he was shocked when Pétain's prime minister proposed it. But no use going into that now, Berlin has given the green light, and the Jewish problem is moving toward its final solution. He hurries out of the stadium, but even when he is out of earshot, Liliane continues to scream, it's unfair to punish her sister, she's always been a good girl.

Her daughter's outburst startles Clara, who has been too absorbed in nursing Gilberte to notice Liliane's mutinous rage. Suddenly Clara is struck by an idea so audacious that it takes her breath away. She looks again at the two girls, one deathly pale, the other red with anger, and makes up her mind before it is too late, before their names are called on the crackling speakers and like the others they have to file out of the stadium to the waiting transports. *"Go to the door,"* she whispers, *"try to slip out."* She arranges her shawl around the child, hiding the yellow star. Lilou looks questioningly at Gigi, from whom she has never been apart in her whole life, not even for an hour. But Gilberte's eyes are turned up in her head, she is moaning as the fever squeezes her body in its relentless grip.

Lilou runs down the steps and skulks near the entrance. Clara's eyes never leave that little figure plastered against the wall, trying to make herself as inconspicuous as possible. A couple of times she is chased away by the guards. But then there is a change of shift, and the new guard lets her stay, it won't do any harm to let the child get a breath of air, the stench inside is enough to make even grown men gag. Liliane waits patiently, but there is no way out of the place without being seen.

Two nuns kneeling over a palsied man speak to him in soothing voices, but it's clear there's nothing more to be done. Slowly they rise to their feet and move toward the entrance. In a moment, they will go past the child waiting by the double doors. Quickly Lilou slips between the nuns; their voluminous skirts swallow her up and sweep her outside the door. The guard sees her leave, but instead of blowing his whistle, he looks away.

Out on the sidewalk, Liliane hesitates. A woman at the *épicerie* across the street beckons, hands her a sweet roll. *"Run,"* she whispers, *"run."* Uncertainly, Liliane crouches in the doorway and licks the powdered sugar with the tip of her tongue. Where should she go?

Clara slumps with relief once Lilou is safely outside. But her relief is mingled with despair as she looks down at Gigi, for whom the end cannot be far. Difficult to say who is suffering more intensely, the child in pain or the mother who watches with helpless anguish and prays for death to come.

By the arbitrariness of chance, its random errors, Clara was mistakenly seized, for this one raid at least the rules were changed to exclude French Jews; and since she was married to an "Aryan," Clara should have been doubly exempt. As a decorated veteran, Samy Fenster was likewise exempt. So was the woman in the fur coat, whose husband had volunteered for the labor camps in Germany. Yet they were all caught up in the net that night. How could Tulard's dossiers prove so fallible, how could there be so many mistakes? Yet to fixate on how some people were moved from one column to another as if it were a simple failure of bookkeeping is to lose sight of a graver error, that it was—all of it— a failure of humanity.

But Clara has no time to waste on questions about how she came here, or where she is headed. She is at the threshold where all falseness falls away, there is time only for essential truths. She knows that one child must die; but the other must live.

Clara turns back to the child in her arms, whose breathing is labored, her face twisted into a ghastly mask of pain as she gathers her strength for the great crossing. A sudden current of air fills that airless space and the child's eyes flutter open. She sees a shadow hovering over her, feels a hand on her burning forehead smoothing back the curls plastered to her brow. She says, *"Papa?"* Clara turns her head around. *"Bernard!"* He has come for them, she always knew he would. *"Help her,"* she says. *"I'm here,"* he says, *"I'm here."*

Together they will their child to die. Yet Gilberte wrestles death for a while longer. After a final struggle for breath, she succumbs at last, her face now smooth, her body still. Clara closes her daughter's eyes, kisses those closed lids, and knows that never in this life will she see either of her girls again. Her wordless keening goes on and on and on until it seems to fill the stadium and overflow into the city and into the world, gathering into that river of lamentation the voice of every mother who has lost her child.

Wherever I go I cannot escape that sound, I will hear it to the end of time. I hear it now as I sit in the park behind Notre Dame, where the Sunday Mass is over on this sixteenth of July in 1989, and the children released from their enforced stillness in church rush at the chittering pigeons that fly up in little puffs of dust. Watching their gleeful play, it strikes me with renewed shock that of the more than four thousand children imprisoned at Vel d'Hiv, not a single one returned alive from the camps. Not one.

Outside the stadium, Lilou crouches uncertainly in the doorway of the *épicerie*, then dashes back across the street. No one at the crowded entrance notices the child trying to make her way inside except the guard who saw her leave. He looks directly at her and Lilou sees the same expression on his face as the woman at the *épicerie*. *"Run,"* his eyes say, *"run."* But she clutches the morsel of bread for Gigi and continues to push her way stubbornly toward him. Another guard comes to the double doors, and in a moment he will see her, too. But just then a woman cries out, *"You wicked girl,"* and snatches her up in her arms, *"wait till we get home, I'll give you what for, running away from school like that."* A few people turn and shake their heads, she's too severe with the child, playing truant at her age, *c'est normal*. The woman doesn't relax her grip as she carries her away, with Lilou screaming for all she is worth: *"Maman, maaamaan!"*

For almost half a century from that July day to this, I searched for the child who was spirited away from the stadium, and everywhere I looked, from the slurry of the past there rose a doleful parade of abandoned children eyeing the world with amazement that it should be so cruel to them, the weak, the defenseless, the innocent.

I hear the forlorn sound of a convent bell as a woman places her baby in a basket and pulls the rope before hurrying away. The infant is sound asleep, and even when the revolving hatch turns and he disappears within those secretive walls, he clutches fast a spray of fragrant muguet tucked into his swaddling sheet to soften the pain of abandonment, and if he survives that stony infancy to wear the red garb of foundlings—les enfants rouges—that will be all his meager patrimony, the memory of the woodland flower.

I think of the children at Vel d'Hiv, taken to transit camps where they were torn from their mothers' arms to be sent to a separate death, pushed into trains with adult strangers randomly assembled to preserve the official fiction that families were traveling together somewhere to the east. The sight of their thin arms piteously outstretched, their little faces sooty from the engine's baleful exhalations, finally awakens the populace to what has been taking place before its unseeing eyes.

But it is the memory of Clara's eyes that rebukes me still, that rebukes us all. That is why all night long I have restlessly roamed the streets, knocking on doors like an uneasy conscience, rattling the windows like a ghost train, beating out the insistent refrain: Do not forget, do not forget, do not forget.

Only now do I push open the sealed door of my imagination to accompany Clara on her final journey. The train belches black smoke as it moves eastward, steadily eastward. For three days and three nights Clara stands in a wagon with a hundred others glued together by sweat, secretions, soil, no window through which to breathe a lungful of air or glimpse an inch of indifferent sky. Finally the locomotive slows down as it pulls up to the camp. It rolls through the archway of a looming tower and stops with a great puffing sigh as it reaches the end of the line.

The locked doors are unbolted and they stagger out, those who survived the journey, stumbling over the corpses of those who died along the way. Bright searchlights turn night into blinding day as guards shout at them to move faster. "Schnell, schnell!" Women are ordered to turn left, away from the men, and Clara staggers into line. Not yet thirty, she moves like an old woman whose limbs have trouble obeying her. In front of a barrack with ventilated louvers, she is handed a towel and a hard sliver of soap. She strips down naked, modesty a distant luxury, and adds her clothes to the immense pile outside the entrance. After the shouts of the guards, the barking of dogs, the sound of whips and pistols, it is eerily silent inside. Shivering, Clara looks up at the showerheads, waiting for a stream of water to wash away the caked moisture in her eyes, the soil in her orifices, but instead of cleansing water, there is only the slow asphyxiating release of gas, the panicked screams of women around her, and she feels her heart beating as erratically as a young stork trying out its wings, flailing, flapping, dropping a long way from the nest atop the chimney, down past the windowbox with its bloodred geraniums, down toward the stones, before she is lifted on a current of air and soars over the green hills of her beloved countryside, out where there are no windows, no bars, it is all air, pure air, stretching out to the blue eye of the horizon.

Sylvie unrolls Clara's paintings to study them again, lingering over each scene. She finally selects one and puts it aside. Would it have comforted Julien to look at the landscape he shared with his sister in happier times? Or would it add to his distress? Like so much else, she can no longer ask him, he will no longer answer.

She stops at a frame shop on the way, then crosses once again toward the Marais, looking not for an unnumbered address at rue Elzévir this time, but for the Center for Contemporary Jewish Documentation at rue Geoffroy-l'Asnier. She enters the courtyard dominated by a bronze cylinder evoking the chimneys of the death camps. Inside the building, a receptionist takes down her name and address, asks if Sylvie is here to be filmed. She shakes her head and says she has an appointment with Ari Wolkowsky.

She is shown into an office that looks as if a cyclone has blown through it, files scattered everywhere, film reels piled on top of each other, and in one corner a single chair against a gray backdrop. A man with hair and clothes as disheveled as his surroundings is setting up a camera across from this makeshift set. Ari Wolkowsky looks up questioningly as Sylvie enters and she says she won't detain him, she just wanted to tell him in person how deeply his story had moved her.

He shrugs. "It's only one of countless stories. For a long time, no one wanted to speak about what had happened. But then suddenly the floodgates opened. Maybe the recent trial of Klaus

Barbie, the man they called the Butcher of Lyon, made people feel that even outside the witness stand, they had a moral obligation to testify. Or maybe it's a growing sense of urgency that if they don't speak now, no one will remember."

"They come to you?"

"Or I go where they are." He points to a map with dots marking his film sites in France, Poland, Israel, America. A thick cluster of dots in Miami.

Sylvie is silent for a moment, trying to incorporate this into her vision of Florida, then she tells Ari how she almost went there last winter, but in the end she couldn't do it, she felt she was leaving Julien behind, he would have called it *illogique*, but logical or not, that's how she felt.

"The heart has its reasons," Ari says.

She nods eagerly. *That reason cannot know.* "Exactly, that's it exactly. And it's just as illogical why I've come to see you. It's about the photo." She tells him the story of rue Elzévir, of Marie and Mathilde, of Clara and the girls. Julien had found proof that Clara died at Auschwitz and Gigi at Vel d'Hiv, but the death of Lilou was unrecorded. It remains a baffling sorrow to Sylvie that Julien never spoke of this to her, but ever since she heard the story from Marie, she has become fixated on the idea that Lilou is still alive, she imagines she sees her everywhere, even in the photo that accompanied Ari's essay in *La Vie Française*.

"The photo," he says. "I know I have it here, somewhere. You know, the funny thing is, someone else called me about that photo, he wanted to talk to me about it. Last summer, I think. But I never heard from him again."

"Julien went into the hospital in August. He never came back home."

Ari Wolkowsky briefly clasps both her hands in his. "I'm sorry."

"In a sense, I've come here today in his place."

"Now, where did I put the photo?" He starts to root through his papers, but Sylvie stops him. She has brought a photocopy, which they study together in silence. Finally Ari says, "A journalist was there to see off his children, they were going to their grandparents' for the summer. It was only when he developed the roll of film that he realized the significance of this photo. His newspaper printed it, and it became iconic proof that the Germans were indeed targeting children."

Sylvie points to a little girl with her face pressed against the window. "I had so recently seen the photographs of Clara's girls at rue Elzévir. And the way this child is reflected in the glass, I was seized with the strange fancy that it was one of the twins. Do you have any idea who she might be?"

He shakes his head.

Sylvie sighs. "Well, it was a long shot."

"I don't know her, but strangely enough I remember her, I even remember her name." He can still recall the pugnacious way she announced it from the moment she boarded the train to everyone who looked at her, the conductor, the guards, the Germans: *"Je m'appelle Christine Boniface de Belleville."* And as they pulled out of the station, he thought bitterly, Why did they take his brother off the train, they should have taken this girl instead, repeating her name so insistently that it was picked up by the rhythm of the train wheels, Christine Boniface de Belleville, Boniface de Belleville, de Belleville, de Belleville, de Belleville.

Well, thinks Sylvie, *that's that, then.* Ari Wolkowsky walks her out, but when she thanks him and shakes his hand, he keeps hold of it and leads her not to the gate but down to the crypt.

"There's something I think you should see. There's no doubt in my mind that Julien saw it, too."

She looks at him in surprise as he gestures to the Tomb of the Unknown Jewish Martyr, a black marble star of David with the eternal flame burning above. "In 1957, the ashes of those who died in the ghettos and the death camps were buried here in soil brought from Israel. It's inconceivable any Jew who was in Paris would have stayed away." Tears start to Sylvie's eyes as she realizes it was around this time that she had first started giving piano lessons at rue de Bièvre.

On the far wall is a Hebrew quotation from the Bible, and Ari reads it aloud: *"Look and see if there is any sorrow like my sorrow. Young and old, our sons and daughters were cut down by the sword."* He looks at her somberly. "Now do you understand why Julien chose to mourn in silence? How does one speak of the unspeakable?"

In the days following her meeting with Ari, Sylvie jumps up every time the telephone rings. He has promised to call if he finds out anything more, but Sylvie does not hold out much hope. What she wants is to make meaning of the incomprehensible, and neither Ari nor anyone else can help with that.

She stares at Clara's framed painting leaning against the mantelpiece. Scenes of Julien's childhood, which he recalled on his deathbed. *Have they come yet, the storks?* And then she realizes what he was trying to tell her so urgently. It wasn't *belle vie* at all, he was struggling to say the word Belleville.

The telephone rings, cutting into her thoughts. She rushes over to pick it up, her heart beating with anticipation. But it is Will, reminding her about their lunch date. "Don't forget," he says, "not a word to Alice."

Alice has already left for her final French class, to be followed by a graduation ceremony and the *vin d'honneur* without which no French *cérémonie* would be complete. Will plans to join her for the festivities, but he has also arranged a surprise celebration afterward with Sylvie and Ana Carvalho at the bistro.

On his way down, he sees Ana Carvalho barring the entry to an apartment on the second floor, arguing with a belligerent couple trying to edge past her. The concierge notices Will and says he should carry on, she has a matter to take care of before lunch. Then she rounds fiercely on a locksmith kneeling by the door and tells him to take his toolbox and get out before she calls the police. He slinks off, but the couple continues to argue in increasingly threatening tones.

"We will come back with a lawyer, Madame, if that's what you prefer," says the man.

"You can come back with President Mitterrand, if you like," retorts Ana Carvalho, "and I'll give you the same answer. The young man is in the hospital for tests, but he *will* be back, he has *not* quit the premises. You cannot force the lock, you have to wait until his death. And I know you would hasten *that*, if you could."

The woman asks her to be reasonable, after all the apartment belonged to their father, they are his legal heirs, they are only claiming what is their own.

"*Raisonnable?* And how *raisonnable* was it for you to come here and persecute your father when he was ill? You said it offended your morals that his companion had moved in, but it was the young man who nursed Monsieur Beaugrand day and night, you two were nowhere to be seen. The least Monsieur Beaugrand could do for him was ensure he had use of the apartment till his death. In any case, it won't be long now, and then you can come back and feast on the carcass. Even vultures have the decency to wait till the body is cold."

The woman looks nonplussed, but Ana isn't done with them yet. "You know what offends *my* morals? That you think because you are *hétéro*, you have a monopoly on affection, but I assure you that young man knows more about love than you ever will." Without another glance in their direction, she sweeps past them on her way to the bistro.

After her lunch with the Americans, Sylvie muses how their coming has transformed her life, not directly perhaps, but by setting in motion a chain of events that she couldn't have imagined three months ago. The folder that fell from Julien's desk, and all that has followed since. But for now her quest has ended, as it began, in silence.

The phone rings, startling her out of her reverie. Ana Carvalho tells her there is someone in the courtyard asking for her, she says her name is Christine Boniface.

Sylvie draws in her breath. Christine Boniface of Belleville. "Send her up."

But Ana Carvalho wouldn't dream of letting the woman into Sylvie's apartment on her own, she's heard too many horror stories about swindlers preying on the old and the defenseless, not that Sylvie is old, and Coco's there to defend her, but still, better to be safe than sorry. And this woman looks a little *toc-toc*, wouldn't surprise her if she's touched in the head.

But when Sylvie opens the door, it is Christine Boniface who eyes her suspiciously.

"I was told you're looking for me," she says.

Sylvie nods to Ana Carvalho, still barring the doorway. "It's all right, Ana."

Reluctantly, Ana moves aside for Christine Boniface to enter. "I'm out here changing the lightbulb, if you need me," she says meaningfully.

But the woman is oblivious of the concierge, her eyes fixed on a framed canvas leaning against the mantelpiece, a landscape of vineyards and hills with three ruined châteaux in the distance. She walks toward it like a frostbitten wanderer toward a fire, then sinks down on her knees and bursts into a howl of wordless desolation.

What Christine remembers most clearly is a woman picking her up and carrying her kicking and screaming all the way to the Grenelle metro station. The woman had put her down on the platform, wiped her face, and said, *"Doucement, ma petite,"* wrapped the shawl tighter around her, and then boarded the next metro. To the child's surprise they got on in front, not the last car meant for those with yellow stars. Once the doors shut, Lilou kept her eyes fixed on her reflection in the glass as the train left the stadium farther and farther behind.

They got off in a part of the city the child had never visited before; the metro stop said Belleville, and the most beautiful thing about it was the calm after the bedlam of Vel d'Hiv. They entered a shabby building with a birdcage elevator that groaned all the way to the third floor. The woman knocked on a door and said, *"C'est moi, Martine."* A man opened the door, a cigarette clamped between his teeth, and the front of his jacket covered with a smattering of ash. Martine ushered the child inside, saying *"Another lost lamb, Arnaud."* He swore under his breath and went back to the papers on his desk. Martine lifted the child into an armchair and brought her some water. Gently she pried open Lilou's fingers, still clutched around the roll, and threw away the mangled piece of bread. "Hungry?" she asked, and Lilou nodded. She brought an orange from the kitchen and peeled it for the child. As the tart juice burst against her tongue, Lilou thought she had never tasted anything so delicious in all her life. She chewed slowly, making each bite last as long as she could. But when she had eaten half, she closed her fingers around the rest to save it for Gigi. Martine and Arnaud were talking in low tones, and then Martine called someone on the phone.

Lilou tried to listen, but Arnaud knelt down in front of her, a pair of scissors in his hand, not a lady's dainty scissors, but big scissors, the kind Aunt Marie used to cut leather in the bindery. *"What's your name?"* he said. *"Liliane,"* she said, *"je m'appelle Liliane,"* and brushed away the cigarette ash from her lap, wondering why Arnaud didn't use the ashtray beside her. She shrank back as he brought the scissors up to her chest and with great dexterity snipped the yellow star off her blouse, muttering under his breath, *"Damn them, damn the stinking bastards to hell."* He gave her the star, then lit a candle and held it out. *"Here,"* he said, *"burn it."* She held the star to the flame, which leapt greedily toward the fabric, and Lilou watched it shrink and curl until it was too hot to hold, then she let it drop into the ashtray, where it continued to burn till it was a charred bit of nothing.

Arnaud blew out the candle, scattering even more ash around the room. Then he told her that she was Christine now, Christine Boniface of Belleville.

"Will I stay with you?"

"No, it's not safe in the city, you must go to the country, to my brother's, if he'll have you. Martine's talking to him now. You'll like it out there, on the farm. When I was a child, I was always happy there, *bien dans ma peau.*"

Lilou tried to imagine this, feeling comfortable in her skin. "Can my sister go, too?"

"Maybe someday."

"When will I come back?"

"Soon, Christine, very soon."

They both called her Christine over and over, until she responded to the name without a moment's hesitation. Arnaud busied himself with forging papers for her, and the next day a woman came to the apartment, everything about her starched, her collar, her expression, even the cloth cover on her Bible. She would take Christine to the farm and leave her there with her counterfeit papers. "Are you ready, Christine?" the woman asked.

"Just a minute," Lilou replied, and went to the bathroom, where she looked at herself in the mirror. Gigi's face stared back at her. *"Christine,"* she said fiercely, *"je m'appelle Christine Boniface."*

On the way to the station the woman told her, "Don't draw attention to yourself, just act like everyone else."

As they waited for the train to arrive, the starched woman clutched her Bible, flinching every time the Germans patrolled past them with their dogs. Christine and she boarded the train without incident, but when the whistle sounded, three German soldiers got on and dragged a stocky man and a young boy from the train. The businessman sitting across from them leaned over and whispered, "Must have been a *passeur*, that fellow they pulled off." Christine was amused by the word *passeur*, what was he smuggling, a little boy? But the woman turned white, and before they came to the next station, she went into the corridor and pulled out a sheet of paper hidden in her Bible. The girl watched in amazement as she tore the list of names into thin strips, then chewed and swallowed each one, and it wasn't until much later that Christine realized that the woman was also a *passeuse*, risking her life to smuggle children to safety.

A city girl like Christine would have stuck out like a sore thumb on a rural farm, but the sheer number of Boniface children provided camouflage, eight already, and another on the way. She was absorbed into the flock, and Madame Boniface told Christine to call her Tante Garance. If anyone asked, she was to say she'd been sick and come to the countryside to convalesce. And as if to prove it true, Christine did fall ill, coughing and shivering, with her temperature spiking so high they didn't know whether to send for a doctor or a priest. But she recovered, and the fever did what forgery could not, made her forget names and places, so when they asked her about the big city, she stared blankly and said, "London?" The younger children laughed and for a while it was a great joke with them to curtsy and call her milady.

They were kind to her, her new "cousins." But kindness was not the same as love. Madame Boniface was a good woman, and she made sure that within their frugal means all the children had enough to eat and warm clothes to wear. She could not guess that what this child was starving for was kisses and words of endearment. When the newcomer wet her bed or awoke screaming from nightmares, Tante Garance silently changed the sheets, left a lamp burning by the bedside. The Bonifaces were a taciturn family, and Christine learned to *act like everyone else*, to say only what was necessary, the virtues of frugality extending even to words. *"Bien dans ma peau,"* Arnaud had said. It wasn't his fault she did not feel comfortable in her skin anymore, because it wasn't her real skin, after all, she had sloughed it off for a forged identity.

"That's all ancient history," Christine shrugs, though it's obvious her childhood emotions have come surging back with the shock of recent discoveries. Anyway, she's married now, she tells Sylvie, has grown children of her own, she and her husband own a pharmacy in a neighboring town, none of the Boniface children had moved far from the farm which belonged to Matthieu since his father's death. All of them gathered there for the holidays, but their reunion this Easter was filled with sadness, for Madame Boniface was ailing and unlikely to recover.

"Before she died, Tante Garance told me what she knew." The approach of death had loosened the reticence of a lifetime, and while her lips moved in prayer, Madame Boniface's mind wandered through the landscape of unsaid things. *Une forteresse sûre est notre Dieu,* and now that she is at the very gates of that mighty fortress, she can't help recalling the day that poor girl, sick and frightened, was delivered to their doorstep like a parcel. When Martine and Arnaud called about the child, her husband had hesitated, told his brother it was too dangerous in these times to shelter a Jew, but she had insisted, had told her husband, we can't turn her away, we Huguenots have too long a memory of persecution. *Love ye therefore the stranger: for ye were strangers in the land of Egypt.* She has never regretted taking her in, especially after what happened to Martine and Arnaud, shot by the Boche for being *résistants.* She can still remember how the girl would cry out in her sleep, this poor scrap of a child that Martine had plucked off the street, with nothing on her but a shawl, where was the shawl now, oh yes, in the attic, Matthieu must fetch it down for Christine right away.

Christine had buried her face in the shawl and the scent in her nostrils released the *génie* bottled up inside and all the banished memories came rushing back from exile.

"Maman," she shrieked, *"Maaamaaaan."*

Christine's husband had been so good with her, so patient as she grappled with these revelations. And she had taken out all her anger on him, poor Gérard. They had contacted the woman who brought her to the farm that July in 1942, but she could tell them nothing more than what Martine Boniface had told *her*, that the girl was found wandering alone outside Vel d'Hiv. They wrote to the Ministry in Paris for information, but nobody could match her up with her family or say where she came from. Then just a few days ago, she got a letter from Ari Wolkowsky, who remembered her name and the station where she got off, and had tracked her down. He had enclosed a photo, and circled the face of a child in the train window. If she was indeed Christine Boniface of Belleville, then she should disregard the letter. But if she was not, he had something to tell her, and he had enclosed his card.

She called him at once, then arranged a trip to Paris. Gérard was ready to accompany her, but she refused. She wanted to go back to the city as she had left it, alone. Rage was bursting out of her skin, the skin it had taken her so long to become comfortable in, but it wasn't even her skin, like everything about her, it was counterfeit. *How could this happen?* she cried. *How could people let it happen? Were they deaf, were they blind, were they insane?*

"I understand why you're angry."

"No, you don't," she had screamed at Gérard. "You don't even know who I am, I'm not Christine at all, I'm Lilou, *je m'appelle Liliane.*"

Hearing those words, Sylvie thinks that for so long Christine's anger has lain within her like a tightly coiled spring. Perhaps it is what saved her; rage impels one forward, grief holds one back.

"What should I call you?"

"Oh, I'm Christine now, for good or ill, what's the point of insisting on my old name, it won't change anything."

"So then you met Ari Wolkowsky?"

"Yes. He told me about you, about the photo in the magazine. So I came here. He said you might have some information. If you'll tell me what you know, I can head back to my family tomorrow or the day after."

"You can stay here, if you like."

"No, I'll find a hotel."

"Come with me," Sylvie says. "I know just the place."

When they are out on the street, Christine seems overwhelmed by the noise, by the crowds. They cross the bridge in silence, and walk through the Marais. But when they turn into rue des Rosiers, her eyes widen, and she looks around wonderingly. "My school," she says, clutching Sylvie's arm. A little further, she points to the old confectioner's shop, now a *salon de thé*. "Madame Cacher," she says, her voice catching in her throat. As they enter rue Elzévir, she drops Sylvie's arm and flies to the blue wooden door and pushes it open, rushes up the stairs, and knocks on the familiar door, and her great-aunts open it and look at her as if she is indeed a revenant, but one of flesh and blood, whom they hold as if they will never let her out of their sight again, and if Marie's joy is mingled with bitterness at all the wasted years since *ce jour-là*, Mathilde's happiness is unadulterated; for her *that day* was then, but here is Lilou, come out of hiding, and this moment, this wonderful moment, this is now.

Sylvie can hardly sleep that night, imagining the scenes and the conversations, the tears and embraces in that apartment with its false ceiling, whose sleeping ghosts she has disturbed. She paces her own apartment, then takes Coco down for a late-night walk, and finds herself passing the offices of the CDJC. She wonders if Ari Wolkowsky is still there, working late. She feels a strong impulse to talk to him again, but the Center is shut, and the guard outside says, "Madame, it's almost midnight."

She doesn't expect Christine back till the afternoon, but barely has she put on the morning coffee when there's a knock on the door. It's evident that Christine has also passed a *nuit blanche*, her eyelids swollen, her voice hoarse. Sylvie leads her in, and looking at the painting, Christine once more bursts into tears.

Sylvie lets her weep. So many tears, so long held back. She pours them both some coffee, and when Christine is more composed, Sylvie says, "I have Clara's things for you."

Christine nods. "Tata Marie told me."

Sylvie finds it moving to hear from this woman's lips—a woman her own age—the childish *tata* instead of *tante*; that's what Lilou would have called Marie, not Aunt but Auntie. She brings out the roll of canvases. "Here, take these, they belong to you."

"I'll look at them later, I can't right now . . . I'm too overwhelmed."

Sylvie nods. "Oh, and this one, on the mantelpiece, let me get it."

Christine stops her. "Keep that, if you want."

Sylvie is grateful for the offer. She would like to have the painting, for Julien's sake.

"What was he like?"

Sylvie wonders what she can tell Christine about the uncle she had never met. That Julien was brilliant, he was generous, he was, quite simply, the finest man she had ever known. How would it comfort her to know all this now? Slowly she says, "Julien loved his sister and he never stopped looking for you."

They are both silent, thinking Lilou's return to Paris was a few months too late for Julien to know that, miraculous as it might seem, she had survived.

Then Sylvie says softly, "He has two children, Charles and Alexandra. I know they'll want to meet you."

A smile trembles on Christine's lips. So she has real cousins now, not just counterfeit ones. But she shakes her head. "Not yet, it's too soon."

"I understand."

"I'm leaving day after tomorrow and taking the aunts with me. I want them to meet my family, my adopted family, I mean." The recent discovery doesn't erase all the years the Bonifaces have made her feel one of them. Ari Wolkowsky had told her she could petition for her rescuers to be posthumously honored as Les Justes, but Christine knows Tante Garance would just have shrugged and said, *No need for a medal, we did what anyone would,* c'est normal.

"There's something else . . ."

Christine looks at her expectantly.

Sylvie shakes her head. "Not yet. Not here."

The next day Sylvie waits for Christine by Julien's grave, and when she comes, Sylvie hands her the wooden box. Finally, she thinks, a legitimate claimant for Clara's jewel case. Her fingers trembling, Christine opens the lid and looks at its meager contents: three pebbles, a lace bonnet, the letter sealed with a drop of wax. She slides her nail under the seal, smooths out the creases, and reads the first words out loud: *My darling girls*. Her voice falters and she tries again: *My darling girls*. Tears blind her eyes, and she shakes her head and hands it to Sylvie. *My darling girls*, reads Sylvie. Her voice trembles as well, but she does not pause, carried along by the urgency of Clara's words.

My darling girls,

How you press me for another story, and another, and another . . . the ones you like best are tales from my childhood, so distant from your lives that they seem like fairy tales, and I find comfort in those dear scenes as well. You are already asleep, and I look at you, your curls glinting in the candlelight, and long to fondle your hair like a miser gloating over his gold. But I am afraid to wake you, so I write to you instead by the sputtering light of the candle. They are rationed now, we can only buy one or two at a time, not a whole box. Everything is scarce this year, even more than last. Too little meat to fill out your cheeks, too little milk to strengthen your bones. Marie does her best with what she can find in the streets, and when I see you choke down sparrow meat and stale bread, I would give anything to serve you my mother's kugelhopf.

I used to eat it fresh from the oven and always burned my tongue because I couldn't wait for the raisins to cool. Those days in Alsace, we had enough bread and enough firewood for the cold nights when Papa would work on his furs, quickly marking them with a blue chalk, then cutting along the lines with his razor, he had a very sure hand, you can't afford to make mistakes with fur. Even when times were hard, Papa always had work, the rich continued to order his coats.

Julien . . .

Sylvie stops abruptly. Seeing his name written on paper instead of carved in stone makes Julien seem suddenly alive. The lines blur before her eyes, and she blinks away her own tears to continue reading for Christine's sake, whose face is bathed with tears as she listens hungrily to her mother speaking to her from beyond the grave.

Julien would read aloud to us, always in French, my father did not allow us to speak German at home even though we were taught German in school until the war ended, the earlier war, I mean, not this one. My father asked us who is the French hero you admire most, and wanting to be first with the answer, I shouted out, Napoleon, Papa, it's Napoleon, but Julien thought for a while and then said Zola, and I could tell Papa was better pleased with my brother's answer than mine.

I loved the summer evenings when women would gather by the fountain of St. Hune—the saint of washerwomen according to local lore—and we children would play in the endless twilight until it was time for bed. But what I miss most are the storks that came every year to Hunawihr. You point to the pigeons on the rooftops and say, we have birds here, maman. Such city girls! Used to manicured parks and signs that say *keep off the grass.* When I was a girl, I ran barefoot on the grass around our house, it was soft and wild and scented with chamomile.

I hated the thought of leaving home, but my mother had enrolled me at Madame Weil's *pensionnat* for Jewish girls in Nancy, where cousin Rebekah had studied. She later married a classmate's brother and my mother told me I must also marry a Jew, friends are all very well, but only Jews are family, no one else stands by you when trouble comes. I wish she had met Bernard, she would know that isn't true.

But I can't blame her for her distrust, not after what happened to Julien. Some boys from our village beat him so badly that he lost sight in one eye. And no one came to commiserate, not any of the women with whom my mother washed clothes in the fountain, not any of the men whom my father had helped when they needed an extra hand with the harvest. Only the schoolteacher stopped by to shake his head and say times were hard and trouble was spreading, we had better find somewhere safe. My father said, "We won't let them drive us from here, we'll fight back," but my mother said, "I can't sleep here another night, this isn't the first time they've attacked us, why wait for the next time, it might be Clara." I cried, "But why would they hurt me?

I haven't done anything!" My father looked at me, then rose to his feet and pulled an old valise from under the bed. "But why, Papa?" I persisted. He stroked my hair and said, "Sometimes people hate you not for what you do, but who you are." "But Papa, who are we, that they should hate us?" "We are Israelites, *chérie*." "But Papa, I thought we were French." "Oh, yes," he said, "we are as French as anyone can be."

My father went into his workshop and rolled up the furs, packing them in the valise to give us a start in the big city. Strasbourg, I asked, because it was the biggest city I could imagine. No, they said, Paris. Paris! At first I was excited and then it struck me that Minou might not like it, but my mother said nonsense, we can't possibly take the cat with us, and then I started thinking how Minou would have taken up with another family by the time we came back. I always thought that we would return, sometimes I think it still. The train ride made me sleepy, but when I put my head down on a bundle, the cat started meowing and my mother slapped me because I had smuggled Minou in place of the fur hat that would have kept me snug that winter.

How I wish I had it now, to bring you a little warmth. I dread the coming winter, there's no wood, no coal, nothing, nothing, nothing, how will we manage?

But you have your own urgent questions: Why can't we play in the park anymore? Why can't we go to the library? Why do we wear yellow stars? Why must we always ride the last car in the metro? Your smooth foreheads are wrinkled with perplexity, and you are right to be puzzled. But even those questions have stopped since your father left and we hid up here. There is only one question which preoccupies you now: "Where is he," you ask, "where is Papa?" I turn my face away, I cannot answer. "In London?" you ask. For you, everyone who is not here is across the Channel, fighting for France. And I say yes, and I would give anything to be by his side. But then I think of you, and I would willingly stay here for the rest of my life if only it would keep you safe.

Oh, my darlings! What good girls you are, uncomplaining even though there is so much for you to lament. You quietly play your childish games and I overhear you whispering to each other about pitchipoi, and I wonder what that is. And then one day I understand it's a special playground where you run freely with the other children, where you find once more everything you have lost, your friends, your toys. Most of all your father, whom you greet with such joy. I feel my heart will burst when I think of Bernard, but I must be strong for your sake, you are all I have left now.

So I close my eyes and I dream of pitchipoi, too. I walk into our little house in Hunawihr, which is just as I remember. My brother is reading by the fireplace, his eyes unharmed. A kugelhopf is baking in the oven, Minou is asleep on the windowsill, and through the open window I can see the ruined fortresses of Ribeauvillé.

Ah, how suffocating this room is, no windows, no light. When will this darkness be over? But then I look at you and I think, for you I would bear much worse. On my knees I pray for God to send all the suffering upon me, but spare my girls.

The candle is almost burned down now, and before it goes out, I hold it up to gaze at you, to look at your precious faces, so beautiful, so innocent. Even when I close my eyes, that is what I see, that is what I will always see, the last thing before I sleep.

Sylvie puts her arms around Christine, who is sobbing uncontrollably. The shadows lengthen around them, alone now among the tombstones. The caretaker walks past, jingling his keys, it's already past closing time, and they can come back another day, his charges aren't going anywhere, not until the trumpets sound on Judgment Day. Christine wipes her eyes and replaces the objects in the box: the letter, the square of black lace, the three pebbles. Then she changes her mind, takes out the stones and arranges them on Julien's grave.

Watching her, Sylvie thinks that one day Christine will know what Julien knew, that no one escapes unscathed, it is the lot of the survivor to bear scars both visible and invisible, but you honor the life you've been spared to live by admitting into it the possibility of happiness. And then she thinks about Isabelle, preoccupied with wills and bequests, rushing to rue Elzévir in pursuit of a valuable painting, but it is Sylvie who has stumbled across the children's true inheritance, the story of their father's past. Julien's silence was meant as a shelter, but might equally one day prove an affliction, just as it has for Lilou, hollowed out for so long by not knowing. They need to know, she thinks, they deserve to know. It is part of their story, part of who they are.

And as she looks around the graveyard, she feels the strangest sensation, her heart expanding within her, growing larger and larger and larger until it seems to contain all these stories that are not separate at all but connected in strange and marvelous ways, herself and Christine and Clara and Julien, and Charles and Alexandra, and Marie and Mathilde, and yes even Isabelle, and all the living and all the dead, and still it continues to expand until it is as vast as the sky and she feels that for this moment, at least, she is what Julien called her, Sylvie, *coeur de lion*.

I feel the sudden loud beat of my stopped heart, a great soaring of my spirit like the swell of the organ that echoed outside the walled church of Hunawihr as the schoolmaster played the music of Bach, giving thanks to a merciful God: Wir danken dir, Gott, wir danken dir.

One of Clara's daughters is no longer "presumed dead"; she is, by some miracle, alive. And it is Sylvie who has found the missing child. For so long I had searched for her in a city which reveals its secrets to those who crisscross it with no fixed purpose; but I could not fool the darkness, I lacked the flâneur's *trademark, loitering without intent. My purpose was unmistakable, I was no stray beam but a searchlight from which the darkness receded, refusing to give up to me the runaway child who had hidden herself so cunningly somewhere in the city that it's as if she never existed.*

I had followed up on every official document, every hazy recollection, every rumor and whisper, but all avenues of inquiry led only to cul-de-sacs of silence. Once I went to an address in Belleville, where I had heard of a couple who forged papers to smuggle dozens of children out of the city. Scarcely daring to hope, I went up the birdcage elevator in search of Arnaud and Martine Boniface. But no one answered when I knocked. I refused to leave. I stood there knocking like a madman. Finally the concierge came up the stairs and asked if I was looking for Monsieur Durand. I shook my head. Monsieur Boniface, I said. She raised her elbow and cocked her finger to mimic a machine gun. "Ta-ta-ta-ta-ta," she said, "fusillé." *Seeing my face, she added, "Your friends died like heroes, they didn't try to hide when the Boche came but went to meet them with their heads held high. Then, ta-ta-ta-ta-ta."*

For me, the trail had ended with the rat-a-tat of a German machine gun.

But then I had come across the magazine a patient had left behind in my office. Flipping through its pages, I had been struck, as Sylvie was, by that haunting photograph. Like her, I thought Ari Wolkowsky might know something more. But before I could see him, I had received the summons which no power on earth can evade and found myself in a hospital room which I would never leave again to stretch out in my own bed with the love of my life lying beside me.

At the very end, I had tried to tell Sylvie: Belleville. She could not make out the word. "Oui, la vie est belle," *she responded.*

But then she picked up the thread that connected her to me and followed it patiently, persistently, the way she worked through knotty passages of music, not by technical skill alone but by a great leap of emotional intelligence, of imaginative empathy. And now it is over, that triumphant search, a great recital performed for no other audience but myself. Brava, chérie, brava!

And then I realize those loud wingbeats, that graceful soaring, is not music at all but the sound of storks as they circle the sky above Hunawihr, gathering their strength for their long journey back home.

For the first time since Julien's death, Sylvie feels ready to leave the city. The seashore, advises Ana Carvalho, but Sylvie shakes her head. Julien and she had always gone together to the coast in Brittany, where he was as carefree as she had ever seen him, talking to fishermen returning with their day's catch, or listening to tales of Breton magic, about the washerwoman of the night who tricks unwary travelers into wringing their own shrouds. His memories found no purchase in this soil and their burden lifted when he was there, literally at the end of the earth, in Finistère.

Impossible to go there without him. A vision rises before her eyes of a clear lake, of reposeful mountains, but she has left it too late, it is almost August and all the hotels are sure to be full.

She walks restlessly around the apartment. She feels the urge to tell Julien all about Lilou, but she can never tell him anything again. *Never again.* The words begin their relentless ostinato, but she shakes her head. She knows where that leads, a dead end. Well, the children will come in September and she can unburden herself of Clara's tragic tale. She could ring them up, or write to them, but no, better face-to-face. If only they were here now!

Sylvie leafs through her music and comes across the late sonatas of Beethoven. Had she been ambitious enough at one time to attempt them? She places the music on the stand, but when her fingers touch the keys, she feels a strange resistance to the piece—not now, not yet—and plays instead the reverberating bass note that begins the barcarolle. She thinks of how Chopin created from undulating rhythms and singing melodies a beauty beyond beauty, an impression of light shimmering on water, of unplumbable depths of yearning. Then in the passage marked *dolce sfogato*, she hears the water's tranquil murmur, it is right, it is natural, that after so long a parting the dead should cease to answer, and the living should cease to weep, and she closes her eyes and stops thinking about anything at all as she becomes one with the music, transparent as the water, and when the theme returns, the water overflows its banks, as boundless and mysterious as the invisible swells of the sea.

She sees Julien clearly before her, lured back to this world by the music that was a prelude to their love, and is now its elegy. *Speak to me*, she entreats him, *speak to me, my darling*, but when she lifts her hands and opens her eyes, that wraith has vanished. It will take more than music to summon him, it will take a miracle.

Then something happens, so strange, so unexpected that it might well be called miraculous. A key turns in the lock, and Coco scampers to the door with a whine of happiness. The hair rises slowly along Sylvie's arms as the door swings open and a beloved face smiles at her, a beloved voice calls her name.

Will sees the door shut on a stranger's back, and the old curiosity flares up in him for an instant. He has made Sylvie his business, but what does it really have to do with him? The amazing story she has told them, that is *her* story about *her* city; he will never inhabit Paris, nor will it ever inhabit him and the threshold he's so eager to cross in an unfamiliar city is only a displacement of his own transition from one stage of life to another back home.

Already the city is beginning to empty out; people are taking advantage of the last weekend in July to start their August vacation early, before the autoroutes are clogged. Will and Alice see several shopfronts already shuttered on their way to dinner, and so many restaurants are closed that tourists have found their way even to their neighborhood bistro. "Their" table is occupied by a Japanese couple, and Will and Alice have to squeeze past them to grab the last empty seats.

After dinner, they stroll around the island before returning to the apartment. Alice turns to say something to Will, but he is preoccupied with his own thoughts. She slips her hand through his arm; what she has to tell him can wait till they are home. And even as she thinks that she realizes she is seeing everything before her, the wrought-iron peacocks, the cobblestone courtyard, Sylvie's lighted window, as if preserved in a photograph or etched in memory; her thoughts have already made the turn for America. Home.

Up in the apartment, Sylvie is comforted by Alexandra's unexpected arrival, as if she had somehow sensed she was needed. And she's glad Alexandra has brought Lucas as well, though he seems strangely withdrawn. He's always been quieter than his cousins, but something is definitely wrong now, she can tell more from Alexandra's manner than from her son's, she's been tense and watchful all evening. Well, Alexandra will confide in her if she wants her to know. And she has so much to tell Alexandra as well, but that story has waited so long, it can wait just a little longer.

Alexandra roots around in the refrigerator, alarmed at how meagerly Sylvie seems to eat, and Sylvie doesn't dare tell her the pork loin is for Ana Carvalho tomorrow. Alexandra cooks it for dinner, and says her brother doesn't eat red meat anymore, he's turned into an old woman, worried about everything, germs, noise, crowds, no one would believe he was once young, let alone a firebrand.

Sylvie laughs at Alexandra's exaggerations, it's not a bad thing Charles is more staid than his sister, he is a banker after all, despite his hot-headed youth, his anarchist friends, especially that red-haired Daniel whom the newspapers dubbed *Dany le rouge*. But she shudders remembering the student protests, the police brutality of those days. Sylvie had worried about his joining the *manifestations*, but Julien said people had a moral obligation to act, and when Charles went to the barricades, Julien stood right there beside him.

All this must seem like ancient history to Luc, the events of 1968 as remote from him as the Revolution. He looks worn out, and doesn't protest when Alexandra packs him off to bed. She calls her husband from the telephone in the hallway, then comes into Sylvie's bedroom and curls up beside her. "If you're wondering why we've come, it's because of Lucas. He's running with the wrong crowd and his father is furious, he wants to send him to military school. But I've persuaded him to let Luc study art. It's what he's always wanted, and in Paris at least there's someone to keep an eye on him."

Sylvie knows how effective Alexandra's persuasions can be; she is an irresistible force, and perhaps she is right, Isabelle will surely take the boy well in hand. But isn't Isabelle still at Vandenesse for the summer? And then she grasps what Alexandra is saying, and is so overcome with emotion that she can hardly speak. It is to *her* that Alexandra has turned, *her* to whom she entrusts her son.

"You don't mind if he stays, do you?"

Mind? She is overjoyed. But won't it be dull for Luc?

"Hardly. When I was his age, I used to wait all week to come here."

Sylvie hides a smile, glad that's how memory's clouded lens allows Alexandra to see the past, their skirmishes forgotten.

"Do you remember how we drove Papa mad with that song we used to sing?"

Yes, she does, the steaming mugs of cocoa, Julien returning from the *boulangerie* with a brioche, begging them to stop, he wouldn't be able to get that song out of his head for the rest of the week, but you could tell from the way he was smiling that he didn't mind at all.

Alexandra hums, *on prend le café au lait au lit*, then bursts into a fit of giggles and can't stop. Woken by the sound, Luc comes into the room. Seeing his mother's face, his own expression lightens and he sprawls at the foot of the bed.

"So how are you getting along with your Americans, Sylvie? Luc is crazy about America these days."

As if she hadn't been the same at his age! She and Charles used to beg Sylvie to take them for hamburgers at Le Drugstore, with deafening music bouncing off all that chrome, and later of course the place was bombed, thank God they had stopped going by then.

"I've been meaning to have them over, but it seems strange to do it now when they're getting ready to leave."

"Nonsense," says Alexandra, "it will be amusing for Luc. I'll go across tomorrow."

Sylvie smiles at her. "No," she says, "I'll ask them myself."

When Sylvie knocks on their door the next day, she remembers how reluctant she had been to divide the apartment and how Alexandra had insisted. A will of iron, that girl. But she was right, after all, having the Americans there has been such a comfort, and after they leave, it's all set up for Luc.

Will opens the door and smiles, delighted to see Sylvie in such good spirits. He cannot get out of his mind the last time she knocked at their door, holding out a piece of paper and looking utterly bereft. "Come in, come in, Alice is in the shower, but she'll be out in a jiffy. Some coffee?"

Sylvie nods absently. She looks around, imagining Luc in the space. *A good idea, isn't it, mon amour?* Apart from the clanging pipes, there is only silence. She wonders if she'll ever get used to it. As she leans out to look at the river, Will shouts a warning but it is too late, the iron railing comes loose from the window frame and sails down into the courtyard. Sylvie braces herself against the wall, but her hands slip and she feels herself falling.

Quicker than he has ever moved, Will springs forward and pulls Sylvie back to safety. She holds on to him, trembling with shock. How often she had dreamed of making that leap, but when fate offered her the chance, she had recoiled, had clung to life. Her heart beating wildly, she buries her face in Will's shirt. He feels the shudders ripple through her and his own breaths come raggedly as he stares over Sylvie's shoulder at the terrifying vision of the sharp iron spikes angled to deter burglars, but from up here their only purpose seems impalement. Just then Alice enters the room and stares at the sight of them clinging to each other like survivors on a raft.

For a moment we remain frozen, an unlikely quartet brought together by the vagaries of chance. The word "quartet" carries me back to the house on rue de Bièvre, the night it all began. And now, at the end, Sylvie has chosen to go on with life. I cannot mask my sudden emotion when she turns her face from me and draws Alice into their embrace. As the three of them grip each other, I am returned to my proper place, outside the circle of the living, once again an observer incapable of harm.

Sylvie says she must leave, they're waiting for her at home; and this time she knows it's true. At the door she turns to look back and sees her life with Julien distinctly again, not obscured by the doubts of the past few months, and it's clear as clear can be why he chose her, why she chose him: for nothing more and nothing less than love. Schumann in his madness had a lucid vision: two rings preserved in the river's silt; Sylvie, too, perceives it clearly now, that love does not end when life ends, but endures beyond reason, beyond breath.

Dazed, Will thinks he could never forgive himself if anything had happened, it was his fault, the rotted frame had slipped his mind. He latches the kitchen window shut and jams a chair under it until the railing can be replaced. "It could have been you," he says to Alice. His knees tremble and he sits down abruptly, feeling as if he has aged in a matter of minutes, has turned into an old man.

Still in shock, thinks Alice. She kneels beside him and murmurs soothingly till the blankness leaves his eyes and his hands stop shaking. He clasps her hand but doesn't say another word.

In a deliberately down-to-earth tone she says, "What did Sylvie want, by the way?"

"She's asked us over."

"You must be thrilled."

He shrugs. His ardent desire to enter a different world seems so remote. Now that his ardor has dimmed and his attention is elsewhere, the invitation has finally come. But it no longer matters.

Will looks at Alice's dear face and kisses her. For him, Sylvie was part of the fantasy that in Paris he would be transported somehow into a different life, but it took those iron spikes protruding from the wall to remind him that the life you have is the one that matters.

Ana Carvalho slips on a cotton glove and runs her hand along the banister, dusting it on her way up to Sylvie's. She used to think nothing of going up and down a dozen times a day, but now she spares her painful bunions by combining several errands into one. Might as well take leave of the Americans while she is upstairs, they will be gone by the time she returns from Hossegor.

Her suitcase is packed, the gaily patterned bathing suit ready for its annual outing, and her cousin Antonio is waiting downstairs to take her to the station, saving her the expense of a taxi, daylight robbery, that's what it is now. A reliable fellow, Antonio, he knows how to take care of her little dears. As for her other charges, August is a quiet time with only a few residents staying on, Madame Sylvie and the Cheroiseys, the judge always takes his holidays in winter, flying to Île Maurice or the Seychelles or somewhere "snob" like that. And of course that unfortunate man on the second floor, who is back from the hospital but will never leave the apartment again, unless by ambulance or by hearse.

Ana Carvalho pauses to catch her breath and swipe at a spiderweb on the railing. It's been almost a year since Monsieur Julien died, where does time go? But at least she needn't worry about Madame Sylvie, it's unlikely there'll be a recurrence of the old madness now that the first extravagance of grief is spent. Thankfully, young Luc will remain with Sylvie while she's away, clever of Alexandra to arrange it so neatly, she's always been clever, even as a child.

Wiping her hands on her apron, she knocks on the door. "I've come to take my leave," she says to Alice, who ignores her proffered hand and gives her a hug. Over her shoulder, Ana Carvalho sees Will riffling through papers, looking for something. *Voilà!* He's found it.

"One of your charges flew up to visit," he says, showing her the orange bird hopping around on his papers.

The concierge squints at the photograph and to Will's astonishment she says she's never seen him before, but adorable little fellow, isn't he? Will smiles and thinks, not all signs and wonders can be explained, it's fitting that some remain a mystery.

He hands her an envelope, and gratified by the thickness of the tip, Ana Carvalho tucks it into her pocket. "*Alors, bonne chance*, enjoy the rest of your vacation. Once the baby comes, you can kiss all that goodbye."

Will stares after her as she leaves and then turns wordlessly to Alice. She puts her hands on his shoulders. "How on earth did she know? I wasn't sure myself until a few days ago."

"You didn't tell me!"

"I was waiting till we were home."

Will is silent, so unlike him that she feels the first prickle of doubt. "You're happy, aren't you?"

He looks at her. *Happy?* He is ecstatic. How can she think otherwise? She puts her arms around him and he rests his cheek against her hair, silent with awe at how the future stretches far beyond his imagining.

On the other side of the wall, they speak of the long shadow of the past. Alexandra listens in silence as Sylvie tells the story of rue Elzévir, relating what she has discovered step by step, from the envelope that fell out of Julien's desk until the heartbreaking scene with Lilou at the graveyard. Alexandra stares off into the distance, it is some time before she can say a word. "When we were children, Charles and I knew Papa's sister had died at Auschwitz, but no details, not how they were picked up, not how they suffered. All our questions were met with vague answers, with warnings not to rake up the tragedy. It loomed so large in our imagination, but we could never speak of it to my father, we felt compelled to join the conspiracy of silence."

Yes, thinks Sylvie, that's how family secrets are forged, on these intimate pacts of silence, and she is still amazed that it has fallen to *her*, Sylvie *la timide*, to break that long silence.

Alexandra shakes her head. "I'm still reeling. What must it be like for Christine?"

"Hard to imagine."

"Should I call her now? Should I drive there?"

"*Doucement, chérie*," Sylvie replies. "It takes time to build a family from scratch."

"Like us?"

"Yes, like us."

Alexandra and Sylvie smile at each other. Luc observes them

with interest, and meeting his piercing blue gaze, Sylvie's heart turns over. So much like Julien, a resemblance that has skipped a generation to show up so markedly in him. And now he knows his love of painting has a direct line of descent as well. As Luc studies the landscape with the ruined châteaux, Sylvie feels a rush of love for Julien's grandson; they are linked by that painting, and she is the link, both receiver and transmitter of memory. Luc sees Sylvie observing him, and a shutter quickly comes down. But before he can retreat, she asks, "This winter, shall we try Florence?" The expression on his face is answer enough.

The next day Sylvie finds herself looking forward to the party with unaccustomed pleasure; no doubt Alexandra's presence accounts for it. She will know exactly how to handle things, she is her mother's daughter after all. Already the dinner is well in hand and she has transformed the apartment with a few deft touches. An old paisley shawl is draped invitingly over an armchair and there are candles everywhere, on the mantelpiece and in the grate. Sylvie admires the new arrangements, but what gratifies her most is that even with Julien gone, Alexandra feels that quai d'Anjou is still *home*.

When Will and Alice knock on the door, Coco greets Alice with transports of happiness, as though he hadn't seen her only that morning. Dogs measure separation by a different clock, thinks Will, looking around the room in surprise. He imagined it with dark walls and opulent draperies, but it is sparely furnished, with uncurtained windows framing magnificent views of the river. Well, he's managed to cross the sacrosanct French threshold that Fabienne talked about, so that's something. The judge and his wife enter on a gust of vetiver-scented cologne, holding a bouquet wrapped in cellophane. Will notices that the French carry flowers differently, not cradled in their arms like a baby but held upside down like a plucked fowl.

Madame de Cheroisey remarks it is *très* jolly to be together like this; she hears Alice is expecting, quite a souvenir to take back from Paris. The judge goes into the kitchen to greet Alexandra. He still can't believe she's a grown woman, seems like yesterday she and her brother were playing their gramophone records all day long. Alexandra whispers that dinner will be very simple on account of the Americans, just some hamburgers and a frozen *gâteau au chocolat* from Picard's. He pales in alarm, but then sees she is pulling his leg: there are artichokes in the pan, duck roasting in the oven, and potatoes prepared correctly, with real butter and cream, not any old butter, but *beurre d'Isigny*, lightly salted, just the way he likes it. He helps her choose the wines, opens the red to breathe, and leaves the white to warm slightly—people make the mistake of serving it too cold, it isn't lemonade—and expertly uncorks the champagne, which he pronounces quite *passable*. High praise for anything not from his own cellars.

Alexandra whisks the salad dressing and the delicate aroma of shallots fills the air. Luc comes into the kitchen for the appetizers, and seeing the look Alexandra gives her son, the judge thinks, some trouble there, drugs, if he had to bet, but it is none of his business. *"Georges-Henri,"* his wife calls out from the drawing room and reluctantly he leaves the kitchen.

Léonie is telling the Americans they must visit their country house in Normandy, mustn't they, *nounours*, and he nods, though he knows very well she wouldn't have volunteered an invitation if there was any danger of their accepting. The judge looks furtively at his pocket watch. He's missing his favorite political show on television, and for what? He can't make out half of what anyone is saying, people mumble terribly. He leans forward to help himself to another *gougère* before Léonie notices. But he is well enough for his age, and poor Léonie sickly as ever, despite being a slave to every fad. The first time nouvelle cuisine made an appearance at his table, he had announced, might as well bury me now, Léonie. She probably would anyway, and without going to pieces, unlike Sylvie. Ah well, he's had his flings, but when push came to shove he chose comfort over passion and stuck with Léonie. He can't imagine how Mitterrand does it, living officially with his wife but going home to his mistress every night, downright uncomfortable all that dodging about. He picks up another *gougère*.

Sylvie observes the judge sitting in abstracted silence, his deafness isolating him as her shyness used to isolate her. She brings over a platter of grapes but he shakes his head and raises his glass. "I prefer them crushed."

"A true connoisseur."

"Speaking of which, do you remember when the Rothschilds bought the Hôtel Lambert on a lark, what, ten years ago, fifteen maybe, and *madame la baronne* had a little at-home for the neighbors? Charming woman, charming. And the wines they served! Romanée-Conti, Gevrey-Chambertin, Puligny-Montrachet, bottles worth as much as her pearls." He is flattered by Sylvie's attention, he can tell when someone is listening or only feigning interest. Léonie doesn't even pretend anymore but fobs him off by saying he should write his memoirs. Maybe he will one day, the recollections of great men are part of the nation's patrimony, not that he is claiming greatness for himself, but he has certainly kept company with the great.

"Yes, I do," Sylvie replies. "I couldn't believe I was standing in the very spot where Chopin used to play."

"And while the baroness was showing the rest of you around, her husband took me for a tour of his cellar. Halfway through, another guest barged in, boasting to the baron about a priceless bottle he had acquired at auction, vintage 1865, liquid gold he called it, meant to be drunk on one's knees. A Sauternes, of course, and not just any Sauternes, but the very finest, Château d'Yquem, a bottle so rare he was willing to bet there wasn't another in the entire city, and would the baron do him the honor of drinking it with him one day? I hid a smile. The baron had just shown me a *whole case* of that very wine, and what an irresistible cue for him to pull out one of his bottles and say, *no time like the present*. But the baron merely smiled and held his tongue. Now, *that's* what I call class, true class."

Sylvie smiles to hear her mother's familiar words in the judge's mouth.

Listening to Léonie de Cheroisey instruct Alice on what to expect in the coming months, Will finds the French attitude to babies bracingly unsentimental. Then the phrase "priceless bottle" catches his ear, and his attention shifts to the judge and Sylvie. Will leans over and asks, "About that article, any chance the Jefferson bottles are genuine?"

"Doubtful. In any case, I'm sure by now the wine tastes like vinegar."

Alexandra calls them to the table and tells the Americans that for the finest French food they must travel to Lyon. The judge objects that the grand cuisine of France comes from Normandy, but yes, the food in Lyon is passable, quite passable. Madame de Cheroisey praises the tarragon mayonnaise, she can tell it's fresh, not from a jar. She breaks off to look warningly at her husband as he helps himself to more potatoes. *"Nounours,* you know you shouldn't . . ."

Irritably he says, "What is it? Speak up, speak up, don't mumble."

Too stubborn to turn on his hearing aid, Léonie thinks sourly, let him suffer from indigestion then if he doesn't want his pills.

Under the table, Coco mulls over his next prospect. Alexandra has already rebuffed him; why do people love the word *non*, so disagreeable to a dog's ears? He rests his face on Luc's knees. The boy succumbs to that wheedling gaze and stealthily drops morsels of food to the floor. Coco is gratified, but not surprised; he has long recognized the generous hand of providence.

The cheese course is followed by an apricot tart, and the judge thinks if they don't linger too long over coffee, he can at least catch the weather report, although he doesn't need *la météo* to tell him it is exceptionally hot, the evidence is plain as the nose on his face, quite purple and painful now but it'll subside once the weather turns cooler; he can't wait for fall when the *coings* show up in the markets, it's wonderful how just one quince ripening on the windowsill can perfume an entire room.

"The clivia is blooming," says Alice. "It's a shame Ana left without seeing the flowers, such a blaze of orange in that dark stairwell."

"Chiaroscuro," murmurs Luc, his thoughts far away in Italy, in Florence.

Chiaroscuro. The word is like a spell, it changes the register of the evening, and conversation retreats from the brightness of company to more contemplative shadows. The candles burn straight and true, there isn't the faintest breeze tonight. So many candles, such extravagance. Sylvie can't help thinking of Clara, writing by the guttering stub of a single candle. How often must Julien have called her to mind, all that youth and promise scattered to the winds. Her attention veers to the play of candlelight on Alexandra's face, on her hair so much like Isabelle's. Ah, that dinner at rue de Bièvre, it has held her in thrall for all these years. But something tonight has loosened the other woman's hold upon her. She might never be entirely free of Isabelle, but for this evening, at least, she no longer feels her presence over her shoulder.

"Hard to believe we're leaving in a few days," says Will.

Sylvie smiles. "Maybe you'll come back to France next year."

"Or maybe you will come to America," Will says. He hopes Sylvie knows Fabienne is not her only friend in Florida.

Luc's face brightens. Florida! *Mot magique.* He looks at Sylvie, and she nods; Florida, why not?

"My father loved to hear Sylvie play," Alexandra says. "He could listen for hours." There is no sign of rancor in her voice, though Sylvie listens closely for it. The pardon she sought from Isabelle has never come, but here is her daughter, forgiving her freely. When Alexandra asks her to play, Sylvie sits down at the piano without hesitation.

The judge, cradling his snifter of brandy, looks at Sylvie's face and for the first time he can understand why Julien chose passion over comfort; leaning forward to listen, Will, too, is struck by how the music reveals her hidden depths.

Maybe it is a trick of the light, but Sylvie can almost see Julien in the chair where Luc sits, his blue eyes opaque, his thoughts far away, dreaming perhaps of a future that must seem as distant to him as foreign lands to her.

Imagine, Julien, America! Italy! Just look at me.

She comes to the end of the piece, and the last note hangs in the air, elongated, endless, sustained not by her foot on the pedal, but by her reluctance to let it die away. But when it does finally fade, no one breaks the silence, and it seems amazing that a world so filled with perpetual motion should be capable of such stillness. Sylvie lifts her hands and thinks that subtle harmonies are the hardest to play, offering satisfactions as deep as they are modest. That's what she must learn now, to be grateful for life's modest satisfactions. And even as she thinks that, life magnanimously unfolds its hand and offers her more:

I'm looking, chérie, *I'm looking.*

I know Sylvie will not come to the window tonight. The living encircle her now, and down here in the shadows I relive the nights when I was among them, how she would glance toward me when the music ended. And I would look at her and look at her, filled with abiding thankfulness that I would see that beloved face every waking morning of my life.

Reluctantly I turn away from her window and make my solitary way to the river. On the stone walls of the pier, I trace my name, the outline visible for an instant and then it vanishes, to be overwritten by other names, other stories. It is inevitable that in time our little lives should enrich collective memory, that breath should become spirit.

And the spirit of the city claims me now as I look down on the river, deep as time. The cathedral across the tip of the island floats like an ark over dark waters. That its towers still rise toward the sky is a miracle. The retreating German army was ordered to burn it down, burn Paris and leave behind its smoldering remains. But even though the bridges were mined with explosives, the German general surrendered to the French without giving the order to detonate. By one of those grace notes that history sometimes provides, the city was saved and here we are, buffeted but still standing.

I think of that cloudless day when Paris was liberated, on the feast day of the king who prayed for France to be rid of its Jews, the Saint Louis for whom the island is named on which I stand, as others did on that August dawn forty-five years ago, when the bells

*of Notre Dame, silent through the long years of the Occupation
pealed out, the sound hovering in the air like a kestrel before
dispersing in ever-widening circles toward the horizon. Then the
cathedral's deep-voiced bell, which had over the centuries intoned
the coronation of kings and the end of wars, fell silent at last,
its reverberating echo lingering in the air like a doubt resolved,
announcing to the world, I AM.*

*Alone tonight in the silence I feel it suffused still by the music,
like a dream that leaves its impress on our already forgetful waking.
I am no stranger now to miracles, and if Lilou can be raised from
the dead by the relentless efforts of the living, then the living, too,
can be lovingly—oh-so-lovingly—awaited by the dead. After the
span allotted to her by capricious Time, one day Sylvie will push
open that curtained door to come to me, and despite all that I have
known, at the sight of her I will finally believe all losses are restored
and sorrows end.*

ACKNOWLEDGMENTS

With love and thanks to Ruth and Arnold Greenfield for introducing my husband and me to Paris, which we love deeply both for its own sake and for theirs.

I'm grateful to Francine Danzon for sharing her recollections of the roundup of French Jews during the Nazi occupation, a family history recounted by her son Marc Danzon in *Le Cordon*; to Hafiz Nouri of Galerie Bamyan for opening so many doors on Île Saint-Louis; to Didier and Marie-Jo Desmet, for allowing us to feel *chez nous* at quai d'Anjou; to Marie Houzelle for her helpful suggestions on the first draft, and to Véronique Schürr McMillan for her invaluable feedback on the final version. *À vous tous, mes remerciements et mes amitiés.*

I'm fortunate to be accompanied on this journey by dear friends who are gifted writers and perceptive readers, especially Anabella Schloesser de Paiz, Rosalind Palermo Stevenson, and Lola Willoughby. I am also grateful to Ellen Levine for early encouragement and sage advice.

Many thanks to Judy Sternlight, whose brilliant suggestions proved to be the turning point in the book's trajectory; to my amazing agent, Marly Rusoff; and to my lovely editor, the inimitable Nan Talese. I'm also deeply appreciative of Carolyn Williams, Todd Doughty, Charlotte O'Donnell, Hannah Engler, Bette Alexander, and the superb team at Nan A. Talese/Doubleday for all the ways in which they have contributed to this book. *Un grand merci* to Emily Mahon for the dazzling jacket, which captures the spirit of *Haunting Paris* even better than I had hoped.

A big thank you to Robert and Peg Boyers for including me in the wonderful literary community they've created through the New York State Summer Writers Institute at Skidmore College; to my mother for fostering a lifelong passion for books; to the wise and generous teachers who have shaped me (though any errors in the book are my own); and, most of all, to MR, last and best of my teachers.

A Note About the Author

Mamta Chaudhry's fiction, poetry, and feature articles have been published in the *Miami Review, Illustrated Weekly of India, The Telegraph, The Statesman, Writer's Digest,* and *The Rotarian,* among others. Much of her professional career was spent as an interviewer, announcer, and program director at television and classical radio stations in Calcutta, Gainesville, Dallas, and Miami. She lives with her husband in Coral Gables, Florida, and they spend part of each year in India and France. *Haunting Paris* is her first novel.

A Note on the Type

Pierre Simon Fournier *le jeune* (1712–1768), who designed the type used in this book, was both an originator and a collector of types. His services to the art of printing were his design of letters, his creation of ornaments and initials, and his standardization of type sizes. His types are old style in character and sharply cut. In 1764 and 1766 he published his *Manuel typographique*, a treatise on the history of French types and printing, on typefounding in all its details, and on what many consider his most important contribution to typography—the measurement of type by the point system.